BLESSED ARE THE MERCIFUL

Also by Al Lacy
in Large Print:

Journeys of the Stranger series:
  Legacy (Book One)
  Silent Abduction (Book Two)
  Blizzard (Book Three)

Mail Order Bride series
(coauthored with JoAnna Lacy):
  Secrets of the Heart (Book One)
  A Time to Love (Book Two)
  Tender Flame (Book Three)

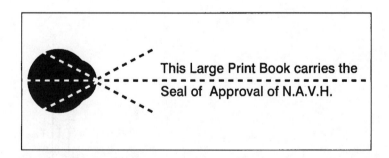

This Large Print Book carries the
Seal of Approval of N.A.V.H.

BLESSED
are the
MERCIFUL

MAIL ORDER #4

Al & JoAnna Lacy

Thorndike Press • Thorndike, Maine

Published in 2000 by arrangement with
Multnomah Publishers, Inc.

Thorndike Press Large Print Christian Fiction Series.

The tree indicium is a trademark of Thorndike Press.

The text of this Large Print edition is unabridged.
Other aspects of the book may vary from the original edition.

Set in 16 pt. Plantin by Rick Gundberg.

Printed in the United States on permanent paper.

Library of Congress Cataloging-in-Publication Data

Lacy, Al.
    Blessed are the merciful / Al & JoAnna Lacy.
      p. cm. — (Mail order bride series ; no. 4)
    ISBN 0-7862-2520-3 (lg. print : hc : alk. paper)
    1. Mail order brides — Fiction. 2. Nebraska — Fiction.
  I. Lacy, JoAnna. II. Title.
PS3562.A256 B55 2000
813'.54—dc21   00-025972

*This book is dedicated to Ken Ruettgers,
our dear friend and Christian brother.
We think the Green Bay Packers should
have retired
#75 when you left the team to enter a new field
of endeavor.
We praise the Lord that He put you with
Multnomah Publishers
to be a helper to the authors.
Thank you for doing such a great job!
We love you, Ken. God bless you!
Al and JoAnna*
PHILEMON 25

Prologue

The Encyclopedia Britannica reports that the mail order business, also called direct mail marketing, "is a method of merchandising in which the seller's offer is made through mass mailing of a circular or catalog, or advertisement placed in a newspaper or magazine, and in which the buyer places his order by mail."

Britannica goes on to say that "mail order operations have been known in the United States in one form or another since colonial days but not until the latter half of the nineteenth century did they assume a significant role in domestic trade."

Thus the mail order market was known when the big gold rush took place in this country in the 1840s and 1850s. At that time prospectors, merchants, and adventurers raced from the East to the newly discovered gold fields in the West. One of the most famous was the California Gold Rush in 1848–49, when discovery of gold at Sutter's

Mill, near Sacramento, brought more than 40,000 men to California. Though few struck it rich, their presence stimulated economic growth, the lure of which brought even more men to the West.

The married men who had come to seek their fortunes sent for their wives and children, desiring to stay and make their home there. Most of the gold rush men were single and also desired to stay in the West, but there were about two hundred men for every single woman. Being familiar with the mail order concept, they began advertising in eastern newspapers for women to come west and marry them. Thus was born the name "mail order bride."

Women by the hundreds began answering the ads. Often when men and their prospective brides corresponded, they agreed to send no photographs; they would accept each other by the spirit of the letters rather than on a physical basis. Others, of course, did exchange photographs.

The mail order bride movement accelerated after the Civil War ended in April 1865, when men went west by the thousands to make their fortunes on the Frontier. Many of the marriages turned out well, while others were disappointing and ended in desertion by one or the other of the mates, or by divorce.

In the Mail Order Bride fiction series, we tell stories intended to grip the heart of the reader, bring some smiles, and maybe wring out a few tears. As always, we weave in the gospel of Jesus Christ and run threads of Bible truth that apply to our lives today.

1

At midmorning on Monday, April 10, 1865, Wanda Perkins left her two-story house in Boston's affluent Beacon Hill neighborhood, humming a nameless tune. She glanced toward the Charles River, blinking at the brilliant sunlight reflecting off its rippling surface.

As she headed up the street, she gave her parasol a little twirl. She and George had dreamed of living on Beacon Hill since he had become a senior vice president of the Massachusetts Bank and Trust Company four years ago, shortly after the Civil War began. It had been only three weeks now since they had purchased their prestigious home — an accomplishment few people in their thirties who had started married life with little money could claim.

Wanda smiled when she saw Geraldine Winkler standing in her yard, twirling her own parasol. Geraldine waved and angled across the sweeping lawn that was beginning to show some green after winter's long months.

Wanda greeted her and fell into step beside her.

"Are you as excited as I am?" Geraldine asked, her eyes flashing.

"Probably more so. At least you were brought up in a neighborhood like this. I'm breathless just thinking about having tea with a member of the family who owns Boston Clothiers!"

"Well, I don't know Elizabeth any better than you do, but I've been told by my neighbors that she's down to earth."

"Mm-hmm. I've been told the same thing. And she's proven it by inviting us to tea to welcome us to the neighborhood." Wanda paused, then said, "They tell me Elizabeth has a live-in maid."

"That's what I hear. And a gardener who lives in a small house behind the big one."

"Oh. I didn't know about the gardener. George said just the other night that when he gets his promised raise in salary this fall, we'll hire a maid."

"That's wonderful! Clyde and I have discussed it, but I think we're probably a year or so away from that. We used most of his inheritance from his father's estate to buy the house."

They turned the corner and looked toward

the Burke house at the far end of the block. It was much larger than either of their homes and had half again as much yard. They hastened their steps and soon turned into the Burke yard and headed for the wide wraparound porch. They could see the gardener working near the rear of the house, cultivating a flower bed for spring planting.

As they lifted their skirts a bit and mounted the steps, the front door opened. A petite woman in her early twenties appeared. "Good mo'nin', ladies. I'm Cleora, Miz Burke's maid. She's upstairs at the moment. Please, come in."

Cleora led them into the large foyer and turned to them with outstretched hand. "May I take yo' parasols?" She placed the parasols in a small container holding a couple of umbrellas and gestured toward an antique padded loveseat. "Please be seated, ladies. I'll let Miz Burke know you is here."

Wanda and Geraldine watched Cleora ascend the grand winding staircase, then let their eyes roam the richly tapestried walls and glistening hardwood floors adorned with thick oriental rugs. A crystal chandelier hung from the high ceiling in the foyer, and various paintings decorated the walls.

The sound of voices came from the second floor, and a moment later Cleora descended the stairs. She told the two women that Mrs. Burke would be joining them in a moment, then vanished down the hall toward the rear of the house.

Within moments, Elizabeth Burke appeared at the top of the stairs, accompanied by another woman. Wanda and Geraldine rose from the loveseat and waited as their hostess made her way down the staircase toward the foyer.

Elizabeth smiled as she approached her guests. "Wanda! Geraldine! I'm so glad you could come." As she spoke, she reached for their hands.

"The pleasure is ours, Elizabeth," Geraldine said.

Elizabeth turned to the woman standing slightly behind her and said, "Wanda Perkins, Geraldine Winkler, this is my sister, Judith Baxter. She's visiting from Philadelphia."

When the women had greeted each other, Elizabeth said, "Ladies, please follow me." As they moved down the hall, Elizabeth said, "I'm very proud of the parlor. It's my favorite room of the whole house. I suppose that's because it's the only room in the house that I designed when Gordon and I had the house built."

When they entered the parlor, Wanda and Geraldine gasped in delight. The room was

13

large, with an elegantly decorated fireplace. Various paintings hung on the walls, and the warm wood paneling and soft flowered wallpaper gave the parlor a mellow, welcoming ambiance.

Cleora came into the room bearing a tray and silver tea service. She set the tea tray on an antique coffee table surrounded by overstuffed chairs and couches.

"Elizabeth," Geraldine said, "why, this is beautiful!"

"That's an understatement!" Wanda said.

"I designed it for me to fit my needs. And it does just that. Well, I think it's teatime." Elizabeth gave her nod to Cleora, who stood quietly by the coffee table. Sunshine streamed through the many-paned windows, sending shafts of light off the silver tea set.

When everyone was seated, Cleora poured the tea into dainty china cups and distributed them to the four women. Geraldine asked Judith about her husband and family in Philadelphia. She soon learned that the Baxters were among the elite in that city.

In turn, Judith said, "Now I'd like to hear about you ladies and your families."

When Wanda and Geraldine had given sufficient information to satisfy the curiosity of their hostess and her sister, Geraldine said to Elizabeth, "Wanda and I are aware that the

Burke family owns Boston Clothiers. We would love to hear about the Burkes, and how it all got started."

Elizabeth's face tinted slightly. "I don't want to bore you."

"You won't bore us," Wanda said. "We're genuinely interested."

"But before you give us the history of the Burkes," Geraldine said, "tell us about your husband and children."

"Well, Gordon is in the Union Army, and we have three children. Adam is twelve, Laura is ten, and Evelyn is eight. Gordon's only living blood relative is his older brother. Sidney and his wife, Darlene, live over on the south side of Beacon Hill."

Elizabeth went on to explain that Gordon's parents, Mitchell and Anna Burke, had come to America from England in 1822, where Mitchell had been in the clothing business with his father since graduating from Oxford University. Mitchell's dream had long been to move to America and establish a clothing business. He started Boston Clothiers in downtown Boston, and with his experience in the business and his ambition to do well, Boston Clothiers was soon a success.

While Cleora poured more tea around, Wanda asked, "So when did Mitchell start branching out?"

"Well, let's see . . . he opened a Boston Clothiers in New York City — Manhattan — in 1829."

"That soon?"

"My husband's father was one of those men who put himself into his business lock, stock, and barrel. He worked about seventy hours a week, Monday through Saturday. Within a year after opening the store in Manhattan, he opened one in Jersey City. Next was Cleveland; then Baltimore. By 1856, there were stores in Chicago, St. Louis, and San Francisco. Mitchell died a couple of years later, and since Sidney and Gordon were his only partners, the business became theirs. Thankfully, all eight stores are doing well."

"So I've heard," Geraldine said. "Are there plans to open more stores in other cities?"

"Yes, but Sidney wants to wait till the war is over and Gordon is home to shoulder the load with him."

"Why is Sidney not with the Union Army?" Wanda asked. "Did he decide not to volunteer because of the business?"

"Not really. If Sidney could have joined up he would have found someone to run the business. But when the war came, Sidney couldn't answer the call to duty because he lost a leg as a child, and the Union Army couldn't use a man with a wooden leg." Elizabeth smiled ruefully. "But with my Gordon, it was a different story. He's always been somewhat of a rakish man. Don't misunderstand me. He loves the children and me as much as it is in him to do so, but there was always a devil-may-care attitude about him. When the war started, he wanted to join up and do his part. But even more, his sense of adventure came to life inside him. According to Union politicians, the war would only last two or three months.

"I pleaded with Gordon not to go, but when I saw how much it meant to him to do his part, I finally gave in. I love my husband dearly and feel that the children and I have been blessed to have him as husband and father. Of course, bless his heart, he set it up with Sidney before he left that if anything happened to him, his half of the company would be mine. Sidney agreed wholeheartedly and even had it set up by the company's lawyers." Elizabeth let out a sigh. "The last time I laid eyes on Gordon was on May 31, 1861, when I stood with many other wives and watched the train pull out."

"Why, that's been almost four years!" Wanda said. "That would mean that your little Evelyn would've been . . ."

"She was only four."

"Does she remember him?"

"Not much. But she's heard so much about him from me and the other children that she talks about him as if she remembers him. Gordon was always kind and patient with the children, and the two older ones adore him. He wasn't always able to spend a great deal of time with them when he was involved in the business, so sometimes they had to love and admire him from afar."

"Well, let's hope this horrible war will be over soon," Judith said. "Those precious children need their father."

Elizabeth's eyes misted over as she said softly, "And so do I."

"You've had letters from him, I assume?" Wanda asked.

"Not many. It's hard to get letters through the lines. I'm so proud of him. In two years, Gordon worked himself up from private to captain. And since making captain, he's been serving under General William T. Sherman."

Geraldine's eyes got round. "Then he was in on Sherman's march on Atlanta last year!"

"He was. Of course we read about Sherman's army burning Atlanta, but I didn't hear from Gordon until it was over, and he was back in Washington for a few days before heading back to the field."

"Too bad he couldn't have come home for a few days at that time, since he was as close as Washington," Judith said.

"He wanted to. He said so in the next letter that came, but General Sherman received direct orders from President Lincoln to head back into another campaign, and they left Washington right away. I guess he won't get home until —"

Elizabeth's words were cut off by loud, jubilant shouts from the street. The women left their chairs and hurried to the window, parting the lace curtains.

"Can you tell what's going on?" Judith asked, trying to get a glimpse out the window. Wanda and Geraldine crowded close behind her.

"They're waving newspapers, and they seem awfully happy about something," Elizabeth said. "Let's go out and see."

The women hurried through the parlor, and Cleora went ahead of them to open the door. The family gardener hurried toward Elizabeth, waving a newspaper. "Miss Elizabeth! Miss Elizabeth! It's the morning edition of the *Boston Globe*! The war is over!"

"Let me see, Jason!"

The gardener handed her the paper, and the other women crowded close.

"Oh, this is wonderful!" Elizabeth cried, running a forefinger over the headlines and the article just beneath. "General Lee surrendered to General Grant in the town of Appomattox Courthouse, Virginia, yesterday afternoon at three o'clock! There is no longer a Confederate Army! The Union soldiers are coming home!"

Elizabeth felt a hand on her shoulder. She turned and embraced her sister. "Oh, Judith," she said, breaking into tears, "he's coming home! My Gordon's coming home!"

Up and down the street neighbors joined together in their yards to celebrate the Union's victory over the Confederacy.

Jason pointed out a paragraph near the bottom of the front page. President Lincoln was quoted as saying it would be many weeks, even as long as two months before all the Union soldiers would be back to their homes. Their families should be patient as they waited for their return.

Elizabeth thumbed tears from her cheeks. "Oh, Jason, it won't be easy to wait for him to come home, but I can be patient!"

"Yes, ma'am. We'll all be glad to have him back."

Someone in the street shouted, "Hey, they must've let out school!" A group of children were running from the direction of the school, and they dashed inside their homes to join elated relatives and neighbors.

Little Evelyn Burke was left behind by her

siblings when they turned into the yard and ran to their mother. Elizabeth folded them in her arms, holding them tight as Adam and Laura cried, "Mama, Papa's coming home! Papa's coming home!"

Little Evelyn bounded up the steps, rushed past Jason, and threw herself between her brother and sister, shouting that the war was over and Papa was coming home. Elizabeth made room for her and hugged all three children as they wept for joy.

A buggy turned up the street, its occupants waving joyfully at the people they passed.

"Oh, look, children!" Elizabeth said. "It's Uncle Sidney and Aunt Darlene!"

The buggy turned into the wide circle drive, and Adam, Laura, and Evelyn ran to it. The five came back to the porch arm-in-arm, then Sidney and Darlene broke from the children and embraced Elizabeth in jubilation.

When emotions had settled some, Darlene said, "Liz, we're going to have a big celebration dinner this evening. Before we left the house I told Maggie to cook up a banquet. Sid and I went to the office and invited our top executives and their families. Everybody's so excited that Gordon is coming home! We'll have to give Maggie till eight o'clock to have it ready. Is that all right with you?"

"Wh-why yes," Elizabeth said.

Evelyn jumped up and down. "Oh, goody! We get to have a party at Aunt Darlene's house tonight 'cause Papa's coming home!"

It had been a long time since there had been an occasion for a celebration this big. The massive dining room table was resplendent with snowy white tablecloths and napkins. The silver was polished to a high sheen, and glowing candles cast a gleam over it all.

The table fairly groaned from the abundance of food. Succulent ham, golden-brown fried chicken, and tender roast beef were the main items, with sweet and creamy mashed potatoes, gravy, stewed tomatoes, corn, applesauce, biscuits, and fresh-baked savory bread.

There was much talk and laughter around the table that night. Even the smallest child had caught the feeling of elation, and spirits were high. Gordon Burke was coming home, and once again Boston Clothiers would have both of its top executives to lead the company.

When everybody at the table was filled almost to bursting, Sidney called toward the kitchen, and Maggie appeared. "Yessir, Mr. Sidney?"

Burke rose from his chair. "Maggie, dear, that was the most delicious meal I have ever eaten. Thank you for doing such a wonderful job to make this celebration even more special!"

There was sudden applause all around the table.

A smile split Maggie's dark face, and she gave a slight curtsy. "I hopes all of you saved some room fo' dessert." With that, she hurried back to the kitchen, and the guests laughed and agreed they would find room.

Moments later, Maggie reappeared, pushing a small cart that bore a four-layer chocolate cake with white frosting, a favorite of her "family."

When everyone had been served their slice of cake, Sidney looked across the table at young Adam and said, "I can imagine how excited you must be, my boy. I know you and your papa used to do things together when he had time."

"Yes, sir. I'm hoping that when Papa comes back he won't be as busy with the company as he was before. I'd like to have more time for us to do 'man' things together."

Sidney smiled. "Well, we've got a larger staff now, Adam. When your papa gets home and is ready to go back to work, I'll talk to him about scheduling time for his son."

Laura leaned toward her uncle. "How about making Papa schedule some 'daughter' time too, Uncle Sidney?"

"I'll have to work on that too, honey," said Sidney, reaching across the table and squeezing her hand.

"Me too, Uncle Sidney?" Evelyn asked.

"You too, darlin'," he said, winking at her. "I'll see that your papa has time for each of you."

2

The following Saturday morning, Elizabeth Burke stood on her wide front porch, kissed her children's foreheads, and said, "Now, I want you to have lots of fun with your friends. But don't forget, I want you home by eleven. That will give you a full two hours to play. I told Mrs. Babcock to shoo you out of the yard when it's time. But if she forgets, it's up to you, Adam, to remember."

The twelve-year-old pulled out the gold pocket watch his father had given him for his seventh birthday and grinned up at his mother. "I won't forget, Mama. We will leave at exactly ten fifty-five."

The Burke children hurried down the steps and ran toward the street. Within a few strides Evelyn was left behind, even though she was running as fast as she could, her long braids flying.

"Adam! Laura!" Elizabeth called.

The two slowed and looked over their shoulders.

"Don't run so fast! Evelyn can't keep up with you. You're always leaving her behind."

Adam and Laura smiled at their mother and put Evelyn between them. They all held hands and hurried on down the street.

Smiling to herself, Elizabeth went inside and climbed the winding staircase to the second floor. When she topped the stairs, she saw Cleora at the hall linen closet, gathering sheets and pillowcases in her arms.

"You can hold my bedroom till last," Elizabeth said. "I'll be in there rearranging the bureau drawers to make room for Mr. Gordon's things again."

"Yes, ma'am. I's gonna do Master Adam's bed first. I already swep' his room. After the bed's done, I'll do the dustin'."

Elizabeth nodded and went on to the master bedroom.

When Cleora had finished making up Adam's bed, she moved around the room, using a feather duster on the furniture and the pictures on the walls. There were six framed photographs of Abraham Lincoln in different poses. Two of them were front page pictures from the *Boston Globe*. One showed Lincoln in front of an army tent with the diminutive General George B. McClellan. The other was a similar background, this time with General Ulysses S. Grant and several other army officers.

Cleora giggled softly while dusting the pictures, unaware that Elizabeth had entered the room. She jumped slightly when Elizabeth said, "What's tickled you, Cleora?"

A smile spread across Cleora's face. "I was jus' thinkin' 'bout these pictures of Mr. Lincoln. There prob'ly isn't another twelve-year-old boy in all the Union states with six pictures of the president on his wall."

"Probably not," Elizabeth said. "But Mr. Lincoln is Adam's hero, as you know."

"Yes'm. I loves Mr. Lincoln, too. He done set my fambly free, an' I loves him fo' that. An' I know that Master Adam has set his heart on bein' a lawyer 'cause what he read about Mr. Lincoln in school all these years inspired him to wanna be a successful attorney jus' like his hero."

"That desire has been in Adam's mind for a long time," Elizabeth said. "Have I ever told you about the time Mr. Lincoln came to Boston back in 1860, when he was campaigning for the presidency and —"

"Oh, yes'm! That was when Master Adam got to shake Mr. Lincoln's hand . . . an' you an' Mr. Gordon had to make him wash his hand."

Elizabeth laughed. "Yes, after we found out he had gone three days without. And the boy was only seven years old!"

"That is some boy you have there, Miz Elizabeth. That is some boy."

"Don't I know it! He has a certain determination about him, Cleora. He was seven when he made up his mind that he wanted to follow Lincoln's example and be a lawyer. He hasn't changed his mind since then, and I'm positive he never will. He's going to go to Harvard Law School and become a lawyer as sure as I'm standing here."

The door knocker clattered downstairs and echoed through the house. "I'll see who it is, ma'am," Cleora said.

Elizabeth followed her down the hall and paused at the top of the stairs. She heard Sidney's voice first, then Darlene's. Cleora invited them in, saying she would fetch Miss Elizabeth.

"I'm right here, Cleora," said Elizabeth, descending the stairs. When she saw their faces, her heart lurched. "Sidney . . . Darlene . . . what's wrong?" Elizabeth reached the last step and saw a folded newspaper in Sidney's hand. "Tell me, what's happened?"

Cleora closed the front door and excused herself.

Sidney raised the newspaper chest high and let it unfold so Elizabeth could see the headline on the special edition of the *Boston Globe* that had just come off the press.

Cleora stopped when she heard her mistress gasp. She turned and hurried toward Elizabeth and saw the shocking headline for herself.

"Let's go into the parlor," Darlene said, moving up to take hold of Elizabeth's arm. "I think we all need to sit down."

"I'll bring some water," Cleora said. She hurried down the hall, tears forming in her eyes.

Darlene guided her sister-in-law to one of the love seats and sat down beside her. Sidney took a seat facing them and quickly recounted the events reported in the paper.

Elizabeth shook her head in disbelief. "But . . . but why?"

"We don't know yet."

Elizabeth touched her trembling fingers to the tears on her cheeks. "I have such love and respect for that dear man. Poor Mrs. Lincoln. What horror she must be experiencing."

"I can't even imagine," Darlene said.

"And their sons," Elizabeth said. "Robert will probably handle it better than Tad. The younger boy and his father are so close." Her eyes widened. "And what of my own son! This is going to devastate Adam, especially if . . . if Mr. Lincoln shouldn't make it." She drew a tremulous breath. "What does the paper say about Booth, Sidney? Since they know he did it, have they caught him?"

"No, but they will. They think he might have broken a leg in his escape."

Cleora entered the room, carrying a tray with a pitcher of water and three glasses. "Here's the water. Mr. Sidney, is President Lincoln gonna be all right?"

"I don't know, Cleora. His doctors aren't giving him much of a chance."

Tears welled up in the maid's eyes. "Oh, I's so sorry." Then to Elizabeth, "If you needs me, ma'am, I'll be upstairs cleanin' in the bedrooms and makin' up the beds."

"All right. Thank you, dear."

Sidney poured water into the glasses and handed one to Elizabeth and to Darlene. The sound of childish chatter and laughter came from the front porch. Elizabeth's gaze swung to the clock on the mantel. It was five minutes after ten.

"Oh my, it's the children. They're home early." She went to the parlor door and took a half-step into the hall. She watched her three young ones troop into the house, one behind the other.

Evelyn ran toward her mother. "Mama, we had lots of fun! We've been talking to Billy and Susie and Kathy about Papa coming home! We're so happy!"

"That's wonderful, honey," Elizabeth said. "But how come you're home so early?"

"Mr. Babcock came home looking sort of upset," Laura said, "and took Mrs. Babcock into the kitchen. He came back out in a minute and said they all needed to talk about something important. He was sorry, but we would have to go home."

"But he was nice, Mama," Adam said. "He asked us to come back again real soon."

Elizabeth bit down on her lower lip. "That's good, son."

Adam frowned as he looked closely at his mother's face. "Mama, are you all right?"

"Are you sick, Mama?" Laura asked.

"I'm not sick. Uncle Sidney and Aunt Darlene are here. Come into the parlor."

"Mama, what's wrong?" Adam said. "Is it something about Papa?"

"No, honey." She put an arm around his shoulders as they entered the parlor together. "As far as we know, Papa is fine and will be home soon."

"Then what is it?"

"Come and sit down," Elizabeth said. "Something bad has happened. Not in our family but to someone we all love and respect."

Laura and Evelyn sat between their aunt

and uncle, and Adam took a seat beside his mother.

Elizabeth took both of Adam's hands in hers and said softly, "It's President Lincoln, Adam. He's been shot."

"Shot?" Disbelief filled Adam's eyes.

"He's still alive, honey. The doctors aren't giving him much of a chance to make it, but as long as he's alive, there's hope."

Silence filled the room, then Adam said weakly, "Who — when — ?"

Elizabeth squeezed his hands. "I'll let Uncle Sidney tell you about it."

Sidney knelt in front of the boy. As he told the story to Adam, Elizabeth watched the fire rise in her son's dark eyes.

Suddenly Adam jumped up from the couch, his fists clenched, and looked at the floor through tear-dimmed eyes. "Mr. Lincoln led this country through that awful Civil War. He . . . he freed the slaves. He's done nothing but good for all of us; especially us northerners. Now the thanks he gets is a bullet in his head!"

Sidney rose to his feet and sent a helpless glance to Elizabeth.

Suddenly Adam whirled about. "I hate that John Wilkes Booth! I hope they catch him and shoot him!"

Sidney laid a hand on Adam's shoulder. "I

know how you feel, Adam. I want to see Booth pay to the ultimate for what he did."

"I'd like to be the one who tracks him down, Uncle Sidney! I'd shoot him in the stomach so he'd die real slow! I'd stand over him and laugh while he clutched his bleeding belly!"

"Adam!" Elizabeth said. "Your hating John Booth will only dry you up on the inside. Don't concentrate on him. Put your mind on Mr. Lincoln, and hope that he gets well."

The boy took a deep breath, then said, "Mr. Lincoln is tough, Mama. He might just fool the doctors and come through it."

Elizabeth wrapped her arms around him. "Just hang on to that hope. Maybe you're right! Maybe Mr. Lincoln is tough enough to come through this."

That night, Adam Burke lay in his bed. Sleep refused to come. He thought about praying but wasn't sure how to do it. He had heard someone pray only one time, and that was when he attended the funeral of a neighbor, and the minister had said a prayer over the grave.

Adam threw back the covers and left his bed. Moonlight filtered into the room through the lace curtains. He stood before the pictures of Lincoln and studied each one, then began pacing from one end of the room to the other.

"Why? Why did John Booth hate Mr. Lincoln so much that he would shoot him like that?"

He lost track of the time and was surprised when he heard a light tap at his door. He grabbed his robe and shrugged into it, tying the sash around his slender waist. It was Cleora. She whispered softly, "Master Adam, is you all right? I can hear you walkin' back an' forth from down in my room."

"I . . . I'm just so upset about Mr. Lincoln, Cleora. I don't want him to die."

"Me either. He's such a good man. All my folk down in Alabama has been slaves fo' so many years. An' now they ain't slaves no mo' 'cause Mr. Lincoln made 'em free. God bless him."

"Yes. God bless him."

" 'Course I's so thankful I was brought up north by my mother's frien's when she died, an' yo' mama and papa give me a job. I has truly been blessed. Adam, is there anythin' I can do fo' you?"

"No, but thank you. I'll go back to bed and try to get to sleep."

"Well, you'd better hurry to sleep, 'cause it's gonna be mornin' in 'bout two hours. G'night."

"Good night," Adam whispered, quietly closing the door.

Sunday morning arrived with a brilliant sunrise that stabbed Adam's tired eyes as it shafted through the windows. He had not slept.

The atmosphere at breakfast was dismal until Elizabeth said, "Now, children, I know we're all concerned about our president, and it is right that we should be. But let's be glad for what's good in our lives. Papa will soon be home."

Her words helped to lift countenances. Elizabeth talked about how Papa always liked for her to fix a picnic lunch on Sunday afternoons in the summertime, and he would drive the family down to Boston Harbor in the horse and buggy so they could have their picnic and watch the sailboats.

Adam and Laura remembered those happy times, but not Evelyn. This made her want her papa to come home all the more. Soon it would be summer, and she could enjoy that adventure over and over again.

That afternoon Laura and Evelyn were sitting on the porch. Laura was mending one of her little sister's rag dolls when Evelyn said, "Look, Laura! It's Uncle Sidney!"

They watched him guide the horse and buggy up the long, curved drive.

"Uh-oh," Laura said. "I think maybe President Lincoln has died, Evelyn. Uncle Sidney looks very sad."

"Shall I get Mama?"

"I'm sure he'll want to talk to her."

Laura went to the edge of the porch to meet her uncle as he reined the buggy to a halt and said, "Hello, Laura. Is the rest of the family home?"

"Yes, sir. Evelyn's gone after Mama. You look sad. Did . . . did Mr. Lincoln die?"

"Yes, honey. He did."

Just then, Elizabeth came outside, holding Evelyn by the hand. Behind her were Adam and Cleora.

"I have a close friend at the *Globe*," Sidney said. "He said he'd let me know if . . . if the president died. Mr. Lincoln died at 7:22 this morning."

"No!" Adam cried. "No!"

He sank to the porch and broke into sobs, burying his face in his hands.

3

On Thursday, April 27, Adam Burke was sitting in class at the Beacon Hill school, gazing out the window while Mr. Meyer explained a math problem at the blackboard. Meyer's voice seemed a mile away to Adam, who stared at the puffy white clouds floating against a cobalt blue sky.

Billy Babcock risked a glance at his friend and saw Adam pull out his gold pocket watch and compare it with the big clock on the wall above the blackboard. They were synchronized perfectly. It was 10:11 A.M.

Adam felt Billy's eyes on him as he slipped the watch back into his pocket. He grinned at his friend and Billy turned his attention back to Mr. Meyer.

Adam again gazed out the window, the teacher's voice distantly touching his ears. Suddenly the distant drone caught Adam's attention.

". . . this problem, Adam."

The boy looked at his teacher blankly. "Uh

37

". . . what was that, sir?"

"I asked if you could solve this problem."

"Well, sir, I —"

"You haven't been paying attention, have you?"

Adam cleared his throat and his face took on a deep shade of red.

When he did not reply, Meyer said with an edge in his voice, "Adam, your mind has been elsewhere since a week ago last Monday, the day after President Lincoln died. Isn't that correct?"

"Yes . . . yes, sir."

Walter Meyer's face lost its scowl. "All of us are mourning the loss of our beloved president, Adam, but life must go on. Everyone in this room is aware that you had the privilege of shaking Mr. Lincoln's hand. A privilege none of us ever had. But he's gone now, and you must get your mind back on your school work."

Adam nodded. "Yes, sir."

The classroom door opened, and the students turned to see Harold Griffin, the school principal, enter and walk to the front of the room. "Mr. Meyer, I have an announcement."

"Of course, sir." Meyer looked at his students. "Class, please give Mr. Griffin your full attention."

"Boys and girls," Griffin said, "I just received word that yesterday morning, John Wilkes Booth was found by federal troops in Port Royal, Virginia. They cornered him in a barn. Booth was given the command to come out and surrender, but he refused. The soldiers, in turn, set the barn on fire. When Booth came limping out, he was carrying a carbine rifle and looked as if he was going to use it. One of the troopers fired, and Booth went down. Before he died, he found the strength to boast about killing the president, saying that what he did was for the good of the country."

Adam turned to Billy and whispered, "Good for that trooper! Booth got just what he deserved!"

One Sunday evening a few weeks later, Elizabeth Burke and her children were sitting on the front porch, waiting for Sidney's buggy. Darlene had invited them to dinner.

While they waited, Elizabeth and the children talked about Papa. For the past three weeks the newspapers had told heartwarming stories of men returning from the war. Some were missing limbs or had suffered other serious wounds but were happily back with their families. These stories intensified their longing for Gordon's return and made each day without him harder to bear.

"There he is, Mama!" Laura said.

All rose to their feet as the buggy turned into the wide circle drive, the horse's hooves beating out a steady clip-clop on the hard-packed earth.

"Everybody hungry?" Sidney asked as he pulled the buggy to a halt.

"We sure are, Uncle Sidney," Adam said, taking his mother by the hand to help her into the buggy. "What's Maggie got fixed for us?"

"Oh, I'm not supposed to tell you, Adam. Darlene and Maggie want it to be a surprise."

When all were aboard, Sidney clucked to the horse and put the buggy in motion. As they headed for the street, Sidney glanced at his sister-in-law. "Liz, you look worried. Something troubling you?"

Elizabeth looked away for a moment, then said, "I read in the papers every day about soldiers coming home to their families, and I ask myself why it's taking so long for Gordon to come home. The children are on edge about it, too."

"That's understandable. But remember what President Lincoln said about that . . . that it might take as long as two months for all the men to return to their homes."

"I know, Sidney, but with every day that passes, it gets more difficult to be patient.

He's been gone for over four years. We so desperately want him home."

"Well, he's being detained for some good reason, I'm sure."

"Even if he can't get away from wherever they have him posted, he could at least send a wire. He has to know that we're anxious."

"Maybe wherever he is doesn't have access to wire service. But he might have already sent a letter and it's just taking time to get here."

Elizabeth was quiet for a moment, then said, "Yes, that's possible."

"Tell you what. If he doesn't come home in another week, I'll see what I can do to trace him."

"Oh, would you, Sidney?"

"Of course." He patted her arm. "Old Uncle Sidney has a few strings he can pull."

Elizabeth smiled at her brother-in-law. "Okay, we'll give it another week. Maybe he'll be home by then."

As the days passed, Elizabeth and her children spent most of their time after dinner sitting on the porch, watching each carriage or buggy or pedestrian that came along.

Every evening, as the sky darkened, Elizabeth gathered her children to her, hugged and kissed them, and spoke encouraging words, even though her heart was troubled and more than a little perplexed.

On Monday evening, May 22, Elizabeth went to the kitchen where Cleora and Jason were eating their supper and asked Jason if he would hitch the mare to the buggy as soon as he had finished his meal.

While the children stayed with Cleora, Elizabeth rode with Jason through the darkening streets of Beacon Hill. When they arrived at the Sidney Burke home, Darlene answered the knock at the door and welcomed Elizabeth and Jason in.

"Is something wrong, Liz?" she asked.

"Only that Gordon isn't home yet. Sidney said a week ago that if we hadn't seen or heard from Gordon by now, he would pull some strings. I think it's time for that."

"I agree. Sidney's in the library; I'll take you there."

"I'll wait here, ma'am," Jason said to Elizabeth.

When Darlene opened the library door, Sidney was seated at his desk with a small stack of papers on one side and several sheets spread before him. When he saw Elizabeth he rose to his feet.

"Hello, Liz. I think I can guess why you're here. Sorry I haven't gotten to you yet today, but I've had some paperwork here that has to be done by morning."

"I understand, Sidney. It's just that I . . . well, I think it's time to ask you to investigate Gordon's whereabouts."

Sidney nodded. "You're right, and in fact I've already begun. This morning I sent a wire to Army headquarters in Washington, to General Earl Howard in the records office. He and I are old friends. I expect to hear back from him right away, maybe even tomorrow. I told him it was urgent."

Some of the worry left Elizabeth's face. "Thank you, Sidney. I appreciate this more than I can say. And the children appreciate it, too."

Sidney gave her a hug. "You just relax now and leave it to old Sid. We'll find Gordon and have him back home before you know it."

It was late morning the next day when Cleora came into the parlor where Elizabeth was sitting in her favorite overstuffed chair, reading a book of poetry.

"Miz Elizabeth, I jus' happened to look out the door an' I saw Mr. Sidney's buggy comin' up the drive."

Elizabeth closed her book and set it aside as she rose to her feet. "Please bring him in here, Cleora."

When Sidney walked through the parlor

doorway, Elizabeth searched his face, but could detect nothing from his expression. She waited for him to speak.

Cleora closed the door behind him, and he said, "I received a wire back from General Howard two hours ago. The army knows that Captain Gordon Burke was seriously wounded in a battle on the banks of the Appomattox River at Farmville, Virginia, on April 7. He said —"

"Please don't tell me he's —"

"No, no! General Howard said Gordon was taken to Potomac Hospital in Bethesda, Maryland, but the Washington office has no more information."

"Oh, I was afraid of this! He died, didn't he? They buried him and didn't even let me know!" She began to sob.

Sidney grasped her upper arms firmly. "Liz, let me finish! As soon as I read General Howard's telegram, I wired Potomac Hospital. They wired me back about an hour ago but didn't give me much, except to say that Gordon was released alive and well on May 3."

"May 3! That was twenty days ago! Something's happened to him. We've got to find him!"

"I think the best place to start is the hospital. Talking to someone there face to face will get us a lot more information than trying to communicate by wire. Surely someone there can tell us where he said he was going after his release."

"You'll go with me?"

"Of course I'll go with you. And so will Darlene."

"Oh, I'm so glad. It will be a real strength to have both of you with me. When can we leave?"

"We're leaving on the train to Washington at eight-thirty in the morning. I already have the tickets. With all the stops the train makes along the way, we won't get to Washington till evening. We'll stay in a hotel tomorrow night and drive to Bethesda Wednesday morning."

"Oh, bless you, Sidney! But I don't understand why someone at the hospital didn't notify me that Gordon was there."

"That puzzles me too, but we'll get some answers when we get there. Be ready in the morning at seven, all right?"

Elizabeth raised up on her tiptoes and kissed Sidney's cheek. "I'll be waiting. Thank you, Sidney."

On Wednesday morning, Sidney pulled the rented buggy into the hospital parking lot and helped his wife and sister-in-law from the vehicle.

The receptionist at the desk smiled at them as they approached. "May I help you, sir?"

"Yes, ma'am. We've come to inquire about a patient who was here from about April 8 till May 3. His name is Captain Gordon Burke."

"And what did you need to know?"

Sidney gestured toward Elizabeth. "This is Mrs. Burke. I am Captain Burke's brother, and this other lady is my wife. We haven't heard from my brother, so I contacted U.S. army headquarters in Washington. When I was told that he'd been wounded and brought here, I wired the hospital and received a return wire that said he'd been released alive and well on May 3."

"I see." The receptionist blinked, looking puzzled.

"We came down from Boston to talk to someone who can give us more information. Can you direct us to the right person, please?"

"Just a moment." She rose from her chair and went down the hall.

Sidney put an arm around Elizabeth's shoulders as they watched the receptionist disappear into a nearby office. Seconds later she returned with a young man she introduced as Joel Hines, the hospital's office manager.

"Hello, Mr. Burke. Elsie says you need to talk to me and that it's very important."

"Yes, sir. It's regarding an army captain who was a patient here for almost a month."

"Please come into my office," Hines said.

As soon as they were all seated, Sidney repeated the story. When he had finished, Hines said, "Let me go look at the records."

When the office manager returned, he was carrying a file folder. "Mrs. Burke, all I can tell you from your husband's record is that he took shrapnel in his head from a cannonball. It required some extensive surgery and three weeks of healing before he could be released from the hospital. The surgeon's notes say that the wound left a slight disfigurement on his face."

Elizabeth closed her eyes and nodded.

Sidney leaned forward, his eyes on the folder the young man was holding. "Is there any indication in the record, Mr. Hines, of where Captain Burke might have gone when he was released?"

"No, sir. There is nothing of that nature."

"Isn't there someone here who might know?"

"Well, he may have told his nurses or someone like that, but it would take some doing to find out who might've been taking care of him the last day or so before he was released. I'm not sure I can help you there."

Elizabeth's lips quivered as she said, "Mr.

47

Hines, this is my husband we're talking about. He has disappeared, and I have three children anxiously waiting for their father to come home. I can't just go home and tell them nobody knows where he's gone."

Hines shrugged. "Ma'am, I'm sorry, but —"

"I want to talk to the head of this institution," Sidney said. "Who might that be?"

"Well, sir, that would be Mr. Glover, the hospital director."

"Fine. Where do I find him?"

"Sir, I really don't think Mr. Glover can do any more than I've already done."

Sidney rose to his feet. "I want him to tell me that. Take us to him."

Moments later, Sidney, Elizabeth, and Darlene were seated before the desk of the hospital director, Vernon Glover, a gray-headed man in his mid-fifties.

"How may I help you?" Glover said with a smile.

Sidney told the entire story again. When he had finished, Glover eased back in his chair and sighed. "Joel is a bit green around the gills yet, folks. I think I can help you. Let me begin by inquiring among my office staff to see who checked Captain Burke out the day he was discharged. I'll be back shortly."

When Glover left the room, Elizabeth put a shaky hand to her cheek and looked at Sidney. "What am I going to do if they don't come up with an explanation?"

Darlene took hold of Elizabeth's other hand and squeezed it tight. "Let's cross that bridge if and when we come to it. I have a feeling Mr. Glover's going to come up with the information we need."

Elizabeth tried to smile. Tears filmed her eyes as she said, "I'm sure glad you two came with me."

"We wouldn't have let you come alone," Sidney assured her.

Soon Vernon Glover returned. "I talked to the office worker who completed the papers and had them signed by Captain Burke when he was released. She said he gave no indication where he might be going when he left us. I'm sorry. I was hoping she would be able to help us."

"What about the nurse assigned to him his last day or so?" Sidney asked. "Maybe he told her something."

"Good point. If she's on duty right now I'll bring her in here and let you ask her yourself."

Less than five minutes had passed when Glover returned, shaking his head. "Wouldn't you know it? The nurse who was assigned to that ward and was attending Captain Burke is no longer with us."

"Mr. Glover," Sidney said, "we're grasping

at straws here. Is it possible there might be some patients still in the hospital who were in the same ward with my brother?"

Glover's eyes lit up. "Of course! There are some soldiers in Ward B who have been with us for quite some time. Let me look into this."

With that, Glover was gone again.

Elizabeth drew a shuddering breath and struggled to control her shaking hands. "Something's wrong, Sidney. I just know it."

"Honey, don't borrow trouble," Darlene said. "Let's wait and see if there's someone who can tell us something that will lead us to him."

When Glover reappeared, he had a nurse with him. He introduced them to nurse Twila Duncan, and said, "Mrs. Duncan came on our nursing staff just after Captain Burke was released, but she tells me there are two soldiers in Ward B who were brought in three days before Captain Burke came here. Perhaps they will have something to tell you."

"Good," Sidney said. "Could we talk to them now?"

"Yes. Mrs. Duncan will take you there."

The trio followed Twila Duncan to a pair of double doors marked Ward B. She led them to a bed where a young man in his late twenties lay.

"Sergeant," Twila said, "these people

would like to talk to you, but first I need to bring Corporal Byars over here so they can talk to both of you together."

The sergeant looked at the visitors and nodded. The Burkes stood in silence while the nurse went to a young man in a wheelchair. She said a few words to him, then pushed his chair up beside the bed.

"Folks," Twila said, "this man in the wheelchair is Corporal Art Byars. The man in the bed is Sergeant Neil Westbrook. I have to get back to my duties now, so I'll let you explain who you are and what you need to know."

Sidney thanked her, then turned to the men. "Gentlemen, I understand you are acquainted with Captain Gordon Burke, who was here for almost a month."

"Yes, sir," Westbrook said. "The captain was in this bed right next to me for the entire time he was here." He gestured to an unoccupied cot. "I got to know him quite well."

"And I did too," Byars said.

"Good. I'm his brother, Sidney Burke."

Both men smiled and shook his hand.

Sidney gestured toward Darlene. "And this is my wife, Darlene."

"Ma'am," they said in unison, nodding at her.

"And this lady is Gordon's wife, Elizabeth."

There was an awkward silence as the two soldiers looked at each other. Then Westbrook said, "Ma'am, I'm — we're sorry, but this comes to us as a complete surprise."

"What do you mean?"

"Well . . . ah . . ." Westbrook looked at Sidney. "Mr. Burke, what we have to tell her is . . . well, is going to be a shock. Maybe we should tell you out of her presence and —"

"Tell me!" Elizabeth demanded, her eyes flashing.

The sergeant took a deep breath and said, "Ma'am, we had a nurse in this ward who was assigned to Captain Burke. Name was Lila Murray. Well . . . we watched a romance develop between them. Neither made any attempt to hide their feelings for each other. Everyone who knew him here in the hospital thought the captain was unmarried . . . as did Miss Murray."

A moan escaped Elizabeth's lips, and she crossed her arms and gripped them tightly, trying to press the pain from her chest.

"I'll get a nurse," Sidney said.

"Ma'am," Byars said, "we're sorry to be the ones to tell you this."

Elizabeth stared at the floor, gasping for breath, as Darlene held her.

52

Sidney returned with nurse Twila Duncan, who said to him, "Grab that chair over there by the other bed."

When Elizabeth was seated, Twila checked her pulse, then bent down and looked in Elizabeth's eyes. Twila asked Sidney to help her get Elizabeth on the adjacent bed. Then she pulled the privacy curtains around the bed and hurried away. She returned with a tin cup and disappeared behind the curtain.

Twila managed to force a little of the sedative from the cup between Elizabeth's tightly drawn lips. Elizabeth choked and gasped, but after several minutes, the contents of the cup had been drained.

Two orderlies came to place Elizabeth on a cart, and Sidney and Darlene followed alongside the nurse to a small, sparsely furnished room outside the ward where they placed Elizabeth on a cot. Elizabeth began trembling all over, and Twila covered her with blankets, tucking them up under her quivering chin.

Finally the trembling began to subside, and Elizabeth's eyelids started to droop. Sidney excused himself, saying he wanted to talk to Westbrook and Byars some more.

Sidney asked the two soldiers if Lila Murray had left her job at the hospital the same day his brother had been released, and they said yes. He thanked them for their help and returned to the small room to find that Elizabeth was asleep. Twila Duncan told them Elizabeth would sleep for a while; if they wanted to get away for a while, she would keep an eye on her.

Sidney and Darlene left the hospital hand in hand and walked to the café they had noticed upon their arrival. They sat down at a table and ordered coffee, strong and black, then Sidney told Darlene what he had just learned from the two soldiers.

For a few minutes they simply sat and stared into space, then spoke at the same time.

"You go first," Darlene said.

"I can't believe Gordon would do something so stupid," Sidney said. "How could he just walk out on Elizabeth and those children?"

"I know, I can't believe it either. But Elizabeth and her children are going to need all the help and support we can give them. Just being angry won't help."

After his third cup of coffee, Sidney released a deep sigh and gave Darlene a sheepish grin as he admitted she was right.

When they returned to the small room in the hospital, they found a droopy-eyed Elizabeth sitting on the edge of the cot, holding her head in her hands. Nurse Duncan was not in the room. Darlene knelt in front of Elizabeth, gathered her in her arms, and held her close for a long time.

When she released her, Elizabeth looked up at Sidney and said, "Thank you both for being here. I don't know what I would've done without you." She drew a shaky breath. "Now I need to get home to my children."

When Elizabeth was able to walk, the three returned to Vernon Glover's office and thanked him for his help. Glover told them he had no idea where Lila Murray went after she quit her job, but he gave them the name of the apartment building where she had lived.

When they arrived at the apartment, the landlord could only tell them that Lila had left quite suddenly. She was with a man in uniform. There was a captain's insignia on his coat, and he had a bandage on his head.

On the train ride back to Boston, Elizabeth leaned on Darlene's shoulder and wept.

Elizabeth walked into the house with Sidney and Darlene at her side, and the children came running to her. All three looked beyond their mother as they hugged her, and asked if their father was with her.

"No, he isn't," she said.

"Why not?" Evelyn asked.

Elizabeth looked at the maid, and said, "Cleora, would you heat up some tea and bring it into the parlor, please?"

"Yes, ma'am. I have some in the kitchen already hot. I'll be right back with it."

Elizabeth guided the children to a brocade couch in the parlor, where the girls sat down with Adam between them. Sidney and Darlene took seats nearby, and Elizabeth pulled up a straight-backed wooden chair in front of the children.

Cleora came in bearing a tray with a steaming teapot and three cups. When she had poured for Elizabeth, Sidney, and Darlene, she left the room.

Elizabeth took a few sips, then ran her gaze over the faces of her children, her mind at a loss as to how to tell them. Noting the fear in their eyes, she took a steadying breath and said, "Adam, Laura, Evelyn, your papa will not be coming home. Ever." Haltingly, she told them what she had learned at the Potomac Hospital in Bethesda, pausing at times to compose herself and to carefully choose her words. "So you see, children, Papa has chosen to go away with this woman rather than to come home to us."

Laura left the couch and rushed into her mother's arms, tears blurring her vision.

Evelyn joined them.

Adam sat staring at his mother and sisters, then suddenly sprang from the couch. Elizabeth reached out and grabbed his arm, but he jerked free and bolted for the door.

"Adam!" Elizabeth cried.

They heard the rapid pounding of his feet as he ascended the winding staircase.

"I'll see to him, Liz," Sidney said, rising from his chair.

Before he reached the parlor door, a sound of breaking glass came from upstairs. Sidney saw Elizabeth start to get up and said, "I'll take care of him, Liz. You stay with the girls."

Darlene joined mother and daughters as Elizabeth held the girls against her, trying to comfort them with the gentle murmur of her familiar voice.

Sidney bounded up the stairs and ran down the hall toward the master bedroom where he heard more glass shattering. When he reached the open door, he saw three windows broken out and Adam throwing his father's bust of Napoleon Bonaparte through a fourth window.

"What are you doing, Adam!"

"I'm throwing away everything my father owned! I don't want to see anything of his ever, ever, ever again!"

Sidney took hold of Adam's shoulders, but he pulled loose from his uncle's grasp, screaming, "I hate him! I don't want anything of his left in this house!"

Sidney reached for him again, and Adam jumped back. "Leave me alone, Uncle Sidney!" He took another backward step, reached into his pocket, and pulled out the gold watch his father had given him. He threw it to the floor and smashed it with his heel. "I hate him! I hate him! I hate him!"

Sidney went to Adam, and this time the boy did not move away. Just as Sidney was wrapping his arms around Adam, Elizabeth, Darlene, and the girls came into the room.

"I hate Papa, Mama!" Adam wailed. "I hate him! I wish he had been killed in the war!"

4

The sun was just beginning its climb into the hazy sky, but its warmth was already heating up the streets of Philadelphia. A short, stubby man of sixty stepped down from a carriage in front of the *Philadelphia Enquirer* building. As he crossed the sidewalk, other *Enquirer* employees were also arriving.

He passed through the double doors beside a younger man, who greeted him. "Have a nice weekend, Mr. Corwin?"

"Not bad, Norm. Would've been better if the weather was cooler."

"Can't disagree with that, sir. But then, it's August. What can we expect but heat and high humidity?"

"That's it, I guess," Corwin said with a chuckle.

He made his way to the second floor and headed for his office. Just outside his door, two men huddled together over some papers. To the older one Corwin said, "Is he ready, Lance?"

"Yes, sir. We worked on it for a couple of hours Saturday afternoon, so our promising young apprentice reporter is ready for his first big story."

"Only with your expert help," Derek Mills said. "I'd be scared stiff to tackle this story without your coaching."

"We all needed help when we first went into the newspaper business, Derek," Corwin said. "This will be a good start for you. With everybody in the city keyed up about this trial, we're printing two thousand extra issues each day the trial lasts."

Derek smiled. "I want to thank you again, Mr. Corwin, for allowing me to write this story. I couldn't ask for a better employer than you, or a better tutor than Lance."

Corwin laid a hand on Derek's shoulder. "You've got the stuff, kid. If I didn't see it in you, I wouldn't have put you with my star reporter. Now, you gentlemen finish up what you're doing and be at the courthouse good and early."

Corwin entered a glassed-in office with lettering on the door that read: JIM CORWIN, EDITOR IN CHIEF.

"All right," Lance said. "Let's go over the basic facts. Tell me what you have so far."

Derek shuffled the papers before him, putting them in order. "Today is the first day of the trial for police officer Seth Coleman, who has been charged with the murder of fellow officer Lawrence Sheldon. Such a charge has never before been brought against a police officer in the state of Pennsylvania. For that matter, it has only happened one time in the history of this country . . . in Bangor, Maine, in the summer of 1797."

"Correct," said Lance. "And in that case the accused officer committed suicide in his jail cell before the trial, leaving a note confessing that he had killed his fellow constable over a woman."

Derek looked at the paper in his hand. "The judge in this trial is the honorable Lucius P. Shagley. The prosecuting attorney is Hansel Vandeveer. The jury is made up of a dozen prominent Philadelphia businessmen. The defense attorney for Officer Coleman is Adam Burke, a dazzling young associate in the Benson, Smith, and Walters law firm. Burke, now twenty-four, graduated from Harvard University Law School in May 1873, and was hired by George Benson, senior partner of the firm almost while still in his cap and gown."

Derek felt Lance's eyes on him. He looked up, caught a look of disapproval, and cleared his throat. "Sir?"

"I wouldn't use the word *dazzling* when

you write it. Granted, Burke is a sharp lawyer for his age, but you really don't need an adjective like that."

"All right. I'll come up with something less potent."

"You need to be careful about that kind of thing until you see how the trial turns out, then go with your flashy adjectives."

"All right, sir."

"And since Burke is young for a lawyer, you're on solid ground to give his age in the first story. But I'd leave out that 'cap and gown' stuff."

"Whatever you say." Derek scratched through a few lines with his pencil and stared at the paper for a moment. "What about if I say that Burke is engaged to the beautiful Philipa Conrad, the spoiled and snobbish only child of Philadelphia's wealthiest and most prominent attorney, Philip Conrad III?"

Lance snorted. "You're kidding, of course."

"No, I'm not kidding. Everybody knows that Philipa is spoiled rotten and sticks her nose up at people she thinks are below her."

"I mean about putting that in print."

Derek laughed. "Gotcha!"

Lance grinned and shook his head.

"Seriously, Lance, wouldn't it be newsy to let the readers know that the defense attorney works for another firm but is engaged to

Philip Conrad's daughter?"

Lance rubbed his chin. "Mmm. I wouldn't put that in unless Burke wins the case for his client. If he does, that'll be chewy stuff for the public."

Derek nodded and made a note to himself.

Lance looked at the clock on the wall. "We'd better get going. You've got the basic things down. We'll work on them some more after we see what happens today. By the way, you didn't mention that Officer Seth Coleman is single. You ought to include that in your first write-up. People want to know about family and that kind of thing."

Derek made of note on the pages, then said, "Officer Sheldon was also unmarried, correct?"

"That's right," Lance said as he closed a side desk drawer. "Coleman has no family at all. Sheldon's parents, Jack and Thelma Sheldon, will be at the trial, along with some cousins. Didn't I give you that information?"

Derek shuffled papers for a moment, then snapped his fingers. "Yes, you did. I've got it right here."

"All right. Let's go."

When Lance Rankin and Derek Mills arrived at the Philadelphia County Courthouse, they spotted reporters from the town's other

63

two newspapers on the courthouse steps and gave a civil nod, acknowledging their presence.

Lance pointed out police chief Mandrake Bennett as they entered the courtroom. Bennett was sitting with several off-duty police officers. On the second row, center section, sat Jack and Thelma Sheldon, along with friends and relatives. Lance and Derek took seats behind the police chief and the other officers.

Ten minutes before the trial was scheduled to begin, the courtroom was packed, and there were people in the hall who had gotten there too late to get seats.

The jury filed in from a side door. Immediately behind them came the accused, Seth Coleman, along with a uniformed officer on each side of him. On their heels was Adam Burke.

A door opened on the other side of the room, and the bailiff came in with prosecuting attorney Hansel Vandeveer behind him. Vandeveer took his seat at a table to the left of the bench, and the defendant and Adam Burke sat at a table to the right. The two uniformed men moved to the door they had entered with the prisoner and leaned against the wall.

The court reporter entered and made his

way to a small desk near the bench, notepad in hand.

There was a murmur of voices across the courtroom, but the sound faded quickly and died out as the door to the judge's chambers opened and the bailiff said loudly, "All rise!"

When the shuffle of feet subsided, the bailiff spoke again: "Court is now in session, the Honorable Judge Lucius P. Shagley presiding."

It was an equally hot day on Wednesday, August 8, and the courtroom was just as packed as it had been the previous two days. Women throughout the crowd used small fans to create a breeze on their faces.

Silence prevailed as the prosecuting attorney walked away from the jury box, having just delivered his final argument before the jury would retire for deliberations.

Adam Burke leaned close to his client and said, "Here goes. We're going to win, Seth. You just hold on."

Seth Coleman tried to smile but couldn't quite manage it.

A few rows back, Lance Rankin focused his eyes on the words his apprentice was scribbling on his notepad. Derek was describing the contrast between the dark-haired, brown-eyed attorney and his blond, blue-eyed client.

Judge Shagley looked at Adam over half-moon spectacles and said, "Mr. Burke, you may now approach the jury to make your closing argument."

Adam patted his client's shoulder and made his way to the jury box.

He gazed at the twelve somber-looking men and said, "Gentlemen, no one in this courtroom envies your position. You have on your shoulders a very heavy responsibility. My client's life is in your hands. We are all deeply sorry over the loss of Officer Lawrence Sheldon, who faithfully wore his badge and served this city well. My concern now is that we not lose another fine officer who has equally worn his badge and served us well."

Hansel Vandeveer leaped to his feet. "Objection! Your honor, Mr. Burke is forgetting that Seth Coleman is on trial for murder. Such a crime would nullify any prior service to the city when Mr. Coleman wore his badge. Mr. Burke is planting misleading information in the minds of the jury."

The judge was about to speak when Adam Burke said, "Your honor, may I respond to Mr. Vandeveer's objection?"

Shagley nodded. "You may."

"Thank you. Your honor, Mr. Vandeveer objects to my statement that Officer Seth Coleman has worn his badge faithfully and served this city well, saying that I am forgetting that my client is on trial for the murder of Officer Sheldon. I am not forgetting that fact at all. But Mr. Vandeveer is forgetting the foundational letter of the law: that my client is considered innocent until proven guilty. Therefore, I believe my statement regarding Officer Coleman's record as an honorable member of our police force plants nothing but the truth in the minds of these gentlemen who comprise the jury. His record stands by itself."

The judge nodded. "Objection overruled."

Vandeveer sat down, a scowl on his face.

Adam turned back to the jury. "Gentlemen, you have heard the prosecution declare that the two witnesses to the murder of Officer Sheldon positively identified my client as the man they saw stab Sheldon to death on the night of July 10. Yet, under cross-examination, you heard both witnesses falter in their answers when I asked them point-blank if they could, without hesitation, pull the trapdoor lever on the gallows to send Seth Coleman to his death for the murder they say they saw him commit.

"You are aware that my client has no alibi for that night, since he was off duty and has sworn under oath that he was home alone at the time the murder was committed. The two witnesses saw the killer stab Officer Sheldon three times, then run away. The witnesses have sworn under oath that it was Officer Seth Coleman they saw commit the murder and run away. Yet they are not so sure that they could pull the lever that would bring about his execution. You can see, then, that there is room for reasonable doubt."

Hardly a sound was heard in the courtroom except for the dull rustle of fans.

"In the prosecuting attorney's closing statement, he wanted to be sure you kept in mind that men in the Philadelphia Police Department know the accused and the victim had not gotten along well. Fine. Let me point out, however, that being at odds with a man is one thing; murdering him is another. And there is no conclusive evidence that Officer Coleman committed the crime.

"As you now retire to contemplate the case and decide my client's fate, please remember that on the first day of this trial, Chief of Police Mandrake Bennett, while under oath, presented to this court the impeccable record of my client as a police officer. Seth Coleman has put his life on the line many, many times in the past three years to protect the citizens of this city. Since there is reasonable doubt as to this officer's guilt, the only right and proper verdict for you to bring back to this courtroom is not guilty."

Burke took a deep breath and let it out. "Thank you for your kind attention, gentlemen. I have no doubt that you will do the right thing."

Judge Shagley addressed the jury about their duty to consider all they had heard from both the prosecution and the defense, and to carefully arrive at their verdict. When the jury was out of the room, Shagley adjourned the court until such time as the jury returned.

Near the back of the room, Lance Rankin whispered to Derek Mills, "Let's go out to the hall and go over a few things. I think it's a bit cooler out there."

They sat down on a bench and Rankin said, "Let me have a look at your notes." Mills handed over his notepad, and Rankin's eyes scanned the notes carefully. After a few minutes he handed them back and said, "Excellent. You're doing well."

A smile broke over Derek's face. "Whew! I'm glad to hear you say that!"

"I'll help you word some of these details so they'll blend with what we've already written for tomorrow's paper. If the jury comes back with the verdict I think they will, we'll have us a knockout of a story."

When Rankin and Mills returned to the courtroom, they glanced at the Sheldons, who were in a hushed conversation with family and friends. At the defendant's table, lawyer and client sat quietly, waiting for the jury to return.

The jury had been out for just over an hour when they filed in and took their seats in the jury box. The judge entered, and everyone in the courtroom rose to their feet at the bailiff's command.

When the judge and the audience were seated, Judge Shagley declared the court once again in session, then turned to the twelve men seated to his left. "Gentlemen of the jury, have you reached a verdict?"

The foreman rose and replied, "We have, your honor."

Shagley looked at Seth Coleman over his half-moon glasses. "The defendant will rise and face the jury."

Coleman stood up, and Burke stood with him.

"Mr. Foreman, what is your verdict?" the judge said.

The foreman looked directly at the defendant. "We, the jury, find the defendant, Seth Coleman, not guilty."

A rumble of approval moved across the crowded courtroom. Seth's knees felt watery as he breathed a sigh of relief and turned to his attorney. "Thank you, Adam. You did an excellent job defending me."

Adam patted Seth on the back. "I was only doing what an attorney is supposed to do. You are innocent, and you had to be declared so."

"No!" came a woman's voice from the group around Jack and Thelma Sheldon. "No-o-o! That man killed my cousin! He ought to hang!" Others in the small group joined her protest, railing at the jury.

Judge Shagley banged his gavel on the desk, shouting, "Order in this court! Order, I say, or I will have this courtroom cleared and those causing the disturbance will be arrested!" Shagley ran his gaze over the crowd then looked toward the defendant and said, "Officer Coleman, you have been duly tried in this court of law and have been found innocent of the murder of Officer Lawrence Sheldon. You are free to go."

The judge banged his gavel on the desk and declared the court adjourned.

Police chief Mandrake Bennett and most of the off-duty policemen hurried to Seth Coleman, congratulating him and saying they knew he was innocent. Other officers went to the Sheldons and talked to them in low tones.

Chief Bennett and the officers who had first gone to Coleman went to the Sheldons and spoke words of sympathy for the loss of their son. When the last officer walked away, the Sheldons headed for the table where Coleman and Burke stood talking to the two guards who had escorted Seth to the courtroom every day.

The couple halted a few steps away, waiting for an opportunity to speak. Seth was standing with his back to them. The two officers shook Seth's hand, saying it looked like the Sheldons wanted to speak to him. Adam stayed close by his client's side as Seth turned and looked at Jack and Thelma Sheldon, who were moving toward him with tears in their eyes.

"We would like to speak to you, Mr. Coleman," Jack Sheldon said. His features were haggard and pale.

"Certainly, sir."

"You know who we are, of course," said Thelma, blinking at her tears.

"We've never been formally introduced, but I know you're Lawrence's parents. I want you to know how sorry I am that he was taken from you. You have my deepest sympathy."

Jack Sheldon took a step closer to him. "My wife and I are Christians, Mr. Coleman. We are taught by God's Word to forgive those who trespass against us. Even though it's hard for us, we want to tell you that we forgive you for killing our son."

72

"Just hold on here," Adam said. "May I remind you that Seth has been tried by judge and jury, according to the law, and that appropriately and legally he has been found innocent of the crime? Both of you should agree with the verdict and conduct yourselves accordingly. Your concern should be to see the real killer tracked down and brought to justice."

"Thelma and I believe, Mr. Burke, that Mr. Coleman is guilty, in spite of his acquittal by the court."

Seth met Jack's teary gaze with steady eyes and said, "Mr. Sheldon, I did not kill your son. Yes, we had an argument. I disagreed with the way he handled an elderly man he brought to the station, but I didn't kill your son."

"And the court has agreed to that, Mr. Sheldon," Adam said. "That settles it, no matter what you believe."

"Mr. Coleman, Thelma and I just want to tell you that we forgive you for killing Lawrence."

Seth drew a sharp breath. "Mr. Sheldon, there is nothing to forgive. I did not kill your son."

"Let's go, dear," Thelma said. "We've told him we forgive him. There's nothing more we can say."

Jack gave his wife his arm, and they left the courtroom.

Adam laid a hand on Seth's shoulder and said, "I'm sorry, but don't let their attitude throw you. You know you're innocent, and you've been duly exonerated by the court. That's all that matters. If those people refuse to accept it, that's their problem."

It was early afternoon when Adam Burke entered the office of the Benson, Smith, and Walters law firm. Secretary Jill Hawkins smiled at him. "Good afternoon, Mr. Burke. Mr. Walters is in Mr. Smith's office, and they would like to see you."

"All right, Jill. I'll go see them in just a minute."

As he headed for his own office, Jill called after him, "Mr. Burke?"

"Yes?"

"Let me be the first to congratulate you. I know it was a tough case."

"Thank you, Jill. It was a tough case, but that fine officer of the law can now have his badge back. That's where my pleasure lies. He's innocent. Now he can get on with his life."

Adam entered his office, laid his briefcase on the desk, and went directly to Bradley Smith's office. He paused at the door, knocked, and called, "Better wake up in

74

there, I'm coming in!"

Smith and Walters were bending over the desk, examining some papers, when Adam entered. Both turned away from the desk, smiling broadly.

"Wake up, eh?" said Eric Walters. "Who can sleep on the job around here?"

Bradley Smith offered his hand first, and as Adam clasped it, he said, "Congratulations, Adam! I happened to run into Lance Rankin and another reporter on the street a few minutes after the trial was over. From what they said, you're going to be a hero in tomorrow morning's edition."

Adam shrugged. "All I did was defend an innocent man."

It was Eric's turn to shake Adam's hand. As he did, he said, "I commend you, my friend, on a job brilliantly and professionally done. If you keep up this kind of work, it won't be long till Mr. Benson will offer you a partnership in the firm. For sure he's going to be very happy when he gets back from New York and learns of your victory in this case."

Bradley chuckled. "Yes, sir, Adam, soon that sign on the door out there will say, Benson, Smith, Walters, and Burke, Attorneys at Law."

At quitting time, Adam Burke went to the

stable down the block where he kept his horse and buggy and headed for his apartment. The air was still hot and humid as the sun lowered toward the horizon. The buggy's top was down, and the breeze felt good on Adam's face.

While driving home, he relived the scene in the courtroom when the jury foreman read the verdict. This was indeed the most important case of Adam Burke's career, and he had won it. He hoped Philipa — and her parents too — would be proud of him. Especially her father.

After a courtship of more than a year, Adam had asked Philipa Conrad to marry him. She now wore his engagement ring, and the wedding was planned for the third Saturday of October.

As the buggy rolled along the streets of Philadelphia, Adam thought of how fortunate he was to be engaged to the only daughter of Philip Conrad III. To marry into such a prominent family of attorneys was quite a feather in his cap.

Philip Conrad had established the Conrad law firm some thirty years ago. Philip II — now retired because of ill health — had inherited the firm upon the death of his father in 1855. Philip III had taken it over upon his father's retirement some thirteen months ago, and the firm was doing better than ever under his leadership.

Adam turned the last corner and headed toward his apartment building. Philipa's parents were happy that she was marrying a successful Harvard law graduate. Today's victory in such a highly publicized case would surely make them even happier that Philipa was going to bring Adam into the family.

He took a deep breath as he drew near the apartment building. Things couldn't be any better. All of his dreams were coming true.

5

Adam Burke smiled to himself as he climbed the stairs to his apartment. Bradley Smith's words echoed through his mind: "Soon that sign on the door out there will say Benson, Smith, Walters, and Burke, Attorneys at Law!"

He inserted his key in the door and moved inside the apartment. Though a partnership in the firm was attractive, he had one burning desire. Upon his graduation from Harvard Law School — which his mother had not lived to see — Uncle Sidney had taken him on a trip to California. Adam had fallen in love with the West and had promised himself that once he was established as a successful attorney, he would go there and set up his own law firm.

He went to the small washroom at the rear of the apartment and splashed water on his face and ran a comb through his hair. Maybe tonight — with today's victory as a springboard — he would reveal his big dream to the woman he loved.

Seth Coleman stood before Mandrake Bennett in the chief's office, his heart light for the first time since he had been arrested and jailed for the murder of Lawrence Sheldon.

Two police captains and three lieutenants looked on as Chief Bennett opened a desk drawer and took out a shiny badge. He pinned it on Seth's shirt, saying, "Officer Coleman, it is with great pleasure that I return this badge to you."

The other policemen applauded, and Bennett gripped Seth's hand. "I'm plenty glad to have you back, son. You will report for duty tomorrow morning at the regular time."

"Yes, sir," Seth replied, a wide smile on his face.

Bennett reached into the drawer again and took out a holstered revolver with a belt wrapped around it. "You might need this, too."

There was just one dark cloud over Seth's joy as he drove his buggy through the streets of Philadelphia toward the boardinghouse where he lived.

Bettieann.

He had been very close to asking Bettieann Ralston to marry him before he was arrested.

His mind went back to the day he was jailed . . .

Seth Coleman sat on the cot in his cell, his face buried in his hands. He heard footsteps echoing down the corridor, and a guard appeared with Chief Mandrake Bennett at his side.

Seth moved up to the cell door and looked at Bennett through the bars. The guard told the chief to tap on the steel door when he was ready to go, then he walked away, leaving the two of them alone.

"I want you to tell me the truth, Seth. Did you do it?"

Seth looked the chief straight in the eye. "No, sir, I did not. Lawrence and I didn't get along, as you know, but whoever those witnesses are who said I stabbed Lawrence, they're mistaken. I was home alone when Lawrence was killed. I didn't do it."

"I believe you."

"Thank you, sir."

"Now, what about a lawyer?"

"I have one, sir, a young lawyer named Adam Burke. He was here a few minutes ago and assured me he'd do everything in his power to see me acquitted. I'm just . . . I'm still in shock, sir. I just can't believe I'm locked up in this jail and have to face a judge and jury for something I didn't do."

"Well, you keep your chin up, son. I believe you're innocent and that justice will be done."

"I sure hope so, sir."

"You just believe it, son. Now . . . I hate to bring this up, but I'm sure you know that it's department policy that until the trial is over I have to put you on suspension without pay."

"Yes, sir."

"When you're acquitted and back on the force, you'll receive all of your back pay." With those words, Bennett reached through the bars, shook Seth's hand, and walked away.

It was early afternoon the next day when two fellow officers, Ray Downs and Cliff Palmer, came to see him.

When they were about to leave, Seth said, "Fellas, I need a favor."

"Name it," Palmer said.

"You know Bettieann . . ."

"Sure. How's she taking this?"

"That's where I need the favor. She hasn't been here yet. Could you guys drop by her house and tell her that I really need to see her?"

"What's her address?"

"314 Baker Street."

"We'll go by there right now," Downs said.

As the officers headed down the corridor, a guard came toward Seth's cell and said, "Your attorney's here to see you, Coleman."

Adam Burke had more questions about the case, and Seth felt even more encouraged than when he had talked to Burke the first time.

It was late afternoon the next day when a guard approached the cell and said, "You've got a couple of visitors to see you, Coleman. Since they're not policemen, I'll have to take you to the visitor's room."

Seth followed a guard to a small booth where he was told to sit on a straight-backed chair. A barred window showed him two chairs on the other side. A few minutes later, the door on the other side opened. Seth saw the same guard enter, and behind him came Claude Ralston and his daughter.

Seth stood to his feet. "Bettieann! Oh, I'm so glad to see —"

The look on her face stopped him cold.

"When you two are ready to leave," the guard said, "just rap on the door. Remember, ten minutes at the most."

"We won't need that long," Claude said. "In fact, we don't even need to sit down."

He moved up beside Bettieann and said, "Seth, this poor girl hasn't eaten or slept for nearly two days. I brought her here so she could tell you what she has to say, and that'll be the last you ever see her. Go ahead, honey. Tell him."

"What a disappointment you have turned out to be, Officer Coleman!" Bettieann said. "Murdered a fellow policeman! I'm so ashamed before my family and friends for ever letting you court me!"

Seth's mouth went dry. "Bettieann, I didn't kill Lawrence Sheldon."

"The papers all say there are witnesses who will swear in court that they saw you do it. Don't lie to me, Seth! You told me yourself that you didn't like Lawrence."

"No, I didn't like him, but I didn't kill him. Bettieann, you've got to believe me! I'm not a murderer!"

"But those two people saw you do it!"

Tears filled Seth's eyes. "They're mistaken. It wasn't me. Bettieann, you told me you loved me. If you love me, why don't you believe me?"

"I did love you, Seth. I truly did. I had such hopes and dreams for us. But after what you did . . ." She turned her back on the barred window and said, "Daddy, I have no more to say to him. Let's go."

Claude gave Seth a hard look and said, "I'm sure glad we found out your true character before Bettieann ended up marrying you."

Seth watched as Ralston put an arm around his daughter and ushered her to the door. Neither one looked back as the guard opened the door for them.

Seth guided the buggy around a corner and blinked at the tears in his eyes. Since news traveled fast in Philadelphia, Bettieann might have already heard about the outcome of the trial. If he could just get a glimpse of her again . . .

The Ralston house came into view, and he could see Bettieann and her mother standing on the porch, talking to a couple of women. He slowed the horse as he drew near the house, pulled over, and stopped.

Seth looked at Bettieann and said, "Have you heard what happened at the trial?"

The look on her face made his heart sink. "Yes, we heard. That fancy-pants lawyer hypnotized the jury, that's all. We know the truth, though, don't we, Seth? Those witnesses saw you do it."

Seth closed his eyes and drew in a ragged breath, releasing it slowly. Without another look at Bettieann, he urged the horse into motion and drove away.

Adam Burke left his apartment, eager to get

to the Conrad home. He scanned the sky as he approached his buggy and decided to leave the top down. Less than fifteen minutes later, he wheeled into the tree-lined circular driveway and drew rein in front of the Conrads' mansion.

Adam smiled at the silver-haired butler who answered his knock. "Good evening, Delmar. And how are you?"

Delmar managed a slight smile. "Just fine, Mr. Burke. Please come in. Miss Philipa is expecting you." Adam stepped inside and Delmar closed the door. "I heard about your success in the Coleman trial, sir. May I be the first in this household to congratulate you?"

"Thank you."

"Mr. and Mrs. Conrad are in the drawing room. I will take you there, then go upstairs and advise Miss Philipa that you are here."

Adam followed the butler through the spacious foyer. When Delmar reached the drawing room door, he tapped on it and said, "It is Delmar. I have Miss Philipa's fiancé."

"Bring him in!" Philip Conrad said.

Candlelight cast a warm glow on the richly tapestried walls and the large paintings that decorated them. A faint hint of beeswax filled the air.

"Mr. Adam Burke," Delmar announced.

Philip stood next to a lavish overstuffed loveseat where his wife, Millicent, was seated. "Do come in, Adam!" Philip said.

The thick carpet muted Adam's footsteps as he moved toward the pair, who were both smiling at him.

Philip Conrad extended his hand. "Young man, it's all over town! Millicent and I are so proud of you!"

"Thank you, sir. It means a lot that you would say that."

"We most certainly are proud of you," said Millicent as she offered Adam her hand. "Philip and I are happier than ever that our daughter is going to marry you."

Adam took her dainty hand in his, bowed slightly, and said, "Thank you, ma'am. It means more than I can tell you to hear it. And may I say you look ravishing this evening."

"Thank you, Adam."

At that moment, Philipa swept into the room. "Adam, darling, what wonderful news! I'm so happy for Officer Coleman, and for you!"

Philipa rushed to him and gave him a brief embrace. Then she looked into his eyes and said, "Darling, I'm so proud of you. In the eyes of most Philadelphians, you stand ten feet tall!"

Adam smiled down at her, drinking in her beauty.

Philipa was a younger version of her mother, with the same high cheekbones, delicate ivory skin, and startling blue eyes. She wore a slipper satin gown that almost matched the color of her eyes.

"Adam," Philip said, "I'd like to discuss the trial with you. From what I've read in the papers, you came up with some excellent tactics." He clapped a hand on Adam's shoulder. "I feel sure that one day soon you'll be made a partner in the Benson firm. Has anything been said to you along that line?"

"Well, sir, Brad and Eric said they expected it to happen, but Mr. Benson hasn't said anything yet."

Philip laughed. "If George Benson doesn't make you a partner pretty soon, I just might make you an offer myself!"

"Well," Philipa said, "we'd best be going." She placed a hand on Adam's sleeve and moved toward the door.

"Have a nice time, children," Millicent said.

Philip and Millicent followed as far as the drawing room door and watched Adam and their daughter disappear into the warm twilight.

Adam drove the buggy to downtown Philadelphia, and Philipa held on to his arm and watched the lamplighters at work along the streets. Soon they pulled up in front of the Royal Crest Restaurant, and a uniformed attendant appeared and called Adam by name. Adam jumped down and hurried to the other side to help Philipa down. An attendant drove away to park the buggy.

Inside the restaurant, Adam and Philipa were met by the host, who smiled and said, "Good evening Miss Conrad, Mr. Burke. Tell me, Miss Conrad, how are your parents? I haven't seen them for a while."

"They're fine, Royce. I'm sure they will be in sometime soon."

When they reached the candlelit table, and Adam had seated Philipa, she said, "Royce must not read the papers or he would have congratulated you, I'm sure."

The waiter came, gave them menus, and returned shortly thereafter to take their order.

Soon they were enjoying a delicious meal. From time to time, people at other tables looked their way, and Philipa enjoyed their admiring glances.

They ate leisurely while Adam tried to work up the courage to tell Philipa about moving west. He listened to her talk about the wedding. Philipa said she hoped Adam's sisters — whom she had never met — would be able to come; Adam assured her they would be there.

Conversation dwindled for a moment. Just as Adam opened his mouth to speak, Philipa said, "Darling, I can't hold it in any longer."

"Hold what in?"

There was a twinkle in her eyes. "I overheard my parents talking last night in the library when they thought I was up in my room. And guess what?"

"I . . . have no idea."

"Mother and Daddy are planning to give us a new house for a wedding present!"

"You mean, build us one?"

"No, it's already built. You remember the big white mansion on the corner, down from our house? With the three bird baths in the front yard?"

"Umm. Yes."

"The people who own it are going to put it up for sale in about a month. Somehow Daddy found this out. He told Mother that he talked to Mr. Jensen — that's the man who owns it — and Mr. Jensen is quite willing to negotiate. So Daddy's going to go back and talk to him tomorrow. He's certain he can strike a deal. The mansion is as good as ours. The Jensens are moving somewhere down south where hired help comes much cheaper than here. So when Daddy buys the house for us, it'll come with a built-in maid, cook, butler, and caretaker. What do you think of that?"

Adam smiled weakly. "Well, I . . . I'm surprised. I really don't expect your parents to give us a house. I would think that we should buy our own house."

Philipa reached across the table and took his hand. "Darling, it would hurt Mother and Daddy's feelings if we turned down their gift. This is their only opportunity to do something like this."

"I don't want to hurt their feelings, but . . ."

"But what?"

"But . . . well, there are a lot of things to consider when you get married and start a new home. You have to go a bit slow in making plans. I don't think we should rush into anything."

Suddenly Philipa's attention was drawn to the front of the restaurant. "Oh, darling, it's the Krantzes!" She waved to draw their attention.

Adam turned in his chair and saw a middle-aged couple smiling at Philipa. The man spoke to the host, and the couple began threading their way among the maze of tables.

Adam leaned toward Philipa. "Who are the Krantzes?"

"You've heard of the Atlantic Coast Construction Company, haven't you? Well, Edgar and Doris are part of the Krantz family who owns the company. They live just two blocks east of us on Frankford Avenue."

Adam nodded. "I've heard the Krantz name ever since I came to Philadelphia, but I didn't realize they were connected with the big construction company."

Edgar and Doris drew up to the table, and Adam stood to his feet. Philipa introduced him, and as Edgar shook Adam's hand, he said, "I've been reading about you in the *Philadelphia Enquirer*, Adam. I commend you for a brilliant job of defense."

"Thank you, sir."

"You know, I felt all along that Seth Coleman was innocent."

"So did most people, sir," Adam said with a smile.

Doris glanced at the host, who was waiting a bit impatiently, and said, "Edgar, Royce needs to get us seated."

The Krantzes politely excused themselves, telling Philipa to give their regards to her parents.

Philipa watched them for a few seconds, then said to Adam, "Edgar and Doris do a lot of philanthropic work. They give to many hospitals and sanitariums, but their favorite charity is the Philadelphia Orphanage."

"That's commendable," Adam said. "My heart always goes out to children who have to be brought up in an orphanage."

He noticed Philipa looking toward the area where the Krantzes were being led by the host.

"The Krantzes are being invited to join Ralph and Louise Zimmerman," she said. "They recently moved to Philadelphia and live in the same block on Frankford Avenue as the Krantzes. Ralph is big in real estate."

"I see."

Philipa took her last sip of tea and smiled at her fiancé. "I'm finished."

Adam signaled to the waiter, who was delivering a tray of food to a table close by.

"Philipa, you remember that the lawyers' convention is starting here next Monday, don't you?"

"How could I forget? Daddy's been talking about it morning and night."

"I'll be tied up all day every day, and on Monday and Tuesday evenings."

"Yes, but on Wednesday evening they have the big dinner. I've been planning on attending it with you ever since you brought it up two months ago."

"Good. I just didn't want you to forget. It will be my pleasure to show you off to lawyers from all over the east coast."

Philipa's features tinted. "I'm glad you feel that way about me."

Adam grinned. "How could I feel any different?"

Adam paid the bill, and they left the restaurant. The attendant brought the buggy, and Adam helped Philipa climb in. They took the long way home.

As they moved slowly through the streets, Philipa gazed at the moon and the stars and said, "I'm so glad the top on this buggy folds down. It sure makes a ride like this more pleasurable."

"It was moonlight rides like this that I had in mind when I bought it."

She snuggled under his arm and kissed his cheek. "You're the crafty one, aren't you?"

Adam chuckled, thinking of the plans he had not yet revealed to her. "I guess you could say that."

6

"Oh, Edgar," Doris Krantz said, "it's the Masons. See if you can get their attention. I'd like to introduce them to Ralph and Louise."

Edgar turned and waved and soon had the Masons' attention. When he pointed to the Zimmermans, Joseph Mason nodded.

"Who are those people, Edgar?" Ralph Zimmerman asked.

"Joseph and Nancy Mason and their daughter, Rachel. They live a few blocks from us . . . nice people."

"My, what a pretty girl!" said Louise, fixing her gaze on Rachel.

"Not only that," Doris said, "she's very charming."

When the Masons walked up to the table, Edgar made the introductions, and pointed out that Joseph Mason owned Philadelphia's most successful brokerage firm.

"Oh, really?" Ralph said. "What's the name of your company, Mr. Mason?"

Joseph reached into his shirt pocket, took

out a business card, and handed it to Ralph. "American Securities Company. The address is here on the card. If I can ever be of service, please come and see me."

"I do a lot of investing," Ralph said. "You'll see me very soon."

"Well, why don't you let me take you to lunch whenever you're free?"

"Well, let's see. Tomorrow's Thursday . . . how about Friday?"

"Friday it is. Why don't you come to my office just before noon and we'll walk to a nice restaurant close by."

"I'll be there."

"Daddy, I really think you should be honest with Mr. Zimmerman," Rachel said.

"Be honest with him about what, honey?"

Rachel had an impish twinkle in her eyes. "Mr. Zimmerman, I hate to tell you this, but my father is the janitor at American Securities. He has these moments when he thinks he's the head of the company."

"Well, Miss Mason, I appreciate this information. Who, then, actually is the head of the company?"

Rachel giggled. "Why, me, of course! If you want to make some investments, see me in my office on Friday. My father even had his name painted on the door and had mine taken off. But this is the kind of thing I've had to put up with since I was nine and became president of the company."

"All right, Miss Rachel Mason," said Ralph, laughing, "I'll be at your office just before noon on Friday."

"Oh! I just remembered that I already have a luncheon engagement on Friday. I'll have to let you go to lunch with my janitor."

Joseph tweaked his daughter's nose and said, "Okay, boss, I'll take Mr. Zimmerman to lunch for you."

There was more laughter, then Doris said, "Nancy, you're still planning on coming to my house next month to attend the fund-raising meeting for the Philadelphia Orphanage, aren't you?"

"Of course. Thursday, September 13. I'm looking forward to it. Is Louise coming?"

Doris glanced at her friend. "I haven't asked her yet."

"Sounds interesting," Louise said. "You can fill me in on it later, Doris."

"Well, wife and daughter," Joseph said, "the waiter is at our table, wanting to take our order. We'd better go oblige."

When the Masons were out of earshot, Ralph said, "Now there's a sharp little gal, that Rachel!"

"Isn't she, though?" Louise said. "Is Nancy not well? She looks a little peaked."

"I was thinking the same thing," Ralph said.

"Nancy was quite ill as a girl," Doris said. "She's never looked healthy since we've known her. Joseph told us one time that Nancy had a very hard time carrying and giving birth to Rachel and was never able to have any more children. She's quite frail and has some bad days."

"Poor dear. She seems to be a very sweet person."

"That she is. And she loves children. She and Joseph give heavily to the orphanage."

"They both love children," Edgar said. "It's too bad they couldn't have had more. They once seriously considered adopting another child, but Nancy's doctors warned them against it unless they were willing to hire a nanny. But Nancy wouldn't do it. Told them that if she couldn't be a mother to an adopted child, they wouldn't adopt one."

"So the Masons found another way to show love to children," Doris said. "They've poured themselves into the work of the orphanage and are quite active in helping to raise money for it, as well as giving very liberally to it themselves."

"Doris, I really would like to come to that fund-raising meeting at your house," Louise said. "You see, I was orphaned at six years of age. I was fortunate to be adopted by a well-to-do family, but most orphans aren't as blessed as I was. I'd like to help raise funds as well as contribute to the orphanage."

"Agreed," Ralph said. "We'll give liberally, I promise."

"Wonderful!" Doris replied. "I have some printed material on the orphanage at home. I'll make sure you get it."

Louise nodded. "And the meeting is at your house on September 13, right?"

"Yes. We'll start about two that afternoon."

"I'll be there."

Seth Coleman was excited about his first day back on the police force. He arrived for duty a bit early, and most of his fellow officers greeted him with smiles and words of encouragement.

When he entered Chief Mandrake Bennett's office, the chief stuck out his hand and said, "Good morning, Officer Coleman! Ready for duty, I see."

"Yes, sir."

Bennett lifted a pay envelope off the desk and handed it to Seth. "Here's that back pay I promised you."

"Thank you, sir." Seth slipped the envelope into his hip pocket.

Bennett noted a look of concern in the young officer's eyes and said, "Hey, is something bothering you?"

Seth nodded. "There is something bothering me. Some of the men gave me the cold shoulder when I came in. Though no one said it, I get the impression they still think I murdered Lawrence."

The chief sighed. "Well, son, some of Lawrence's closest friends are finding it difficult to accept his death. But they'll get over it in time."

"I understand the difficulty of getting over his death, sir, but why give me the cold shoulder? The very legal system they work for has exonerated me of the crime."

"You're right. And those men who shunned you will wake up to that fact shortly and realize how wrong they've been."

"I sure hope that happens soon, sir. It's pretty hard to work with other policemen who think I murdered one of our own."

When Seth went out on the street, he found that some of Philadelphia's citizens had not accepted the jury's verdict either.

By the end of the day on the following Monday, Seth entered his apartment very discouraged. He sat in an overstuffed chair by the window that overlooked the street and watched the traffic below. People were going about their normal lives, but his life had been anything but normal since the day of his arrest.

After a few minutes, he went to a dresser drawer, took out an envelope, a pen, and some paper, and sat at the kitchen table. He addressed the envelope to the Chief United States Marshal's Office in Washington, D.C., then wrote the letter, asking for an application to become a deputy U.S. marshal.

The next morning Seth mailed the letter on his way to the police station.

On the evening of August 15, Adam Burke and Philipa Conrad were seated at a table with her parents and other lawyers and their wives, enjoying a lavish meal.

The convention had proven profitable and enjoyable for the three hundred lawyers who had gathered in Philadelphia to sharpen their skills, learn from one another, and enjoy the social functions that went with it.

Everyone knew there was to be a special after-dinner speaker that evening, but the leaders of the convention had kept it a secret. George Benson, who was chairman of the convention, had not divulged the speaker's identity even to his partners in the firm.

When the meal was over, Benson stood to his feet, lifted his voice above the rumble of conversations that filled the room, and called for attention. Adam helped Philipa position her chair to face the head table, then turned his chair around. He glanced at the head table and saw a familiar face next to his boss, then leaned close to Philipa and whispered, "I just saw the speaker for the first time. It's Dr. Manfred Welles, my favorite professor at Harvard!"

"Oh, really? I recall you mentioning his name to me several times."

"Brilliant man," Adam said.

Welles spotted Adam, and when their eyes met, they smiled and nodded at each other.

George Benson finished his introduction of Manfred Welles, and several attorneys — including Adam Burke — quickly rose to their feet, applauding. Soon the entire crowd was standing and applauding enthusiastically.

Welles smiled and waited patiently for the applause to run its course. When everyone was seated, he thanked them for the warm welcome and began recounting some of his experiences with law students at Harvard. Pointing to Adam, Welles told of an experience in class that had made it clear to him Adam was going to be an outstanding attorney.

Philipa reached over and took Adam's hand, whispering, "He's talking about my future husband! I'm so proud of you, darling."

Adam raised her hand to his lips and kissed it softly.

Dr. Welles looked at Adam, then said to the crowd, "Chairman Benson is Adam Burke's boss, folks. During dinner he told me of Mr. Burke's success thus far in his firm, especially the case he recently won involving a Philadelphia police officer who had been falsely accused of murder."

There were cheers and applause.

"I have to tell you, folks, that except for my help, Mr. Burke would never have made it in the legal field. He would probably be pushing a broom in some Boston warehouse!"

Everyone laughed.

Welles went on with his speech, addressing the problems facing lawyers and challenging every lawyer present to serve his clients better than ever before.

When the speech was finished, the crowd applauded vigorously. George Benson made a few remarks and then announced the end of the convention.

Adam took Philipa by the hand. "Come on, honey, I want you to meet Dr. Welles."

They had to wait a few seconds for others who had reached Welles first, but soon Adam was able to introduce his former professor to his fiancée. Welles greeted Philipa warmly, saying he always knew Adam would find a beautiful and charming young woman to marry. He was also impressed when Adam told him that Philipa was the daughter of Philip Conrad III.

"Sir," Adam said, "I notice that Mrs. Welles isn't with you. I hope she's not ill."

"Oh, no. Martha would've come with me, but our youngest daughter, Patricia, is about to give birth, and Martha felt she should stay with her."

"I don't blame her. Please greet her for me when you get home, sir."

"I'll do that."

"So when are you putting the ball and chain on this young man?" Welles said, looking at Philipa.

"October, sir."

"We sure would be honored if you and Mrs. Welles could come," Adam said.

"We'd love to come, Adam, but it might not be possible."

"Oh?"

"Mmm-hmm. Say, my train doesn't leave until late afternoon tomorrow. I'm staying at the Pennsylvania Hotel. Could you meet me at the hotel dining room at noon? I'd sure like to spend a little time with you."

"I've got a court date in the morning, sir, but the judges in this city like to eat at noon, so I'm sure there'll be an adjournment at about eleven-thirty. I'll look forward to having lunch with you."

"Wonderful!" Welles shook hands with Adam, told Philipa how glad he was to have met her, and turned to other people who were waiting to talk to him.

At noon the next day, Adam Burke and Manfred Welles sat at lunch, enjoying their time together. After talking about Adam's days at Harvard, Welles said, "Last night when you said you would like for Martha and me to come to your wedding, I said it might not be possible. I'd like to explain what I meant."

"Good. You've had me wondering about that."

"I haven't told anyone here about it, Adam, but I recently resigned my position at Harvard."

"You . . . you resigned your professorship, sir?"

"That's right."

"But you're too young to retire."

"I turned fifty-one in May, Adam, but my resigning at Harvard doesn't mean I'm retiring."

"Well, good, I'm glad to hear that. What are you planning to do, sir?"

"Let me preface my answer by first telling you that several years ago I took Martha on a trip to Cheyenne City, Wyoming. We had some friends who moved there, and they asked us to come visit them. Well, we did . . . and I fell in love with the West."

Adam inched forward on his chair. "Really, sir?"

"I've had a hankering to move out to the wide open spaces ever since."

Adam smiled. "So you're going out west?"

"That's right . . . to Grand Island, Nebraska. We had to cross Nebraska to get to Cheyenne City, and that big sky and the openness of it captured me. I have a lawyer friend who has been in Grand Island for some fifteen years. The town has grown steadily, and so has my friend's practice. He wrote me a couple of months ago, asking if I would come out and become his partner. I took him up on it. This is why I couldn't commit to coming to your wedding."

Welles looked closely at Adam and said, "You seem excited about something I've said. What is it?"

"Well, sir, right after I graduated from Harvard, my uncle in Boston took me with him on a trip to California. Those wide open spaces captured me, too. I see the western frontier as a place where a man can breathe free. I've made up my mind that I'm taking Philipa out there to start our married life. I'm going to find a growing town and establish my own law firm. The way people are moving west, I'm sure if I choose the right town, I can build a successful firm. It's my dream."

"I have no doubt you'll do fine, Adam. At my age I'm glad I don't have to start from scratch. The partnership sounds great to me. But you're just the one to build your business from the ground up."

"Dr. Welles, how about your wife? Is she as excited about moving to Grand Island as you are?"

"Well, she wasn't too excited about it at first. But when she saw how much it meant to me, she said she would gladly move out there."

"I'm sure that means a lot to you."

"I'll say." Welles paused. "And how about Philipa? Is she happy about your plans?"

"Well, sir, I . . . ah . . . haven't talked to her about it yet."

"Isn't the wedding set for October?"

"Yes, sir. The latter part of October, but I know it's not very far away. The reason I haven't talked to her about it yet is because living out West will be vastly different from living here in Philadelphia. It will be quite a change. I . . . I just haven't found a way to bring it up to her."

"Well, Adam, you need to do that soon. But from what I could see last night, that girl adores you. If a woman loves her man, she'll go along with his big dream."

Adam grinned. "That's what I think, sir."

Welles snapped his fingers. "I just thought of something."

"What's that, sir?"

"Before I tell you, have you got some growing town in mind?"

"I've done a little reading, but I haven't set my mind on any particular location yet. I figured that once I told Philipa about it, I'd get down to business about just exactly where to go. What were you going to tell me?"

"It just came to me. When my friend in Grand Island wrote about coming out there, he mentioned that North Platte, Nebraska, is in dire need of a law firm. The people there have to go all the way to Grand Island for legal help. You ought to seriously consider North Platte."

"I will, sir. Thank you for telling me about it."

"Let me write down the name of the law firm in Grand Island. I want you to write and let me know wherever you end up. Will you do that?"

"I sure will, sir. And if it's North Platte,

maybe we can see each other once in a while."

The next day, after getting some help at the county courthouse, Adam wrote to Ben Colter, sheriff of Lincoln County, Nebraska, for information about North Platte.

7

Seth Coleman entered police headquarters and headed for Chief Bennett's office with an envelope in his hand. Two officers were coming down the hall toward him.

"How was your day, Seth?" one of them asked.

"One of the quiet kind. Nice to have a quiet one now and then."

"For sure," the other officer said. "Everything back to normal for you?"

"Not quite," Seth said as they passed in the hall.

"Little more time yet?"

"Yeah, I suppose."

Seth drew up to the chief's door and knocked, and he heard a muffled command to enter. Seth opened the door and paused, setting his gaze on the man behind the desk. "Would you have time to see me, sir?"

"Sure," said Bennett, laying down a paper in his hand. "Come in and sit down, Seth." He leaned forward, placing his elbows on the desk. "What can I do for you?"

"I hate to say this, Chief, but . . . I'm still having a problem with the treatment I'm getting from some of the men on the force."

"I take it it hasn't improved?"

"Oh, two or three of the men have quit giving me dirty looks and will at least speak to me. But other than that it's gotten worse. It's not much better with the people out there on the streets, either. Sir, I really think I need to move somewhere else to go on with my career as a law officer."

"I'm sorry to hear that, Seth. I still think that in time this attitude will disappear."

"Sir, I'll be honest with you. I'm just not willing to give it any more time. I don't mean to contradict you, but the way I see it, the problem is only going to get worse. These people have their minds made up that I murdered Lawrence Sheldon, and nothing is going to change that. I've got to get out of Philadelphia."

"I know you don't have family to be concerned about, but you do have friends here. Would it be that easy just to pack up and leave? Besides, where would you go?"

Seth laid the envelope on the desk.

"What's this?" Bennett asked.

"It's a letter from the U.S. marshal's office in Washington. I wrote and asked for an application form. I'm going to apply to become a deputy United States marshal. They sent me an encouraging reply and the application form. They've also enclosed papers for you to fill out. I have to have your recommendation in order to proceed with the application."

Bennett took the papers out of the envelope, gave them a quick once-over, and said, "I hate the idea of losing you, Seth, but I assure you, you'll get the highest recommendation from me. But won't you reconsider staying?"

"I really need to get away from here, Chief. There's more to it than you know."

"What do you mean?"

"Well, I was about to ask the young lady I've been courting for some time to marry me. But —" Seth swallowed hard. "But when I went to jail she turned against me and wouldn't believe me when I told her I was innocent. Nothing changed when I was acquitted. She still thinks I murdered Lawrence."

"I'm sorry about this. You're still in love with her, aren't you?"

Seth nodded.

"Well, it seems to me that if she loved you like you thought she did, she'd believe you."

"Yes, sir. I . . . I just need to get away from here, sir."

Bennett sighed. "I understand. Like I said,

I hate to lose you, but I'll fill out this report and send it to the U.S. marshal's office right away." As he spoke, he handed the envelope and its other contents back to Seth.

Seth rose from his chair and reached across the desk to shake Bennett's hand. "Thank you for understanding, sir. You've been very good to me."

Bennett gripped his hand firmly. "I'll miss you, Officer Coleman."

"I'll miss you too, sir. And please know that until I leave, I'll strive to be the best officer you have on the force."

"I have no doubt of that."

Seth stepped out of the chief's office and headed for the front door. Hank Moldow and Keith Dailey were just coming on duty, and when they drew abreast of him, they stopped.

"Well, whattya know, Keith?" Moldow said. "Here's Lawrence Sheldon's old pal. I wonder if he misses him like we do."

"I doubt it," Dailey said.

"I don't have time for this," Seth said. "Kindly get out of my way."

Moldow sneered. "He wants us to be kindly toward him. You know . . . like he was toward Lawrence."

"I said I don't have time for this." Seth started to move past them.

Dailey started to say something but stopped

when four officers came through the front door. When they were out of earshot, he said, "So you don't have time for this, eh? Lawrence's time on earth was cut short, wasn't it?"

"Yes, it was," Seth replied, "but not by me."

Moldow smiled. "Marvelous what a sharp lawyer can do with a jury, isn't it?"

"Get out of my way."

"Why don't you make me?" Moldow said.

Seth's right fist connected solidly with Moldow's jaw. Moldow was down on his back in a split second, dazed and wondering what had happened.

Seth ducked Dailey's fist and smashed a wicked uppercut to Dailey's jaw. The blow lifted the man off his feet, and he joined his friend on the floor.

"What's going on here?" came a familiar voice from behind.

Moldow rubbed his jaw and said, "Chief, I don't know what got into Coleman. We were talking to him all friendly like, and he up and punches both of us, taking us by surprise."

"That's right, Chief," said Dailey, rising unsteadily to his feet.

Bennett's face flushed and his eyes narrowed. "Both of you are liars! I've been watching this scene from my office door since it started. I heard every word. And I saw exactly what happened. Moldow, Dailey, I want your badges and your guns right now. You two are on suspension until you face the internal affairs committee for what you did to Officer Coleman!"

Dailey rubbed his jaw. "But, sir, we —"

"You heard me! I want those guns and those badges this instant! You're on suspension!"

"Chief Bennett, sir," Seth said, "may I . . . may I ask you not to do this? I'm willing to forget it if you will."

"Officer Coleman, I appreciate your attitude, but the conduct I just witnessed is inexcusable, and it's not going to be tolerated in this department. These two men must be disciplined."

As the officers handed Bennett their guns and badges, he turned to Seth and said, "I understand even better now why you made the decision that brought you to my office today."

The next day, dark clouds were hovering over Philadelphia. The air was hot and muggy, and though the wind was picking up, it did little to cool the air.

Adam Burke left the courthouse after a long, tedious day in court. When he reached the stable, he glanced up at the heavy clouds and took the time to put the top up on the buggy. He drove through the streets of the city and felt closed in by the tall buildings on every side. For the last few days, Adam had rushed home in eager anticipation of the letter he was expecting from Sheriff Ben Colter. If the letter held what he thought it would, he would soon be free from the confines of Philadelphia.

Adam arrived at his apartment and hurried to his mailbox. He sifted through the envelopes until his eyes fell on one from North Platte, Nebraska. He rushed inside the apartment and set his briefcase on the table, dropping his other mail beside it.

Adam noticed in the upper left-hand corner that it was from William C. Dauntt, chairman of North Platte's town council. He tore open the envelope and took out the letter.

Dauntt explained that Sheriff Ben Colter had passed Adam's letter on to him. He told Adam that the town had no lawyer at all. The people of North Platte were traveling to Grand Island to get legal advice or help, a distance of a hundred and twenty miles. Dauntt encouraged Adam to come and establish his law firm as soon as possible, assuring him that he would have plenty of clients in a hurry.

Adam let out his pent-up breath and shook the letter excitedly. "Yes! Yes! This is what I've been waiting for and dreaming about!"

Adam read the letter again, then carefully placed it back in the envelope and went to the washroom. He had a dinner date with Philipa tonight. He would tell her of his dream during dinner.

It was pouring down rain as Adam pulled the buggy up in front of the Conrad mansion. He opened his umbrella and bounded up the front steps. The wind was whipping the rain about as he lifted the door knocker and let it fall.

Delmar opened the door. "Good evening, Mr. Burke. Please come in out of the weather." Adam stepped inside, and Delmar took the umbrella. "I'll keep this here for you, sir." He placed it in a cane and umbrella holder and headed down the hall. "Follow me, sir. Mr. and Mrs. Conrad are in the library. Miss Philipa hasn't come down yet."

Philip and Millicent Conrad greeted Adam warmly. Philip smiled as he said, "We heard about your masterful handling of the Gregory Stedman case, Adam. You are to be congratulated once again."

"Yes," said Millicent. "We're very proud of you."

"Thank you," Adam said.

"So, Adam," Philip said, "has George Benson offered a partnership to you?"

"No, sir." Adam's eyes darted to the library door, hoping to see Philipa coming through it. He thought he heard the rustle of her skirt.

"Well, he'd better hurry or I'm going to make my future son-in-law an offer he can't refuse."

Suddenly Philipa swished through the door. "Daddy, dear, why don't you just go ahead and make Adam the offer? I say let's keep it in the family. It would be wonderful to have my husband a partner with my daddy! George Benson's loss would certainly be your gain."

"You know why I haven't made the offer yet, sweetie. Your old father still has ethics about him."

Philipa kissed Adam's cheek. "Hello, darling." She turned to her father and said, "How much longer will your ethics make you wait before you offer Adam a partnership?"

"Well, I figure to give it another month. If George hasn't made Adam an offer by then, I'll meet with him and tell him I'm about to make a partnership offer to my future son-in-law, and give him a chance to respond. If he doesn't, Adam will be offered a very lucrative partnership in the Conrad firm."

Philipa sighed. "Well, I hope Mr. Benson won't make the offer. I understand about your professional ethics, Daddy, and I appreciate that you're a man of principle, but it sure would make me happy if my husband was my father's partner."

"I'd love to see that too," Millicent said.

"Me too," Philip said. "But I have to shave this face every morning and look myself in the eye. Understand?"

Mother and daughter glanced at each other and smiled.

Adam seated Philipa at their table in the restaurant, then moved to the opposite side and sat down. After the waiter took their order, they talked about the day's events until the food came. Adam's stomach was so jittery he could hardly eat. By the time dessert came, he was almost nauseated. When the meal was finally over and they ordered fresh cups of coffee, Adam said, "Sweetheart, I . . . ah . . . I—"

"Yes, darling?" she said, smiling sweetly.

"I want to talk to you about something very important."

"All right. I'm listening."

"You remember Dr. Manfred Welles, my Harvard prof? Well, he told me just a few days ago that he has resigned from Harvard to become a partner with an old friend in a law firm in Grand Island, Nebraska."

"He what? Adam, you're kidding!"

"No. He was excited about it when he told me."

Philipa laughed and shook her head in amazement. "Well, you never know what some people will do. How could he ever give up his position at Harvard and leave the Boston area for such a remote, dried-up, dismal place like the plains of Nebraska?"

Adam was quiet for a moment as he stared into his coffee cup. Then he said, "Philipa, I . . . I have something I want to discuss with you."

"Good," she said. "Let's get our minds off Nebraska."

"Well, we can't exactly do that."

"Do what? Get our minds off Nebraska?"

"Yes. I have a letter from the chairman of the town council in North Platte, Nebraska, that I want to show you."

"You know someone in North Platte?"

"Not exactly. But I'm going to get acquainted with him when we move there."

Philipa squinted at him. "When we what?"

"Let me tell you what I've had in mind for some time, then I want you to read the letter."

"I don't think I want to hear this." Philipa squeezed her hands together until the knuckles were shiny white.

"Please, Philipa. Hear me out, will you?"

She made an effort to relax and nodded.

Slowly and carefully, with his heart in his throat, Adam told his fiancée about the dream that had long been in his heart to go to the West and establish his own law firm. He explained about the trip he had taken with Uncle Sidney and how the West had captivated him with its ruggedness and wide open spaces. Dr. Welles's decision to move to Grand Island and his mention of North Platte needing a law firm had encouraged him to look into it seriously. With that, he placed William Dauntt's letter into her hand and said, "Now, read this."

Philipa's mouth went dry as she read the letter. She swallowed with difficulty and struggled to keep her outward calm as she placed the letter back in Adam's hand and said, "It . . . was nice of Mr. Dauntt to write to you."

"Do you see what I'm saying, honey? I need to cut a new swath in life. Philadelphia has lots of lawyers. I'd like to go where I'm really needed. And you saw what Mr. Dauntt said about the people of North Platte having to make a hundred-and-twenty-mile trip to Grand Island for legal advice and help. That's a two-hundred-and-forty-mile round trip! I'm needed in North Platte. Can you see that?"

Philipa stared at him but did not reply.

"Look," Adam said, "I'm tired of big city life. Philadelphia is stifling me. I need the wide open spaces. You've never been out west but I'm sure you'd love it, too. A person can . . . can breathe out there!"

Suddenly Philipa broke into a laugh. "It's not April first, but you really are pulling a joke on me, aren't you, Adam? I know you couldn't pass up the opportunity that's going to come from Daddy if Mr. Benson doesn't make you a partner. Either way, you'll have a wonderful career ahead of you. You are kidding me, right? Either partnership will be much more lucrative than having your own law firm in North Platte or any of those smelly, dried-up Western cow towns."

"No, Philipa, I'm serious. Sure, getting started in North Platte would be a little tough, maybe, but you saw what Mr. Dauntt said about my having plenty of clients in a hurry. It wouldn't be long till I was bringing in a very good living. And even if I never make the kind of money I would in a partnership here, I'd still rather live out west. Besides, as far as money is concerned, I have a third of the estate Mom left my sisters and me. We'll never hurt financially with money coming in from Boston Clothiers for the rest of our lives." Adam leaned closer. "Honey, here's what I want to do. Let's move the wedding date up to mid-September. I'll write to Mr. Dauntt and tell him we'll be there shortly after we get married. How's that sound?"

Philipa put a hand to her mouth and pressed the tips of her fingers tightly against her lips.

"Now, honey, I know you're worried that North Platte might not have the kind of house we'd have if we stayed here. But as soon as we get to North Platte, I'll draw a chunk of cash out of the bank and build you a big, beautiful house that'll knock your eyes out! What do you say?"

Philipa took her hand away from her mouth, drew a shaky breath, and said, "Adam, I . . . I need some time. This is all so sudden."

"Of course. I understand. You take a day or two to think it over."

At the same time Adam and Philipa were having their conversation at the restaurant, Philip and Millicent Conrad were sitting in their library while rain beat against the windows.

Millicent was crocheting, and Philip had just picked up the evening edition of the *Philadelphia Enquirer*. He scanned the front page and said, "Looks like they're finally going to hang that killer, Jake Wilson."

Millicent looked up from her work. "Oh? Well, it's about time. How long has it been since he was arrested?"

"Says here the murders were committed on the night of July 8. He was arrested on the eleventh. That's more than six weeks ago. He went to trial on the twenty-fourth and was told by the judge that he'd be executed at the state prison within a week. But you remember . . . there were some legal complications that developed right after the trial."

"I never did understand what they were. So when is Wilson going to hang?"

"Six o'clock tomorrow morning."

Millicent nodded. "Sometimes the wheels of justice turn slowly, but eventually they do turn."

"You're right about that, dear."

As the evening moved on, the sound of the storm eased off.

Philip was on the last page of the newspaper when the front door opened and closed. Delmar's voice was heard in conversation with Philipa, then all was quiet. Philipa's parents waited for their daughter to enter the library, but when several minutes had passed and she had not appeared, Philip left his chair and went to the hall. When there was no sign of his daughter, he called out, "Philipa?"

There was no response. He called to her again, then started toward the staircase. He halted when he saw Delmar coming from the kitchen area.

"Didn't I hear Philipa come in, Delmar?"

"Yes, sir. Mr. Burke walked her to the door

and left immediately. Miss Philipa spoke to me but seemed upset. Didn't she come into the library?"

"No, she didn't."

"She probably went up to her room, then, sir."

Philipa paced from one end of her spacious and lavishly decorated bedroom to the other. "Adam Burke, how could you do this to me? Do you really think I would leave Philadelphia for some dusty little cow town in Nebraska? How dare you! Do you really think I would leave my family, my friends, and my social life to shrivel up and waste away in the dull, boring existence you have planned for me out there in that no-man's land? Well, Mr. Burke, you've got another think coming!"

There was a tap on the door. Philipa stopped pacing and forced herself to calm down. She hurried to open the door when a second knock came.

"Oh, hello, Mother . . . Daddy."

"Honey, are you all right?" Philip asked.

She put fingertips to her temple and said, "Well, I developed a headache at the restaurant, so I came on up here to take some powders. I was going to come down to the library in a moment."

"We were worried," Millicent said. "Delmar

124

said you seemed upset when you came in."

"I'm sorry. It was just the headache. Adam just walked me to the door but didn't come in. He told me to tell both of you good night. I didn't mean for Delmar to think I was upset."

"Well, just so we know you're all right, dear," Millicent said.

They kissed her good night and left.

Philipa lay awake till the wee hours of the morning. Before finally falling asleep, she decided that the next time she and Adam talked she would just lay it on the line, tell him she didn't want to live in Nebraska. Tell him straight out that if he loved her he wouldn't take her away from Philadelphia.

8

To Jake Wilson, the Pennsylvania State Prison was not merely quiet, it was eerily still. He lay on his cot in the tiny cubicle on death row, staring into the darkness. The silence about him seemed to have substance. He sat up and put a trembling hand to the nape of his neck. When he took his hand away, his palm was moist and cold.

He got up from the uncomfortable cot and went to the barred window that overlooked the rolling hills beyond the prison walls. A slight breeze touched his face, and the few clouds that drifted overhead were a pale silver with reflected light from a half-moon. Countless stars twinkled against a vast reservoir of darkness.

Nausea knotted Wilson's stomach. This was the last time he would ever see the night sky, the moon, the stars. Shortly after sunrise they would come for him and take him to that dismal corner of the prison yard where the gallows stood like an evil monster, waiting to

126

drop him through a trap door to the end of a rope.

Jake Wilson wasn't sure what would happen to his soul, but somehow he knew down deep inside that he had to go out into eternity and face God. He felt a strong desire to clear his conscience before they hanged him.

He turned away from the window and shuffled back to the cot and sat down. No sense in lying down. He couldn't sleep.

He thought of the plunge through the trapdoor of the gallows. He fought the terror churning in his stomach and folded his arms across his chest, closed his eyes, and rocked back and forth. He lost track of time, and when he finally opened his eyes, dawn was a pale ghost light on the eastern horizon. His last day on earth. Where would he be this time tomorrow?

The sound of a steel door opening at the end of the long corridor brought Jake's head around. The door closed, then echoing footsteps grew louder. Presently, a guard bearing a food tray stopped in front of Jake's cell. Jake could barely make him out in the vague light coming from the outside window. The guard peered through the door and said, "Got some breakfast for you, Jake."

"I ain't hungry, Arlie."

"Some of 'em eat heartily before — well,

you know. And others don't want anything. Prison rules are that we bring your last meal. But there's no rule that says you have to eat it."

"Arlie, listen. I've gotta see Warden Miles."

"You'll see him. He always walks a man from his cell to the gallows. Along with the chaplain, that is."

"No, I mean I've got to see him before then. I . . . I have somethin' very important to tell him."

"Chaplain Donaldson will be here first. You can talk to him."

"No! I've got to talk to the warden, Arlie! I'm telling you, it's important!"

"He's still in bed at this hour. I can't disturb him."

"You've got to! Please. Get him here so I can talk to him!"

"All right! All right. His house is about two miles away. I'll send someone over there."

A half hour later, Arlie appeared, stuck his key in the lock of the cell door and said, "All right, Jake. The warden's in his office. Let's go."

Jake picked up the copy of the *Philadelphia Enquirer* that lay on the small table in his cell, folded it, and stuck it under his arm. "Thanks, Arlie, I really appreciate this."

Warden Chester Miles was standing at his office window, looking at the sunrise, when

Arlie ushered Jake through the door. Miles turned from the window and set steady eyes on the condemned man. "I understand you have something important to discuss with me before you die."

That same day, Officer Seth Coleman entered police headquarters, escorting a handcuffed man. He paused at the desk and said to the sergeant, "Bill, this is Mr. Cummings. He was caught stealing groceries at Weberly's Market. Do you have an empty cell, or should we put him in with someone?"

"We can give him private accommodations," the sergeant said. "I'll take him back and lock him up. We can book him after you see the chief."

Seth frowned. "Pardon me?"

"Chief Bennett told me he wanted to see you whenever you came in. I guess since it's lunchtime you could go eat then see him when you come back."

"Well, if he wants to see me, he comes before my stomach. I'll see him now."

When Seth entered the chief's office, Bennett rose from behind his desk and said, "Seth! I was hoping you'd come in before the end of your shift."

"Sergeant Gunderson said you wanted to see me."

There was a glint in Bennett's eyes and a smile curved his lips. "Yes. Sit down."

Seth eased onto the chair in front of the desk. Bennett returned to his desk chair and leaned forward with eagerness etched on his face. "Seth, I have some wonderful news for you!"

"Well, sir, I sure could use some of that."

"About half an hour ago, a messenger from the state prison delivered this letter to me from Warden Miles." Bennett picked up a white envelope from his desk. "He says in here that before Jake Wilson was hanged this morning, he asked to talk to him. Wilson confessed to Warden Miles that it was he who stabbed Lawrence Sheldon to death. He didn't want to die with it on his conscience."

"Well, what do you know!"

"Wilson told Miles that Sheldon had arrested him on a minor charge a couple of years ago, and Wilson did six months for the crime. He hated Sheldon for it, and when the opportunity came, he stabbed him in revenge. Of course, that wasn't the reason he was in prison. He'd murdered those two women two days previously in the Rittenhouse Square district. There were witnesses to those killings, if you remember the story, and Wilson was hunted down and arrested three days later . . . the very next day after he murdered Sheldon."

Tears misted Seth's eyes. "Sir, this is the best news I've had since I heard that jury foreman say 'Not guilty'!"

"Well, soon everyone will know. Warden Miles is going to tell the story to a reporter for the *Enquirer*, and Wilson's confession will be on the front page of tomorrow morning's edition. That should settle anybody's doubt about you. So let me ask you something."

"Yes, sir?"

"Since everybody in Philadelphia will know by noon tomorrow about Jake Wilson's confession, will you stay on the force and forget the deputy U.S. marshal idea?"

Seth didn't reply immediately, then he said, "Chief, I very much appreciate that you want me to stay, but I really want to go ahead with those plans. I just feel it's what I'm cut out for."

"Well, I sure hate to lose you, but I understand, son. A man has to do what a man has to do."

"I'm glad you understand, sir."

"But if for some unforeseen reason you should be turned down by the U.S. marshal's office, will you consider staying?"

"You're persistent, sir. I'll say that for you."

"I know a good lawman when I see him. If

131

you were in my shoes you'd feel the same way about Officer Seth Coleman."

"Thank you, sir. If I get turned down, I'll make my decision then. If by then I still think I should leave Philadelphia, I might ask you to recommend me to a police department in another city. But, sir, please know that I deeply appreciate your wanting me to stay."

When Seth Coleman arrived home that afternoon, he found a letter in his mailbox from the Chief U.S. marshal's office in Washington, D.C. Its contents thrilled him, and he wanted to share the news with someone. He had thought of his friend Adam Burke earlier, wanting to let Adam know about Jake Wilson's confession. He would go to Adam's apartment and share both bits of news with him.

Seth pulled his buggy up in front of Adam Burke's apartment and climbed down, then saw Adam coming down the street in his open buggy.

"Hello, Seth!" Adam said with a wave. "To what do I owe this pleasure?"

"I have some good news to share with you."

"All right. I'll put away my horse and buggy and be right back."

Moments later they entered the apartment,

and Adam directed his friend to sit down in the parlor. "All right. Let's hear this good news."

Seth scooted to the edge of his chair. "I know you keep up with what's in the newspapers, Adam, so I'm sure you're aware that Jake Wilson was hanged at the state prison this morning."

"Wilson's hanging has something to do with your good news?"

"Yes, as strange as that sounds. Before they took him to the gallows this morning, he confessed to the warden that it was he who stabbed Lawrence Sheldon to death!"

"What? Really?"

"Really. It'll be in tomorrow morning's *Enquirer*, but I wanted you to hear it from me before you read about it in the paper."

"Seth, this is great news! I can't tell you how happy I am for you! This will shut the mouths of all those doubters. You can finally have some peace about this thing."

"Believe me, that's going to feel good. I . . . ah . . . I have some other news to share with you. I'm going to leave Philadelphia."

"To do what?"

"I'm going to become a deputy U.S. marshal. I sent an application to the office in Washington, and I've been accepted. Just got my acceptance letter in the mail today. I'm to

133

report in at the Washington office on September 3 to begin my training."

"So tell me, was this application sent in because you wanted to get away from the doubters here who still thought you killed Sheldon?"

"Well, it helped to put it in motion, yes. But actually I've wanted to get into that branch of law enforcement for some time. I'm really happy about it."

Adam smiled. "Then I'm glad for you. Guess I should fill you in on what's happening with me."

"What's that?"

"Well, Philipa and I are going to move our wedding date up about a month because we're moving to North Platte, Nebraska."

"Nebraska!"

"Yes, sir. I took a trip out west right after I graduated from Harvard. Those wide open spaces have beckoned to me ever since. It's been my dream to go out there somewhere and set up my own law firm."

"Well, a man should follow his dream, Adam. That's what I'm doing by becoming a deputy U.S. marshal. So tell me more."

"I've been in contact with the chairman of North Platte's town council. He tells me the town is on the grow but has no law office. The people have to go all the way to Grand Island

— one hundred and twenty miles away — to get legal help. That's where I'm going to open my own law firm."

"Sounds like quite the adventure. I hope you and Philipa will be very happy in North Platte."

"Thank you."

"Guess we won't be seeing each other anymore, Adam, but I'll make it a point to see you once more before I leave for Washington."

The sun was rising when Joseph Mason stepped onto the front porch of his mansion and picked up the morning paper. He waved to a neighbor a few yards down and turned to go inside.

Upstairs in the master bedroom, Nancy Mason was seated in front of the mirror at her dressing table, applying the last touches of rouge to her cheeks. The powder and rouge didn't completely hide the pallor of her skin, but it did help some. She was feeling better than she had the last couple of days and was looking forward to her busy day. The Masons were not only on the board of directors at the Philadelphia Orphanage, but Nancy worked one day a week as a volunteer. That was Nancy's greatest joy — the highlight of her week. She only wished her health would allow her to put in more time there.

"Ready, Mother?" Rachel asked from the open bedroom door.

Nancy laid down the rouge brush and smiled at her daughter's reflection in the mirror. "I'm ready."

They locked arms and headed down the wide hallway toward the winding staircase.

Joseph entered the kitchen, newspaper in hand and drew a deep breath. "Ahh . . . Millie," he said to the middle-aged cook, "it sure smells good!"

"I hope it tastes as good as it smells, Mr. Mason."

"Well, if it doesn't, it'll be the first time!"

"Good morning, Daddy, Millie!" Rachel said as mother and daughter entered the kitchen arm in arm.

Millie returned the greeting over her shoulder as she stood at the stove, transferring scrambled eggs from a skillet into a bowl.

Joseph laid the morning's edition of the *Enquirer* on the table at his usual place and said, "My, don't my girls look gorgeous this morning! You could almost pass for sisters."

Mother and daughter smiled at each other as the family sat down at the table and Millie began filling their plates.

"Honey, you're not eating this good food

with much enthusiasm," Joseph said after a few minutes. "Are you having a bad day?"

"Mama, maybe you'd better not go to the orphanage today," Rachel said.

"Oh, I'm fine. The last couple of days have been a little rough, but I'm better today. My appetite isn't back yet, but I'll be able to go to the orphanage."

Joseph looked at her questioningly, but Nancy smiled at him and said, "Really, honey. I'm fine."

He gave her a tentative smile, then filled his mouth with scrambled eggs and unfolded the newspaper. The headline caught his attention:

CONDEMNED MAN CONFESSES MURDER OF OFFICER LAWRENCE SHELDON BEFORE GOING TO GALLOWS!

"Well, look at this!" he said, holding up the paper so his wife and daughter could see the bold print.

"Well, isn't that something," Rachel said. "Who was it, Daddy?"

"I don't know. Let me see here . . ."

"I'm so glad to hear this," Nancy said. "So many people around here have spoken their doubts about Officer Coleman's innocence, in spite of the jury's verdict. I've never felt he did it."

"I have to admit I had my doubts, Mama," Rachel said. "It was —"

"You remember that man who killed the two women in the Rittenhouse Square district back in July?"

"Is he the one?" Rachel asked.

"Sure is. Jake Wilson. They executed him yesterday morning at the state prison, but before they put his neck in the noose, he confessed to the warden that he was the one who killed Officer Sheldon. It was a grudge thing."

"Well, that should put a stop to the talk that Officer Coleman got away with murder," Nancy said. "Just goes to show you we humans are but frail creatures quite capable of error."

9

Seth Coleman arrived at the police station that same morning for duty. He passed through the double doors and headed down the hall. When he rounded a corner, there was a crowd of officers gathered in front of Chief Bennett's office, some in uniform and others in street clothes. Bennett was standing in the doorway.

Suddenly every man turned and looked at Seth, and they all began applauding. Chief Bennett threaded his way through the press while the applause grew louder.

When the noise settled down, Bennett said, "Officer Coleman, when the news of Jake Wilson's confession reached your fellow officers, they gathered here to show you their support."

One officer in uniform said, "Many of us thought the jury handed down the wrong verdict. All of us who doubted you are truly sorry and ask your forgiveness." Several policemen nodded in agreement.

"Fellas, I admit it wasn't easy to get the cold shoulder and to hear some of the accusing remarks," Seth said. "It hurt pretty deep. But since you're man enough to confess you were wrong, and you're asking my forgiveness . . . I'm man enough to forgive you. Consider it done."

There was more applause, then one of the officers said, "Seth, let me say for those of us who never doubted you, we're just happy that you've finally been cleared. You're an excellent police officer and a great guy!"

When the applause started up again, Chief Bennett took a step closer to Seth and said, "Officer Coleman, as you know, we've got men here who need to get out on the streets, including yourself. But before we break up this meeting, there are two men in my office who would like to see you, and they want to say something to you in front of all of your fellow officers." Bennett looked behind him and said, "Tell them to come out."

The two witnesses to the murder of Lawrence Sheldon stepped out of Bennett's office. The officers made a path for them, and when they approached Seth, they had tears in their eyes. Seth shook their hands, assuring them they too were forgiven.

The meeting broke up, and as Seth headed for the street to begin his shift, he found Hank

Moldow and Keith Dailey waiting for him. The two men had just been reinstated after receiving a reprimand from the internal affairs committee.

"Seth," Moldow said, "Keith and I just want to say we're sorry — and to thank you for the kindness you showed us when you could have shown us scorn."

Seth shook hands with them and said, "I hold no grudges, guys."

Claude Ralston sat at the breakfast table, clutching his morning edition of the *Philadelphia Enquirer*. His eyes ran over the headlines for the dozenth time since he had read the story to his wife and daughter. The two other chairs at the table were unoccupied, and the food on the plates and the coffee in the cups had grown cold.

Claude could hear sobs coming from Bettieann's bedroom. He shook his head and mumbled to himself, "How could I have been so wrong?"

Finally, he folded the paper, dropped it on the table, and shoved back his chair. When he reached his daughter's bedroom, he tapped on the door and then stepped inside. Bettieann lay face-down across the bed, her body quaking. Lillian sat beside her. Lillian looked up at her husband and shook her head, tears running down her cheeks.

Claude started to speak, but Lillian touched his arm and said, "Let her cry it out."

He nodded and sat down in a chair next to the bed.

When Bettieann finally stopped crying, Lillian pressed a clean hanky into her hand, and she sat up, sniffling.

"Oh, Papa, how could I have been such a fool? How could I have been so wicked and so mean to poor Seth? He told me he was innocent, but I wouldn't believe him! I told him that attorney had hypnotized the jury. How horrible of me!"

Claude squeezed her shoulder tenderly. "Honey, your mother and I are as guilty as you are. We didn't believe him either."

"I know, but Seth was in love with me. I'm sure he was on the verge of asking me to marry him. He trusted me when I told him that I loved him. Then I cut his heart out! I told him I stopped loving him when I found out he had been arrested. And that wasn't true! I didn't stop loving him. I thought I had, but I've known I still love him ever since he came by the house to see me!"

"Honey," Lillian said, "if you still love Seth, you need to tell him."

Bettieann brushed the hair from her eyes and shook her head. "He wouldn't believe me, Mama. And besides, I can't face him. Not after what I said to him . . . and did to him. I'd be too ashamed to look him in the eye."

"But if you really do still love him," Claude said, "you ought to find the wherewithal to go face him. Tell him how sorry you are . . . that you still love him. You owe him that much."

Tears filled Bettiann's eyes again. "I owe him a lot more than that, Papa, but I just couldn't face him! I'm a coward, too, I guess."

Lillian patted her arm. "Let a little time pass. Time has a healing balm of its own. When you feel better about yourself, you can go to Seth and talk to him."

That evening, Seth Coleman returned to his room at the boardinghouse after eating supper with the other boarders in the dining room. He sat down in the overstuffed chair by the front window and looked down at the traffic on the street below.

"Ah, sweet relief!" he said. "No more suspicion-filled eyes at the station, on the streets, or at the table here in the boarding house." He closed his eyes and whispered, "But, oh, Bettieann, I still love you. I'd be so happy to hear you say you still loved me. I'm sure you've heard about Jake Wilson's confession by now. If I could only —"

There was a knock at the door. Seth went to answer it, his heart pounding like a triphammer. His heart sank when he saw Jack and Thelma Sheldon standing there.

"Officer Coleman," Jack Sheldon said, his voice barely audible, "we need to talk to you. Could you spare us the time?"

Seth felt a desire to slam the door in their faces but pushed the urge away. "Certainly," he said, his voice calm and steady. "Come in."

He led them to the love seat and invited them to sit down. Then he turned the overstuffed chair away from the window and positioned it facing them. "What can I do for you, Mr. and Mrs. Sheldon?"

Jack cleared his throat and fidgeted with his hands, then said, "Thank you for letting us see you."

Seth nodded but said nothing.

"Officer Coleman, we . . . we learned today about the confession of Jake Wilson. We realize how wrong we were to accuse you of killing our son even after the jury acquitted you. Thelma and I have come to ask your forgiveness. We want you to know that we're truly sorry for the way we acted that day in the courthouse."

"We mean that sincerely," Thelma said. "Will you forgive us?"

Seth stared at them for a long time. "That moment in the courtroom when you would not believe I was innocent of Lawrence's death was a very painful one, Mr. and Mrs. Sheldon. For days afterward the scene came back to me, and in my mind I could see your accusing eyes. I remember you saying that you're Christians, and that even though I did kill your son you had forgiven me."

"We were so wrong, Officer Coleman," Jack said. "Christians are far from perfect, and we proved that to you."

"We had to ask the Lord to forgive us before we could come and ask the same of you," Thelma said.

"I know you were going through a horrible experience that was tearing your hearts out," Seth said. "Sitting in the courtroom throughout the trial had to be a terribly painful thing. Maybe if I had been in your place I would've done the same thing you did. So let me say that I appreciate your coming to see me, and I appreciate your willingness to admit you were wrong in the way you treated me. Mr. and Mrs. Sheldon, I forgive you."

Thelma pulled a hanky from her purse and wiped away the tears streaming down her face.

Jack thumbed his own tears away, and said, "Thank you, sir. If you had not forgiven us it would have weighed on us the rest of our lives. Are you aware of what the Bible says about people who show mercy to others?"

"Well, I'm not sure."

"It says a lot about it, but I have a particular passage in mind. Do you have a Bible, Officer Coleman?"

"Yes, it's in my bedroom closet. I'll get it."

Seth returned with the Bible, and said, "This was given to me when I was a boy." He handed it to Jack. "I was nine years old at the time."

"Looks in pretty good condition. Do you read it much?"

"Well, no, I don't. I suppose I haven't looked inside it since I was a teenager."

Jack opened the Bible to the New Testament. While he was flipping pages, he said, "Officer Coleman, do you believe this Book is the Word of God?"

"Yes, sir. I was brought up in Sunday school and church. I . . . ah . . . got away from church when I was seventeen. My parents were killed . . . well, you don't want to hear my family history. Anyway, what was it you wanted to show me?"

Jack flipped a few more pages. "Here . . . Matthew 5:7. Jesus says, 'Blessed are the merciful, for they shall obtain mercy.' "

"Yes, I recall that verse."

"You see, Officer Coleman, you —"

"Call me Seth, sir. You too, Mrs. Sheldon."

Thelma smiled for the first time since entering the apartment.

"All right . . . Seth," Jack said. "Mercy is what you showed to Thelma and me. Jesus said that the merciful shall obtain mercy. He said that if we are merciful to others we'll have mercy shown to us when we need it."

Seth smiled. "That's good, isn't it?"

"Sure is. And of course as guilty sinners before God, all of us are in need of His mercy. The whole human race has sinned grievously against God, including me and Thelma, including you. Right?"

Seth rubbed the back of his neck. "Yes, sir. I remember Sunday school lessons and sermons that made me feel so guilty for my sins."

"That's because whenever we hear the Word of God taught or preached, it isn't long until it shines its light on our sins. We learn quickly that God hates our sins, though He loves us. It was God's marvelous love that caused Him to send His Son to the Cross. He died for sinners so that we could be saved. He paid the price that God — in His holiness, righteousness, and justice — demanded for our sins."

Seth remained silent, but he was listening carefully to Jack's words.

"By dying and then raising Himself from the grave, Jesus provided the one and only way for guilty sinners like you and me to find mercy from God. Salvation is ours when we repent of our sin and believe that Jesus did all that was necessary to save us." Jack searched Seth's face, then said, "From what you told us a minute ago, Seth, you've heard the gospel before."

"Yes, sir."

"Have you ever sought God's mercy and forgiveness through Jesus Christ and His shed blood?"

Seth slowly shook his head. "No, sir. I came close to being saved when I was about fourteen years old. An evangelist was preaching at our church and he really got to me. I almost walked down that aisle to be saved, but I was afraid of what my friends at school would think of me if I became a Christian."

"Seth, just as Thelma and I wronged you and needed your mercy, you've wronged God and need His mercy. There is no mercy from God apart from His Son."

Seth's hands began to tremble. "Yes, sir. You've brought it all back to me tonight. I've been a fool to go on in life as a lost sinner. I want to be saved, Mr. Sheldon."

"Well, Seth, Romans 10:13 says that whosoever will call upon the name of the Lord shall be saved."

"Will you help me do that?"

Thelma wiped tears as her husband knelt with Seth Coleman beside the love seat and led him in prayer.

The following Sunday, Seth attended the Sheldons' church, publicly professed his faith in Christ, and was baptized. The congregation swarmed him after the service, not only to let him know how happy they were that he had been saved but to express their joy that his name had been cleared by Jake Wilson's confession.

During that week, Adam Burke handled one court case after another. Every night he had to prepare for the next day's case. There had been no time to talk with Philipa.

On Friday night, August 31, Adam's busy week had come to an end and he sat at a table in one of Philadelphia's finest restaurants, looking past a pair of flickering candles at the woman he loved.

"I'm sorry about neglecting you this week, honey," he said.

Philipa warmed him with a smile. "You don't have to apologize. I'm a lawyer's daughter, remember? I've seen Daddy under that kind of pressure many times over the years. I understand."

"I'm glad you do." He took a bite from his plate. "You've had more than a few days to think about the Nebraska venture we discussed. How do you feel about it now?"

"Well, darling, I certainly appreciate a man with your drive and the courage to step out on your own. But this is such a big step."

"I know. But a turtle never gets anywhere without sticking his neck out. And I really want to get to North Platte. If we're going to change the wedding to the middle of September, we've got to move on it quickly."

Philipa made no attempt to hide the fire in her eyes. "We can't change the wedding date. Everything is planned! This is going to be a big wedding. It's got to stay as we have it now."

"But Philipa, we can't wait very long. Some other attorney is liable to move into North Platte ahead of me."

Philipa put a hand to her forehead. "Will you take me home, Adam? I'm developing a headache."

"Of course. Let me get the waiter's attention . . ."

When they reached the Conrad mansion, Adam walked Philipa to the door. The porch lanterns illuminated the couple with a yellow glow.

Adam took Philipa's hand and said, "I won't come in. I want you to take some powders for that headache and get to bed." He kissed her tenderly, then pulled back and looked into her eyes. "Are you angry with me? You seem distant. Have I done something wrong?"

Philipa looked down for a moment, then raised her eyes to look at Adam. "I wish you'd reconsider this move to Nebraska and let Daddy make you a partner."

"But Philipa, my heart is in the West. It's drawing me like a magnet draws iron."

Philipa touched her hand to her forehead again. "Let's talk about this later."

"All right. Later."

Philipa's kiss was a bit warmer this time. She went inside and closed the door, waiting until she heard Adam drive away, then went to the library where she found her parents in their favorite chairs, reading.

"Have a nice time, dear?" Millicent asked.

"Of course." Philipa replied. Then, moving to stand over her father, she said, "Daddy, couldn't you go ahead and make a partnership offer to Adam? It would make me so happy if he was part of your firm."

Philip reached out and took her hand. "I'd like that myself, honey, but I really have to give George Benson a little more time."

★ ★ ★

Adam climbed the stairs in his apartment building and found Seth Coleman waiting for him at the top.

"Hello, Adam," he said, smiling broadly. "I'm leaving for Washington in the morning and I wanted to tell you good-bye."

"So soon? I thought you didn't have to report in until Monday."

"That's right, but I want to get settled in a boardinghouse before then."

"Oh, sure. I'm not thinking well tonight, am I? Come on inside, Seth."

"I can only stay a few minutes."

When they sat down, Adam said, "I know you'll make a good federal lawman. Any idea where you'll be placed once the training is over?"

"Not really. Could be anywhere in the country. How are your plans working out for going to Nebraska?"

"I'm working on them every day. As soon as Philipa and I can settle on a new wedding date, I'll be able to work out the details."

"I'm sure you will, Adam." He paused for a few moments, then said, "Before I go I'd like to tell you what happened to me tonight. I . . . I'm sure you've heard about Jesus Christ dying on the cross."

Adam's brow furrowed. "Well, yes."

"I was talking to . . . well, you remember Jack and Thelma Sheldon?"

"Of course. How could I forget them?"

"They came to my room the other evening to ask my forgiveness. When I told them I forgave them, they started talking to me about the Lord and the forgiveness I needed for my sins against Him. I was raised in Sunday school and church, Adam, so what they were saying wasn't foreign to my ears. But when they asked me if I'd ever repented and believed the gospel, I couldn't say that I had. So I asked the Lord Jesus Christ to come into my heart and forgive me of my sins. I'm a Christian now."

Adam was silent for a moment, then said, "Seth, if this makes your life happier, I'm really glad for you."

Seth wanted to say more, but instead, he rose to his feet. "Well, my friend, I've got to be going. If I ever get near North Platte, I'll drop in and see you."

Adam grinned. "You do that, Seth."

10

On Saturday morning, Seth Coleman stood in front of the boardinghouse with three trunks and a couple of pieces of hand luggage, waiting for his ride to the train station. When the buggy came around the corner and pulled up to where he stood, Seth helped the driver load the baggage and then climbed into the backseat. On impulse, he leaned forward and said to the driver, "Would you do me a favor?"

"Certainly, sir."

"Would you swing down to Spring Street? Just follow Spring till you get to Eleventh, then you can cut south and go on down to the station. That be all right?"

"Sure. Did you want to stop somewhere on Spring?"

"Ah . . . no. I just want to go by a particular house for a last look."

"Fine by me."

When the Ralston house came into view, Seth felt his heart quicken. But there was no one in the yard or on the porch. He gazed longingly at the house while the buggy moved past.

At the station he boarded the train to Washington, D.C., and took a seat by a window. Tears filled his eyes, and a lump formed in his throat as the train chugged out of the depot.

"Good-bye, Bettieann," he whispered.

That same afternoon, Adam Burke left the county courthouse after successfully defending a client against a lawsuit and headed back to the office to finish some paperwork. He passed through the double doors of the Benson building and went up to the law offices. As he passed the reception desk, Jill Hawkins looked up and said, "Mr. Burke, Philipa was here about an hour ago. When I told her you were in court, she asked me to give you a message."

"All right. What did she say?"

"That I should tell you she is going to Newark with her mother and won't be able to take in the ballet with you tonight."

"Newark? Oh, that's right. She has an aunt who lives there."

"Yes, her mother's sister has taken ill, and Mrs. Conrad wanted Philipa to go with her."

"That's too bad. I met her Aunt Bertha

once. Nice lady. Did Philipa say anything more?"

"No, sir. Only that they might be gone for several days and she'll let you know when she arrives home."

"All right, Jill. Thank you."

Adam sat down at his desk and decided to postpone the paperwork until early the next morning. Right now he needed to send a wire to William Dauntt in North Platte.

The next morning, Adam was concentrating on some law briefs when Jill entered his office and laid an envelope on his desk. "A telegram just came for you, Mr. Burke."

"Thank you. Is the messenger waiting in case I want to send a return wire?"

"Yes, sir."

"I'll read this and be right out."

As soon as Jill shut the door behind her, Adam ripped open the envelope. A smile spread across his face. He took out a sheet of paper, dipped his pen in the inkwell, and wrote a quick message to tell William Dauntt he would be coming to North Platte before the end of October. He would send another wire when he had a firm date of arrival.

Lillian Ralston awakened in the deep of the night and looked around the dark bedroom.

Claude's soft, even breathing was reassuring. She rolled over and started to go back to sleep. Then the sound came again. Lillian eased out of the bed, trying not to disturb her husband, and slipped into the hall. She moved across the hall to Bettieann's room and went inside.

Bettieann tossed and turned and moaned in her sleep. Lillian groped her way to the bedstand and found the lantern and matches. She fumbled with the glass chimney, then laid it aside, struck a match, and fired the wick. She leaned over Bettieann and shook her daughter's shoulder. "Bettieann! Bettieann! Wake up, honey."

Bettieann gave a tremulous cry and opened her eyes. "Oh, Mother! I was having a horrible dream!"

"Seth?"

The girl began to cry and turned her head away.

"Honey, these nightmares seem to be getting worse."

"They're nightmares, all right. I can't stand this any longer! I was dreaming that Seth had fallen in love with another woman and . . . Oh, Mother, what am I going to do?"

"Honey, you've been nothing but miserable ever since we learned that other man had confessed to killing Lawrence Sheldon. You've been eating your heart out over the way you treated Seth. I think you need to go to him. Tell him how wrong you were . . . that you still love him . . . and ask him to forgive you."

Bettieann sniffed and shook her head. "I can't. I just can't, Mother! I couldn't face him!"

"I think you'll have to," came Claude's voice from the open door. "You'll not have any peace until you talk to him."

"Your father's right, honey," Lillian said. "You need to swallow your pride, go to Seth, and tell him how you feel. If he turns you away, at least you'll know you did the right thing."

"And at least you'll know whether there's any hope for the two of you to get back together," Claude said. "If there isn't, then you can close that chapter of your life and get on with it. The way you've been moping around here, something's got to be done."

Bettieann wiped her tears with the corner of the bed sheet. "All right. I'll go see him. If he's still on the day shift he'll be home about five-thirty."

The next afternoon, Bettieann walked to the boardinghouse, her stomach churning. When she stepped inside the building, no one was in the hall, so she went to Seth's door and stood there for a few moments,

158

taking deep breaths. She raised a trembling fist and knocked on the door.

Seconds passed, but there was no sound of footsteps inside.

Bettieann knocked again.

When there was no response, she took a step back from the door and looked both directions down the hall. She thought about leaving a note but quickly dismissed the idea as too impersonal. She would have to catch him at another time.

On Tuesday morning, September 11, a wire came from Philipa Conrad to Adam Burke's office. Her aunt had been through surgery and was doing better. Philipa and her mother would be home on Wednesday afternoon, and she would love to go out to dinner that evening. Unless she heard differently, she would be ready at seven o'clock.

On Wednesday evening, Delmar greeted Adam in his usual manner and invited him in. Philipa rushed into his arms the moment he stepped inside. She kissed him on the cheek and said, "Darling, we have a surprise for you. Mother and Daddy are taking us to dinner tonight. That's all right, isn't it?"

"Why, of course," he said, forcing a smile. "It'll be delightful to dine with them." He saw her parents at the top of the winding staircase and whispered, "But could I take you to dinner tomorrow night? Just the two of us?"

"Oh, I can't, darling. I'm already committed to Lorraine Bates and Barbara Mullins for tomorrow night. We're going to a fashion show downtown."

"The whole evening?"

"Well . . . yes. We have to leave about six o'clock to make it to the restaurant in time to eat before the fashion show starts at eight."

"Friday, then?"

"Of course. Friday will be fine."

Adam Burke awakened the next morning to a brilliant sunrise. He sat up in bed and stretched, opening his mouth in a wide yawn. He had slept fitfully, consumed with the need to talk with Philipa about their move to Nebraska. Tomorrow night the issue had to be settled so he could wire William Dauntt the next morning and tell him when they would arrive. Dauntt had offered to help locate space for his office and would need time to work on it.

Adam shaved and put on a clean white shirt and took a suit from the closet. He glanced at the photograph of his mother that stood on the dresser and picked it up. "Mama, if you were here I know you'd put your blessing on my decision to go to North Platte. You'd want your son to follow his dream and be happy."

He thought of the terrible unhappiness his mother, sisters, and he had suffered when his father deserted them. Over the years Adam had tried to keep from thinking about Gordon Burke, but once in a while memories of his father crowded into his mind. Each time those memories came, his hatred for the man grew stronger. His loathing took a giant leap when his mother died, a broken-hearted woman.

He pushed thoughts of his father from his mind and kissed the picture. "I love you, Mama."

It was just past one o'clock at the Mason home when Nancy stood before the full-length mirror in the master bedroom, dressing her dark, upswept hair.

She had gotten up at the normal time and enjoyed the breakfast Rachel fixed, since Millie was away for a few days to attend a family reunion. But Nancy had returned to the bedroom to lie down for a few hours afterward. The meeting today at Doris Krantz's house was a vitally important one for the orphanage, and it was imperative that she be there.

Rachel had brought her a light lunch at noon,

and by twelve-thirty she was feeling some-what better. As she put finishing touches on her hair, she heard footsteps in the hall and saw her daughter's reflection in the mirror. She pushed in the last hairpin and turned to face Rachel, putting on her best smile. "Do I look all right, honey?"

"You look positively beautiful, Mama. But you also look rather peaked. I think it would be best if I cancel my shopping date with Sylvia and go to the meeting with you."

"Now, Rachel, I'll be fine. Sylvia's your best friend and you need some time with her. You really have no reason to be at the meeting. I want you to have a fun day."

Rachel hugged her mother, a tinge of worry showing in her eyes. "All right, if this is the way you want it."

"I'll be fine."

Moments later, Rachel stood beside her mother on the front porch as gardener Cecil McIntire drove the buggy from behind the house and pulled up to the steps.

Nancy hugged her daughter. "You have a good time, honey. And don't worry about me."

Rachel kissed her mother's cheek and watched as Cecil took her hand and led her down the steps and into the buggy. Nancy glanced at Rachel and said, "The meeting is over at five. If you get home before I do, go ahead and start supper."

"All right, Mama. I love you."

"I love you too."

Minutes later, the buggy neared the Krantz estate, and Nancy admired the large three-story, red brick residence. The mullioned windows were hung with deep jewel-toned silk draperies. A wide porch stretched around three sides of the mansion. Mums and daisies in large ornate pots decorated the steps at the bases of the banisters, and flowers of various descriptions nestled along the sides of the house.

A sweeping circle drive led up to the mansion that looked like a many-faceted ornament in the center of the parklike grounds. Every blade of grass was neatly trimmed, as were all of the shrubs. The flower gardens that dotted the yard were gloriously bright in their many-hued splendor.

Cecil helped Nancy from the buggy. With a parting comment to him to pick her up at five, Nancy turned to Doris Krantz, who was standing at the open door. They entered the drawing room, and Nancy was pleased to see such a good turnout. There were more women in attendance than ever before, and she was amazed when Doris told her there were seven more women coming.

Within a few minutes the other women arrived, and the meeting began.

As the afternoon progressed, plans were made to raise more funds for the Philadelphia Orphanage than had been raised the previous year. A sizable amount was pledged by the wealthy women present. Everyone was jubilant with the results of the meeting and chatted happily when it was teatime.

This was not a court day for Adam Burke, and as he labored over various legal documents in his office, he finally decided he would go home early, change clothes, and drive to the Conrad mansion and ask for a few private moments with Philipa. Certainly they could come to an agreement within half an hour. That would give her plenty of time to dress for the evening.

The day had been clear until midafternoon, then dark clouds blew in from the west. When Adam left his apartment, he glanced at the clouds and thought about putting the top up on his buggy, then decided he would be home before any rain fell.

Adam turned into the Conrads' circle drive and saw a crew of men putting down a new layer of gravel. He drove the buggy around behind the mansion and parked it near the back porch. He hurried back to the front of the house and bounded up the porch, greeting the men spreading the gravel.

Millicent was in the hall when Delmar let Adam in. She came toward him, saying, "Philipa's up in her room getting ready to go to the fashion show, Adam."

"I know she's leaving at six. I need to talk to her, so I came early enough to have a few minutes with her."

"Is she expecting you?"

"No, ma'am. But it's very important."

"Then I'll go up and tell her you're here."

Philipa's bedroom was the picture of femininity and substance. A large cherry four-poster bed sat between two huge bay windows, each with its own window seat. The bed was covered with a blue crocheted spread and white lace overlay. The windows were hung with gauzy white curtains and blue silk draperies. The wide window seats were covered with the same shade of blue in an intricate brocade pattern, and an abundance of small blue-and-white pillows were strewn across each seat.

Philipa stood before a full-length mirror framed with gold inlay. She studied her reflection and was pleased with what she saw. She plucked at the curls that dangled on her forehead, trying to give them a little more life.

Millicent knocked and stepped inside. "Adam is here to see you, dear."

"Adam? I wasn't expecting him."

"I know. He said he needs a few minutes alone with you, and that it's very important."

Philipa sighed. "All right. I'm not quite ready to put in an appearance. Tell him I'll be down in a few minutes."

Philipa had a determined look in her eyes as she left her room and headed down the hall. When she reached the staircase, she saw Adam waiting for her at the bottom of the stairs. Halfway down the stairs, she said, "I had no idea I would see you today, Adam. I'm surprised you're not in court or at your office."

"This wasn't a court day. I decided to take part of the afternoon off."

As she reached the bottom step, Adam said, "I like your hair styled that way. You should wear it that way more often."

"Thank you. Mother said you wanted to talk to me in private."

"Yes, I do."

"All right." She glanced through the windows at the side of the staircase. "Doesn't look like it's raining yet. Let's go out on the back porch."

When Adam and Philipa stepped out on the back porch, the sky was black with clouds and the wind was blowing, but the way the chairs were recessed into a cove, the wind barely touched them. The smell of rain permeated the air. Adam seated Philipa, then sat down facing her.

"Well," she said, "what did you want to talk about, darling?"

"I need to coordinate our arrival in North Platte with Mr. Dauntt, honey. I wired him a few days ago and he wired me right back. There's still no law office in the town. The door is wide open for me to become North Platte's only lawyer, but we dare not wait any longer than necessary. We need to agree on a date of departure from Philadelphia as soon after the wedding as possible."

Philipa began to fidget with her engagement ring, turning it round and round on her finger. "Adam, I'm really hoping Daddy will make you a partnership offer soon."

"But I'm not interested in a partnership with your father. I want to build my own firm. And it seems to me that if a woman loves her man she will follow him to the ends of the earth if necessary."

"Oh? Well, it seems to me that if a man loves his woman he won't make her leave her family and friends to go where she'd be bored stiff!"

"Look, it's my job as a husband to provide

for my wife. You've got to let me do it my way."

"Your way is stupid. You've got to get this fool notion out of your head."

Adam's cheeks turned red. "Fool notion? Just because I want to get out of the big city and cut out a career in the West doesn't mean it's stupid! If that's the case, there are a lot of stupid people moving west to find a better life!"

Philipa shrugged. "You said it; I didn't."

Lightning slashed the dark sky, and thunder shook the porch.

"A person only gets one time to live his life on this earth, and I want to realize my dream."

"Well, go ahead! Realize your dream! But you'll do it without me. I'm telling you right now, Mr. Adam Burke, I'm not leaving my family, my friends, and my social life for some . . . some stinking backwoods cow town. That's no dream, it's a nightmare!"

11

Multiple bolts of lightning shot across the dark sky as a buggy pulled into the Mason driveway at precisely 4:45. The resounding thunder rattled the buggy Rachel Mason rode in with Sylvia Coffman and Sylvia's fiancé, Leon Dressler, who had driven downtown to pick them up and now was delivering Rachel to her home.

The wind whipped the trees along the driveway and in the yard as the buggy rolled up to the front porch. Rain noisily peppered the buggy's top.

Leon jumped out and hurried around to the other side. "I'll help you carry your packages in, Rachel," he said, then helped her out of the buggy. They carried her packages onto the porch, bending their heads against the wind and rain.

"Bye, Rachel!" Sylvia called from the shelter of the buggy. "Thanks for going with me!"

"I enjoyed it!" Rachel shouted back.

She laid her packages on a marble decorative table beside the front door and reached into her purse for the key. Leon banged the door knocker.

"Won't do any good, Leon," Rachel said. "Cecil has gone after my mother by now."

She turned the key in the lock and Leon followed her inside with an armload of packages. He laid them on a bench in the vestibule and went back for the rest of them. When he had brought the packages inside, Rachel thanked him and said good-bye. She brushed rainwater from her face and clothing, then headed for the kitchen to start supper.

Rachel lit a lantern in the kitchen and began taking food and supplies from the pantry. She carried these to the cupboard and looked out the kitchen's rear window. Lightning flashed, and she noticed the buggy under the lean-to shelter beside the barn. She couldn't see the barn door from the window but she could hear it banging in the wind.

Rachel went out the back door onto the porch and paused at the steps. "Cecil!" she called toward the barn. "Cecil!"

Suddenly Rachel saw a dark form lying on the ground near the barn door. She dashed off the porch and knelt beside the elderly gardener. By the light of another lightning flash she could see that his face was blue.

A tiny whimper escaped her lips as she took

hold of his arms and began pulling him toward the house. She struggled to get him up the steps and out of the rain. She saw lantern light in the kitchen window of the house next door and hurried in that direction.

Just then, Joseph Mason drove his buggy around the back of the house and saw his daughter waving and calling to him, her clothing soaked and her hair matted to her head.

"What's wrong?" he shouted, pulling rein.

"It's Cecil! I found him lying on the ground at the barn door. I think it's his heart. I have him on the porch."

"We'll have to get him to the hospital. What about your mother?"

"Cecil was supposed to pick her up. She's still at Krantzes."

"No time to go get her now. Get in the buggy, honey! We'll take Cecil to the hospital, then go after your mother."

Teatime at the Krantz house had ended at five as buggies and carriages began arriving to pick up the ladies. Myron the butler was preparing one of the Krantz buggies to take some of the older ladies to their homes.

"Would you like to go with Myron, honey?" Doris said to Nancy. "He'd be more than happy to take you home."

"Thank you, Doris, but I'm sure Cecil will be here any minute."

The Krantz buggy was the last to pull away, leaving Doris and Nancy alone. They sat in the drawing room at the front of the house and watched for Cecil. When 5:15 came, Nancy said, "I think something has detained Cecil. I really need to be getting home. Would you have a raincoat I could borrow? I'll just walk."

"Walk? It's raining cats and dogs out there!"

"I'll be all right if you have a raincoat you can let me use."

"Of course I do, but I really don't want you to go out in this storm. Why don't you wait till Myron gets back? He can take you home."

"No telling when he might get back. I really should be going."

"Oh, dear. Edgar is working late at the office this evening. He won't be home till after seven. I hate to see you walk, Nancy."

"It's just a couple of blocks. I'll be fine."

"Well, all right. If you insist. The raincoat is in the foyer closet."

They walked up to the foyer.

"I feel so terrible, Nancy," Doris said while helping her into the raincoat. "I wish there was a way I could get you a ride home."

"No need to fret. I'll be home in no time. Thanks for the use of the coat. I'll get it back to you soon as I can."

As they walked toward the door, Doris said, "The way it's storming out there, you're going to get wet in spite of the raincoat."

Nancy patted Doris's arm. "Even if I get a little wet it'll be worth it. I'm so glad we were able to raise so much money today. And the plans we've made will bring in a whole lot more. Well, here I go. Bye-bye now."

Doris opened the door and Nancy pulled the hood up over her head. They embraced, and Nancy stepped out into the storm. She hurried toward the street with darkness closing in on her.

"So that's it, Philipa? No matter what, you won't leave here to go with me?"

"No, I will not!"

"Well, you're not made of what Mrs. Welles is, are you? She didn't balk when her husband told her he wanted to go to Grand Island and become a partner with his old friend. She had to leave the fancy life in Boston to do it, but she loves her husband enough to follow him."

"Don't judge me by somebody else!" Philipa said. Only her anger kept her from breaking into tears.

"Well, I guess that settles it then. I'm going to North Platte!" Adam stomped off the porch and headed toward his buggy. The horse stood with its head bent against the wind and rain.

"Adam, stop!" Philipa screamed. "Come back here and talk to me!"

He paused and looked back over his shoulder. "If you won't go with me to Nebraska, there's nothing to talk about." He moved on toward the buggy.

"Adam!"

Once more he stopped and looked back.

Philipa's hair was wet and hanging in her face. "If you leave now, Adam, it's all over. Do you hear me?"

"I hear you. And I'm leaving."

"Don't ever come back! I never want to see you again!"

He lifted a foot to climb aboard his buggy.

Philipa pulled off her engagement ring and threw it at him. It landed in the mud at his feet. Adam gave her a look of disgust and ground the ring into the mud with his foot.

"I hate you!" Philipa screamed.

Adam climbed into his buggy. Philipa was still screaming as he drove around the corner and trotted the horse down the long driveway to the street.

Adam Burke had been this angry only once before in his life — the day he found out his father had deserted his mother. When he reached the street, he snapped the reins and put the horse to a gallop.

Nancy Mason was only a block from the Krantz house when the storm grew worse. The rain came down harder and the wind lashed at her ruthlessly. She bent her head against the onslaught and hurried on, clutching the hood close to her neck and lifting her skirts out of the damp.

She came to Washington Avenue and looked both ways before hurrying across. The street lamps along the way had not been lit, and she stumbled when she reached the sidewalk on the other side.

She paused a moment at the intersection of Oak Street and Franklin Avenue, less than a half-block from her home, as a massive lightning bolt slashed the dark clouds. Then she stepped off the sidewalk into the street just as a long roll of thunder roared in her ears.

Adam Burke raced his fishtailing buggy down Franklin Avenue, the fierce wind driving the rain into his face. A massive lightning bolt slashed the dark clouds overhead as he neared the intersection at Oak Street. Thunder boomed, and Adam felt his rain-blinded horse jerk to one side, followed by a thump as the buggy wheel on the right side seemed to roll over something.

In his anger, Adam paid little attention to what was going on around him. He raced on down Franklin, snapping the reins to make the horse go faster.

Nancy Mason lay half-conscious in the mud. The pain in her head was excruciating. Where was she? She tried to move her arms and legs, but couldn't. She recalled lifting her skirts and stepping into the street. She remembered turning her head toward a sudden sound. The next thing she remembered she was lying in the mud. Her head hurt terribly. Why couldn't she move her arms and legs?

"Help me! Somebody help me!"

There was nothing but wind, rain, and thunder to answer her.

She cried out again, but her voice was so weak she knew it wasn't carrying far. She gingerly tried to raise her head to look around, but the blinding pain stopped her.

After a few minutes she was able to move her right arm, then her left. With the same effort she soon was able to move both legs. But when she tried to get up, agonizing pain shot through her body.

"Oh, dear God!" she moaned weakly. "Send someone to help me!" She gathered what little strength she had and called out, "Joseph! Rachel! I . . . I need you! Help me!"

She felt herself sinking into blackness. Just before she lost consciousness she heard voices, and her dull eyes caught a glimpse of lantern light coming toward her.

Rachel Mason slumped in the chair, her hair and clothing soaked, and watched her father pace back and forth in the hospital waiting room. The doctors had told them Cecil's condition was critical. It was his heart. They couldn't say more until they had done a thorough examination.

"It's my fault, Rachel," said Joseph, running fingers through his hair.

"Daddy, how could it be your fault?"

"He's been complaining of chest pains for weeks. When I offered to take him to the doctor he said he'd had the pains before but they always passed. I should've put him in a buggy and taken him to the hospital right then."

"But you can't blame yourself, Daddy. It wasn't your responsibility to force Cecil to go to a doctor."

Joseph began pacing again. "Maybe I've been working him too hard."

"No, he has plenty of time to rest between his little jobs. Daddy, you mustn't blame yourself for this."

Joseph paced silently for a few minutes, then stopped and said, "He's just got to pull through. Cecil's . . . well, he's not only our gardener and handyman, he's one of the family. He's been with us a long time."

"Yes, before I was born. He's family as far as I'm concerned, Daddy."

Joseph's hands were shaking. "I need a good stiff drink."

Rachel jumped off the chair and looked him square in the eye. "Don't say that, Daddy! You haven't had a drink in three years. Certainly you don't want to go back to the bottle. You almost lost your business because of alcohol. Please, don't even mention drinking again!"

Joseph ran a shaky hand over his face. "I'm sorry, honey. I just . . . I still get a craving when I'm upset. I'll be all right if Cecil makes it."

"And if he doesn't?"

"Well, I —"

"Daddy, what did whiskey ever do for you? Sure, when you got drunk you forgot your troubles for a few hours. But when you sobered up your troubles were still there. And you had a hangover to boot. Don't take yourself and Mama and me back to that horror. Please!"

"I'm sorry, Rachel," said Joseph, taking her

in his arms. "I shouldn't have said it. I won't turn back to the bottle, even if Cecil should die."

"Promise?"

"Promise. We should've left a note for your mother. I'm sure Doris has provided a ride home for her by now."

"Mm-hmm. Mama has to be worried about Cecil. She won't know what to think if she finds the other buggy in its place but no Cecil."

"And us gone, too. I should've taken the time to leave a note."

"You couldn't, Daddy. We had to get Cecil to the hospital as fast as possible. Maybe for Mama's sake you ought to go home and let her know what's happened. I can stay here."

"I'll bring her right back with me. At least one of us will be here in case one of the doctors comes out to give us any news."

Even as Joseph was speaking, the door opened and Dr. Donald Walker, who had been the last to talk to Joseph and Rachel, came in.

"From what we can tell, Mr. Mason," Walker said, "Mr. McIntire is going to be all right."

Joseph closed his eyes in relief. "Oh, thank God!"

"I won't go into detail now, but we've got

him past the crisis. It's his heart, yes, but he has quite a constitution and there's every indication that he'll pull through this. It really wasn't what we call a coronary seizure, which at his age might have taken him instantly. But it was serious enough that we'll keep him here for at least a week and watch him closely."

"I'm just so glad it wasn't any worse. Thank you, Doctor."

Walker smiled. "I love it when I can give good news. You two can go on home now. Come back tomorrow afternoon. Mr. McIntire will be able to talk to you then, I'm sure."

Joseph put an arm around Rachel's shoulders as they stepped into the long hallway and headed for the outside door.

"I'm glad when we tell Mama what happened we can give her the good news to go with it." Rachel paused for a moment, then said, "Daddy, I've been at Cecil's side so many times all these years while he was doing yard work. I helped him a lot, too."

"Yes. I used to call you my little tomboy."

"I can do the gardening till Cecil gets better."

"Aw, honey, I don't want you to worry about the yard. I can hire someone else till Cecil's back on the job."

"Well, whatever you say. But I sure would be glad to —"

She stopped speaking when orderlies came through the front door wheeling an unconscious woman on a cart. A pair of well-dressed men followed.

Joseph glanced at his daughter at the same moment she gasped, "It's Mama!"

12

The sight of Nancy lying unconscious under a blanket, with blood oozing from a large bump near her temple, and her hair and face caked with mud, froze Joseph Mason in his tracks.

He felt Rachel grasp his sleeve as he lunged forward and said, "Wait! That's my wife!"

The orderlies halted the cart as the two men behind stepped up to Joseph.

"How did you know these men were bringing her in, sir?" one of the orderlies said.

"I didn't! My daughter and I have been here with the family gardener, who collapsed earlier this afternoon. Wh-what's happened to my wife?"

One of the well-dressed men spoke up. "We found her lying in the street at the intersection of Oak and Franklin. My name's Martin Reid. My friend here is Bill Jessup. We were passing through that part of town when we saw her. We put her in my buggy and brought her to the hospital as fast as we could."

"Daddy, she seems to be breathing all right," said Rachel, letting go of his sleeve.

Joseph leaned over and tenderly pushed damp strands of hair from Nancy's face. In a soft voice, he said, "Nancy, it's Joseph. I'm here and so is Rachel. We love you."

There was no response from the still form beneath the blanket.

Rachel caught a look on the orderlies' faces and put a hesitant hand on her father's arm. "Daddy, we need to let them take Mama so the doctors and nurses can care for her."

"Yes, of course. I'm sorry. Please, go ahead."

The orderlies rushed the cart down the hall. Joseph and Rachel followed while Reid and Jessup hurried to keep up with them.

"Sir," Jessup said, "your wife carried no identification, otherwise we would have tried to contact you."

"My name is Joseph Mason, and this is our daughter, Rachel. I own the American Securities company downtown. I want to thank you gentlemen for bringing Nancy to the hospital."

"We're just glad we happened along, Mr. Mason," Jessup said.

The orderlies stopped abruptly at a pair of solid double doors. One of them pointed to a small room across the hall and said, "You can wait in there, Mr. Mason. A doctor will be in touch with you shortly, and there'll be someone else who will want to get some information from you."

"All right." Joseph looked down at his wife. "Please tell the doctors we want to know her condition as soon as possible."

"Yes, sir. You and your daughter wait right in there." With that the orderlies wheeled the cart through the double doors.

Joseph turned to the two men. "You say you found her in the street at Oak and Franklin? She was just lying there unconscious?"

"Yes, sir," Martin Reid said. "We think she was struck by a vehicle."

Rachel's face lost color. "You mean somebody hit her and left the scene?"

"That's what it looked like, ma'am," Jessup said. "There sure wasn't anyone around when we spotted her."

"I can't believe someone would be so callous as to hit her and leave her lying there," Joseph said.

"I guess it happens, sir," Jessup said. "Mr. Mason, Marty and I have to leave. We'll come back tomorrow and see how she's doing."

"Wait a moment," Joseph said. "Let me write down your names and addresses. I may need to get in touch with you." He took a pencil and a slip of paper from his pocket and wrote down the information as Reid and

Jessup gave it to him.

When the men had left, Rachel said, "Come, Daddy. I think we need to sit down."

She led him into the small room that had a couch and two uncomfortable looking chairs. She gently guided him onto the couch, then sat down beside him.

After a few minutes, Rachel hunched over and wrapped her arms about herself. She stared at the floor as she said, "I wish Aunt Esther were here, Daddy. We need her to pray for Mama."

"My sister may carry things too far when it comes to her religion, honey, but I have to admit she does know how to get hold of God. I wish she were here, too."

Tears slipped down Rachel's cheeks as she pictured how her mother had looked on the cart. Suddenly she became aware that her father was shaking violently. Then he let out a great sob and covered his face with his hands.

Rachel put her arms around him. "Daddy, she'll be all right. Don't cry. I'm sure Mama is going to pull through this." She rose from the couch to grip his shoulders, giving him a little shake. "Daddy, listen to me! You need to get hold of yourself. Mama is going to need all the support we can give her. She'll need strength from both of us to help her overcome her injuries."

Joseph focused on Rachel this time and drew a shuddering breath. He nodded slowly. "You're right, honey," he said in a whisper, wiping tears from his cheeks. "How could this horrible thing have happened?"

"I don't know. Apparently she was walking home because Cecil hadn't come to pick her up."

"But why didn't someone else give her a ride? Krantzes have a butler. There had to have been a good number of women at the meeting. Someone could have given her a ride."

"I don't understand it either, Daddy. She shouldn't have been out in that storm by herself. And I can't fathom that the person who hit her just drove away, leaving her lying in the street."

A woman came in carrying pencil and paper. "Excuse me. I'm Gail Lockyer. I'm in charge of records and admittance. Are you the relatives of the lady who was brought in a few minutes ago?"

Joseph nodded.

"I need to get some information from you."

When Gail Lockyer left them, Joseph and Rachel sat in silence, holding hands. She looked at her father and said, "Daddy, we must believe she's going to pull through this. We —"

The door opened and a man in a white

smock came out. "Mr. Mason? I'm Dr. Richard Alban."

"How is she, Doctor?"

"Still unconscious. The orderlies gave me what details they could. Mrs. Mason was run down by some kind of vehicle. It struck her head, and the wheels went over her when she went down. She has some broken ribs. The large lump at her temple tells us she took quite a blow. The vehicle must have been moving at a good clip."

Rachel struggled to keep her voice from quavering as she said, "Doctor, do you have any idea when she might regain consciousness?"

"She will regain consciousness, won't she doctor?" Joseph said.

Alban lifted his shoulders slightly. "We can't tell for sure, but I have to be honest with you. Two other doctors have examined her with me, and we're in agreement. There is little hope that Mrs. Mason will survive. We're afraid there might be extensive brain damage."

A tiny whimper escaped Rachel's lips, and Joseph slumped back on the couch.

"I wish I had better news for you. But I don't want to give you false hope."

"We wouldn't want you to lie to us, Doctor," Joseph said. "But Rachel and I can't leave here. We have to stay until Nancy either . . . leaves us or shows a turn for the better. That is possible, isn't it? She could fool us and come out of it?"

Alban tried to smile. "Stranger things have happened, I'm sure. I'll let you know of any change. We're going to be working on her for some time yet. We're not giving up, but we have to face the facts we have so far."

Rachel and Joseph thanked the doctor. When he was gone they clung to each other in fear and sorrow.

After several minutes Rachel spoke. "What kind of a low-down person drove that buggy or wagon or carriage that ran Mama down? I don't understand how anybody could do such a thing! How could he just heartlessly drive away and let her lie there?"

"I don't know, honey. I don't know."

Adam Burke wheeled his buggy into the alley behind his apartment house and jerked on the reins. He put horse and buggy in the barn, then trudged through the mud and driving rain into the apartment building. When he entered his apartment and slammed the door, he felt lower than he had ever been. He and Philipa had shared so much together. They had spent so much time talking about their future, about the children they would have, about how happy they would be.

And now it was over.

In addition to his hurt and anger, Adam was cold and wet. He thought about a hot bath, then dismissed the idea. It would be too much trouble right now. He went into his bedroom and peeled off his wet clothes and briskly dried himself off.

He put on an old comfortable pair of corduroy pants and a well-worn sweater. As he was pulling on dry socks, his gaze fell on the photograph of Philipa in a gold-edged frame. She was smiling at him.

He pulled on his slippers and walked to the dresser. "Don't smile at me, woman! You've been a thorough disappointment. I wonder now what I ever saw in you." He picked up the frame. "How could I have been such a fool, Philipa? Oh, I saw little signs of your self-centeredness, but I was so head over heels in love with you that I overlooked it. But there's no overlooking this! You said you never wanted to see me again. Fine. You never will."

He rushed from the bedroom, carrying the photograph, and went to the small kitchen. There he lifted the lid of the trash receptacle and dropped the photograph into it.

He built a fire in the cookstove and pulled the coffeepot onto the grate to reheat it. It was left over from breakfast and would be strong. *Good,* he thought. *Just what I need.* He went to the tiny pantry, took out some bread and cheese, and cut off a couple slices of bread and some chunks of cheese.

When the aroma of coffee filled the room, he poured a steaming mug of it and carried it with the bread and cheese into the living room. He placed the plate and mug on a small table beside his favorite chair, lit the lantern, and turned it down to a soft glow.

His attention was drawn to the sound of the rain on the roof and the windows. It was beginning to let up. He couldn't recall hearing any lightning or thunder in the past few minutes either.

He took a big bite of bread and cheese and sipped the strong, hot coffee, and let his weary mind go over the scene on the back porch of the Conrad mansion. He could still hear Philipa's high-pitched voice telling him that she hated him.

"How could I have been so blind?" he said aloud. "Why didn't I see her for what she really was? Too much in love, that's what I was. And that love isn't gone yet, either. That's why it hurts so much." He took another sip of coffee. "Maybe — just maybe I've been spared a lifetime of misery. It might never have worked."

When Adam finished his simple meal, he washed cup, plate, and knife, and put them away. He went back to the comfortable chair and replayed the argument with Philipa. After a while he laid his tired head against the back of the chair and closed his eyes.

It was close to midnight when Adam awakened. He roused himself enough to leave the chair and go into the bedroom to take off his shirt and pants and climb into bed.

But sleep eluded him now.

He began to think about what he would do next. First thing would be to talk to George Benson and give his notice. Benson was out of town but would be back in a couple of days. As soon as he had told Benson of his plans to go to Nebraska, he would make train reservations, then wire William Dauntt and tell him when he was coming. He was going to North Platte even if there was no office space available. When he got there he would work something out, even if he had to have a small building built.

The more he thought of his move to North Platte the more excited he became. There was nothing to keep him in Philadelphia now. He finally fell asleep, thinking about the wide open spaces and his new life in Nebraska.

It was a beautiful rainwashed day that

greeted Adam when he stepped out of the apartment building the next morning and headed for the small barn and corral to hitch his horse to the buggy. There was a touch of fall in the air.

When Adam entered the law office, he was greeted by Bradley Smith, Eric Walters, and Jill Hawkins. He greeted them in turn and tried to cover his weariness and the hurt Philipa had put in his heart.

"So what did you think of that storm yesterday, Adam?" Smith asked.

"It was a good one," Adam replied. "I was about ready to trade my buggy in for a boat."

Walters gave an appreciative chuckle and said, "Well, people, I've got to meet a client at his office over on Fifth Street in about twenty minutes. Guess I'd better pick up his file and scoot."

"I've got a long hard day at my desk," Smith said. "So what's on your schedule, Adam?"

"I've got to be in court at ten o'clock. I'm defending a client who's in a real sticky lawsuit."

A half hour later, Jill came into Adam's office. "Here are your morning papers, sir," she said, laying three newspapers on a small table beside his desk.

"Thank you, Jill."

Adam worked on his plan of defense for another half hour, then left for the courthouse. He waved at Jill and Bradley Smith, who were in conversation at her desk.

When Adam was gone, Jill said, "Mr. Smith, does Mr. Burke seem all right to you?"

"What do you mean?"

"He just isn't himself today."

"I didn't notice anything."

Jill snickered. "Of course not. You men have no intuition at all!"

"My mother could always read me no matter how hard I tried to cover what was going on inside me." He chuckled. "I thought when I left home to get married those days would be over. But my wife reads me even better than Mom did!"

Jill was alone in the office at two o'clock that afternoon when Adam came in, carrying his briefcase.

"How did it go?" she said, giving him a bright smile.

"Just fine. We won."

"Isn't that how it is every time Adam Burke takes a case?"

"Not quite. I've lost some too, Jill."

"Well, not many." She paused and squinted at him. "Mr. Burke, I don't mean to be nosy, but . . . well, you're just not yourself today. I can tell that something's bothering you."

"Oh, you think so?"

"Mm-hmm."

"And exactly what makes you think so?"

"Woman's intuition."

Adam's face tinted. "Jill, I won't fib to you. I'm carrying something pretty heavy, but I just can't talk about it right now. Thank you for caring enough to ask, though."

Jill smiled. "I've got two good listening ears if and when you want to talk about it."

"Thank you. Well, I've got a stack of work waiting for me in my office. Best get to it."

Adam entered his office and closed the door behind him. He set his briefcase on the desk and took out the folder from the case he had just won in court, filing it in the cabinet behind him. He glanced down at the newspapers Jill had placed there. The one on top was the *Philadelphia Enquirer*. He was about to turn to some work on his desk when his eye caught small headlines near the bottom of the front page:

WIFE OF JOSEPH MASON
RUN DOWN BY
UNKNOWN DRIVER

Adam picked up the paper and read the

first few lines. They told of a tragic incident last evening during the violent rainstorm in Philadelphia's affluent district, at the intersection of Oak Street and Franklin Avenue.

When those words registered, Adam's breath hitched in his chest.

Two men had come along in a buggy and found Mrs. Mason lying in the intersection, bleeding and unconscious. They had taken her to Ben Franklin Memorial Hospital.

The victim was the wife of Joseph Mason, owner of American Securities Company, one of Philadelphia's most prominent brokerage firms. She was struck down at approximately 5:45 to 6:00 P.M. by an unidentified vehicle. The driver had left the scene.

Adam recalled his wild drive home after his argument with Philipa. A wave of nausea washed over him.

Doctors at the hospital said she was in critical condition, and as of nine o'clock last night she had not regained consciousness. Chief of police Mandrake Bennett said there was no way to identify the person or persons who struck Mrs. Mason then left the scene. There were no eyewitnesses to the incident, and the rain had obliterated any clues that might have been left in the muddy street.

Adam laid the paper down and pressed his face into his hands.

There was a tap on the door.

"Yes, Jill?"

"I have a telegram for you, sir." She handed him the yellow envelope. "Mr. Burke, are you all right?"

"Yes, I'm fine."

"You're very pale, sir. Can I get you something? Water? Something else?"

"Ah . . . no, thank you. I —"

"Why don't you go to the lounge and lie down for a few minutes? You're white as a ghost."

Adam swallowed hard. "Tell you what, Jill. I'm really not feeling well. I think maybe I should go home and lie down."

"Maybe you ought to see a doctor."

"No need for that. I'm sure I'll be all right if I can get some rest. I really haven't been sleeping lately."

"Yes, sir. But I'll be glad to get a doctor here if you'll give me permission."

"No, thank you, Jill. I just need to go home for the rest of the day. I'll be fine by morning. I have a court date at nine o'clock, but I'll come into the office first."

Adam's knees felt weak as he climbed into his buggy and headed home. The intersection of Oak Street and Franklin Avenue drew him like a magnet. He drove slowly through the intersection and eyed the very spot where his

196

buggy had struck Nancy Mason.

When Adam arrived at his apartment, he washed his face with cool water, then lay down on the bed. Tears came, and he wept over what he had done, crying out, "Oh, dear God in heaven, don't let her die! Please . . . don't let her die!"

He finally gained control of his emotions and sat up on the side of the bed. He remembered the telegram Jill had handed him, and he pulled it out of his pocket and tore open the envelope.

It was good news from William Dauntt. He had located a nice office for him and had put some money down to hold it. The office was occupied at the moment but was being vacated within a week.

Adam wanted to shout for joy, but Nancy Mason was so heavy on his heart that the shout turned into a moan.

It was not his fault! Why should he put a black mark on his career by going to the police and confessing that it was he who ran Mrs. Mason down? Besides, she had stepped into the path of his buggy. There was nothing he could have done . . . or could do now. Even if he turned himself in, it wouldn't change Mrs. Mason's condition.

He would think on it for a day or so and see what happened to Mrs. Mason. His life had already been torn apart by Philipa. He didn't need it shredded any more. A great future lay ahead of him in North Platte. He must not allow anything to take that from him.

13

At ten o'clock on Friday night, Joseph and Rachel were sitting beside Nancy's hospital bed. Joseph gently squeezed his wife's hand. "Sweetheart, please wake up. Please come back to me."

Neither Joseph nor Rachel had slept since arriving at the hospital the night before. They had eaten only a few bites of food at the hospital lunch room. Yet the thought of leaving Nancy's side never entered their minds.

Head nurse Alice Drummond came into the room, glanced at her patient, then looked at father and daughter. "Mr. Mason," she said in a tender tone, "you and Rachel need to go home and get some rest."

Joseph looked up at her. "We can't do that, ma'am. We can't leave her. What if she wakes up and we're not here?"

Alice laid a hand on Rachel's shoulder. "Listen to me, both of you. I've been a nurse for thirty-one years, and I know exhaustion when I see it. You've been here for over twenty-eight hours now and neither of you slept a wink last night. You're going to collapse, and then what good could you do for Mrs. Mason if — when she wakes up? The best thing you can do for this dear lady is to go home, have a decent meal, then get yourselves a good night's sleep in your own beds. You'll be much better for it, and much better prepared to help Mrs. Mason when she regains consciousness."

"She's right, Daddy," Rachel said.

"All right, ma'am, we'll do it on one condition," Joseph said.

"And that is?"

"You promise to send someone to the house if there is any change. Good or bad."

"It's a deal. If there's any change, you'll have someone knocking on your door."

"All right," Joseph said. "And though the doctors say our gardener is doing well . . . if he should take a turn for the worse, we'd want to know that right away, too."

"You have my word on it, sir."

Joseph squeezed Nancy's hand and kissed her cheek and said, "We'll be back in the morning, sweetheart."

Rachel kissed her mother's forehead and lovingly stroked her hair before following her father to the door.

Rachel was quiet for several minutes while

Joseph drove the buggy through the dimly lit streets, then said, "Daddy, wouldn't the police let us know if the person who ran Mama down turned himself in?"

"I'm sure they would. Chief Bennett as much as said so."

"If he was a decent person his conscience would've gotten the best of him by now. He'd have been at the police station this morning to confess." Rachel's anger suddenly turned to grief and she bent over, putting her face in her hands. Joseph laid a hand on her back and patted her gently.

"Come on, honey," he said, "sit up. We're almost home."

When they turned into the driveway, the sight of home gave a lift to their spirits.

"I'd just like to fall into bed," Joseph said when they entered the house.

"I know, Daddy, but Mrs. Drummond was right. We need to eat something before we retire for the night. It's been too long since we've had a real meal."

They lit a couple of lanterns in the hall, then went to the kitchen. While Joseph built a fire in the cookstove, Rachel scoured the pantry for something nourishing.

"How about bacon and eggs, Daddy?"

"Sounds good to me."

Soon the kitchen was filled with the aroma

of frying bacon. Rachel steeped a pot of tea and sliced large pieces of bread, slathering them with butter. Joseph set the table, and in a little while they sat down with plates full of food.

"Poor Mama," Rachel said, "she's had enough trouble in the past to do her for a life-time. And now this."

"When you say the past, are you talking about bringing you into the world?"

"Well . . . that and her childhood too."

"But your mama never thought of your birth as 'trouble,' you know that. She was so delighted to have you she would've gladly gone through it again."

"I know, you've told me that before. And it makes me love her all the more. Still, I wish she could've been spared some of the struggle she's had to put up with."

Joseph and Rachel cleaned up their plates and emptied the teapot, and Rachel put the dirty dishes and utensils in a large pan and added water. She was too tired to wash them. That would have to wait till morning.

Father and daughter extinguished lanterns as they went down the hall and made their way up the familiar stairs. Joseph stopped at his bedroom, and Rachel kissed his pale cheek and told him good night.

In her room she lit a lantern and poured

water from a pitcher into the wash bowl. After washing her face she ran a brush through her thick hair, then doused the lantern and crawled wearily between the sweet-smelling sheets. She fell asleep asking God to spare her mother's life.

In his own room, Joseph was struggling with the strong desire for a stiff drink. But there was no whiskey in the house; he would have to face the night on his own. Though his mind and body were spent, sleep was a long time coming.

Adam Burke awakened on Saturday morning after a near sleepless night, a hollow feeling in his heart. He pondered his move to Nebraska and figured it would be a little over three weeks before he would actually arrive in North Platte.

After a bit of breakfast, he sat down and wrote a letter to William Dauntt, explaining his plan. He enclosed a check to cover the first two months' rent on the office space and enough to cover the cost of a boardinghouse room for the same amount of time.

Adam briefly explained that the wedding he had planned didn't work out. He would be coming alone.

At Ben Franklin Memorial Hospital, Alice

Drummond had just arrived for the change of shift and was talking to Dr. Alban at the nurses' station when a young nurse came running down the hall. "Dr. Alban! Mrs. Drummond! Nancy Mason is waking up! Mary Nall is with her, and she asked me to come and tell you!"

Dr. Alban and Alice Drummond hurried down the hall and entered Nancy's room. Her eyes were dull as she looked at their faces.

"Has she said anything yet?" the doctor asked.

"A little," Mary said. "Her speech is slurred, and as you can see by her eyes, her mind is hazy. But she asked for her husband and daughter."

Dr. Alban leaned down close. "Nancy, I'm Dr. Richard Alban. Can you talk to me?"

Nancy's eyes closed as she swallowed with difficulty, then she opened them and said, "D-o-c-tor, is . . . Jo-seph here? Ra-chel?"

"They will be here shortly."

"I was about to change this bandage on her head," Mary said. "Shall I go ahead, Doctor?"

"Hello!" came a voice at the open door. Doctor and nurses turned to see Joseph and Rachel looking a bit more rested.

"Jo-seph?" Nancy said.

"Mama!" Rachel darted to the bed. "Daddy, she's awake!"

Nancy's dull eyes brightened a bit as Joseph and Rachel bent down and kissed her.

"How long has she been awake?" Joseph asked.

"Only a few minutes, sir," Mary answered. "I was checking her vital signs when she opened her eyes and looked at me. It took her a few seconds, but she was finally able to ask for her husband and daughter."

"Oh, Mama!" Rachel said. "It's so wonderful to see you awake!"

"Miss Nall needs to change the bandage on her head," Dr. Alban said. "If you'll give her time to do it, then you can come back and stay in the room."

Joseph put his face close to Nancy's and said, "Sweetheart, Rachel and I will be back as soon as the nurse has changed your bandage. All right?"

Nancy smiled weakly and said, "I . . . love . . . you."

Joseph squeezed back the tears and said, "I love you too, sweetheart."

Nancy slowly turned her gaze to Rachel. "I . . . love . . . you."

"I love you too, Mama. With all my heart."

Some twenty minutes had passed when Dr.

Alban came into the small waiting room and sat down facing Joseph and Rachel.

"I must tell you that I'm amazed at this," he said. "Amazed and very pleased. Nancy is awfully weak, so let me caution you not to make her talk. Just let her know you're there. If she chooses to talk, fine. But don't keep her awake if she wants to sleep."

"We understand, Doctor," Joseph said.

"I did question her a bit. She doesn't remember walking home on Thursday. In fact, she doesn't remember being anywhere on Thursday. Of course, this means she doesn't remember what happened at the intersection, so she can't tell us anything about it."

"I guess we'll never know exactly what happened," Rachel said. "Unless the person who ran her down comes forward and turns himself in to the police." There was a bitter edge to her next words. "But then if he was going to do it, he'd have done it by now."

Alice Drummond appeared at the door. "Mr. Mason, there's a Derek Mills here from the *Enquirer*. He would like to interview you."

"May I go to my mother, Mrs. Drummond?" Rachel asked.

"Of course."

"Daddy, I'll be with Mama when you're through with the reporter."

"All right, honey. I'm sure I won't be long."

★ ★ ★

Joseph and Rachel stayed with Nancy for the day and into the evening. They let her sleep as much as she needed and talked to her briefly each time she awakened. Her responses were slow and sometimes incomprehensible, but Joseph and Rachel's elation grew with each word she uttered. When the nurses came in to give Nancy her medicine for the night, she was able to tell Joseph and Rachel to go home and get a good night's sleep.

On Sunday morning, Adam Burke left his room after breakfast and picked up the Sunday edition of the *Philadelphia Enquirer* in the lobby of the apartment building. He returned to his room and searched the paper for news about Nancy Mason.

On page three, an article by Derek Mills said that Nancy had regained consciousness on Saturday morning. Dr. Richard Alban, the physician in charge of Mrs. Mason, spoke with caution, but he believed that his patient was on the road to recovery.

Adam laid the paper down and massaged his temples. "Thank God she woke up."

Throughout the day, Adam thought of the distress Nancy Mason's family had endured. By sunset, his conscience was eating away at him, and he decided he needed to go to the hospital and talk to Nancy and her family. Surely the Masons wouldn't press charges when he explained to them what had happened.

Adam decided he would leave home early in the morning and stop at the hospital to see Mrs. Mason on his way to the office. Then he would talk to George Benson and give him notice that he would be leaving the firm in about two weeks.

Joseph and Rachel were at the hospital early Sunday morning and were elated to see Nancy more alert than she had been the previous evening.

Alice Drummond came into the room and told Joseph there had been some visitors, but Dr. Alban had left orders that no one could see Nancy except her husband and daughter. The receptionist was keeping a list of the names so the Masons would know who had come.

"Do you know why Cecil didn't come to get me?" Nancy asked suddenly.

Joseph quickly leaned over the bed and studied Nancy's face. "Is some of what happened that evening starting to come back?"

"I . . . I guess so. Not much . . . though I remember waiting for Cecil to come get me. But he never did."

"That's because Rachel found him unconscious at the barn door, and we had to bring him here, to the hospital. We were just leaving when we saw you being brought in on a cart."

"Oh."

"Rest now. You need to get your strength back, then we can talk about what happened that night."

When night fell and the hour grew late, the nurses came in with Nancy's bedtime medicine. After she had taken it, she set loving eyes on her husband and daughter and said, "It's time for my family to go home and get their rest."

Joseph leaned down and kissed her tenderly on the cheek. "We'll be here in the morning, honey."

Nancy smiled. "How is the company going to survive if you're not there tomorrow?"

"American Securities will make it all right."

Rachel kissed her mother and said, "You rest good now. I love you, Mama."

Nancy smiled. "I love you too, my precious little girl."

Joseph and Rachel entered the hospital early on Monday morning with buoyant spirits. But as they drew near Nancy's room, a doctor rushed out of the room and ran down the hall the other direction. They could hear distressed voices coming from the room.

When they reached the partially open door, Joseph saw Dr. Alban, Mary Nall, and another nurse working on Nancy.

Mary caught sight of them and left the bedside to head them off. "I'm so sorry. She's taken a turn for the worse. We're doing all we can."

Just then the doctor who had run from the room a moment before pushed past them and hurried to the bed.

"I have to get back to her," Mary said. "We need you to go to the waiting room for now. Please . . . don't give up. Dr. Alban will come and see you once we get her stabilized."

"Is she going to make it?" Joseph asked.

"As I said, we're doing all we can. Now I must get back to my post."

Rachel took hold of her father's arm. "Come on, Daddy."

A man and woman were just leaving the waiting room, holding on to each other, as Joseph and Rachel approached the door. Rachel guided her father to the couch and sat down beside him.

Joseph stared at the floor and mumbled, "She isn't going to make it. I know she isn't going to make it."

"No, Daddy," Rachel said, squeezing his

arm. "She will! You must believe that! We have to —"

Dr. Alban appeared at the door. "Mr. Mason . . . Rachel . . . I'm so sorry. We couldn't save her. She took a turn for the worse about half an hour ago. She began mumbling incoherently while Miss Nall was checking her vital signs. We know now that the blow she received when the vehicle struck her was more severe than we thought. There is every indication that she died from a brain hemorrhage."

Father and daughter sat like statues, unable to move or speak.

Alban wiped tears from his eyes. "I . . . I have to tell you that if by some miracle Nancy had lived, there is a good possibility she would never have been normal. I know she showed what seemed to be great improvement, but with the damage done to her brain, she no doubt would not have been the same as you knew her. Please know that my heart goes out to you. And if there's anything I can do for you, I want you to let me know."

"Thank you, Doctor," Rachel said through tears. "I know you and the others did everything you could to save my mother. Can we . . . can we go into her room? Just the two of us? We need some time with her."

"Certainly. Wait here a moment and I'll come get you."

Rachel wrapped her arms around her father and said, "Daddy, we still have each other."

Joseph nodded but did not speak.

Dr. Alban came back to the waiting room and said, "All right. Take your time, and let us know when you're finished."

Rachel stood up and reached for her father's hand. "Come, Daddy. We can go in with Mama now."

They entered the room, and Joseph halted just inside the door. Rachel went to pull the sheet from her mother's face, and with tears gliding down her cheeks, she bent over and kissed her mother's brow. Abruptly she turned away, great wracking sobs convulsing her.

Joseph remained by the door, staring at the lifeless form on the bed. After a few minutes, Rachel went to her father's side and firmly grasped his arm. "Come, Daddy. Sit down over here by the bed."

She guided him to a chair near the head of the bed and gently made him sit down. He stared vacantly at the floor.

After what seemed like a long time to Rachel, she heard her father gasp. She turned to see him lift his head, his eyes overflowing with tears. He rose from the chair and stood over Nancy's body, then leaned down and gathered her into his arms. The floodgates opened and Joseph gave way to his anguish.

When his weeping subsided, he gently laid Nancy down and stared into her face.

"Daddy, we should go now," Rachel said, taking hold of his arm.

He turned toward her, and there was a glassy look in his eyes. Rachel gently but firmly led him from the room.

Alice Drummond was standing a few feet from the door. "Are you going home now?" she asked.

Rachel nodded, and Alice went with them to the front door of the hospital. As they walked, Rachel told Alice she would get back to her as soon as they had contacted a mortician to pick up the body. Alice helped Rachel get her father into the buggy, then watched as the young girl put the horse in motion.

When they arrived at the house, Rachel accompanied her father up the stairs to his bedroom and helped him lie down on the bed.

"You just rest, Daddy," she said. "Maybe you can sleep."

Joseph nodded without speaking.

Rachel then went to her room, sprawled across the bed, and wept. Some time later, she heard the old grandfather clock in the downstairs foyer chime four times, and she got up and went to check on her father. The bed covers were awry but there was no sign of him.

When she reached the first floor, Rachel heard a familiar tinkling sound in the kitchen. She ran down the hall and found Joseph Mason sitting at the table, pouring whiskey into a glass.

"Daddy!" she gasped. "Where did you get that bottle?"

"At the liquor store, that's where."

"Daddy, don't! That whiskey won't bring Mama back!"

Joseph put the glass to his lips and poured the amber liquid down his throat.

14

On Monday morning, Adam Burke stopped at the Ben Franklin Memorial Hospital before work. His heart was in his throat.

The receptionist looked up at him and smiled as he approached the desk. "May I help you, sir?"

"Yes, ma'am. You have a patient here . . . Mrs. Nancy Mason. What room is she in, please?"

The receptionist's smile faded. "Sir, Mrs. Mason took a turn for the worse earlier this morning and died a little over an hour ago."

It took a few moments before Adam could speak. He finally said, "I . . . I'm sorry to hear that."

"Are you a member of the family? If you are, we can let you go to the room. Mr. Mason and his daughter are there now. I'm sure they could use some comfort."

Adam's voice faltered. "No . . . I'm not a family member."

Adam's whole body was quaking and he

could hardly breathe as he drove his buggy from the hospital. *I killed Nancy Mason!* The words were loud and accusing in his mind. Adam pulled the buggy to the side of the street and stifled the cry in his throat by pressing his hand to his mouth.

"Adam," he said aloud, "it *wasn't* your fault. Get that into your head."

He took a deep breath, and after a few moments put the horse in motion once more and turned his thoughts to his next task — a talk with Mr. Benson.

"Good morning, Mr. Burke," Jill Hawkins said, smiling. "Have a nice weekend?"

"I've had better," he said, forcing a smile. "Jill, when Mr. Benson comes in, will you tell him I need a few minutes with him as soon as possible? It's very important."

"How about right now? He was here already when I came in. I think he'd have time to see you before he gets his day started." She left her chair and went to Benson's office door.

Adam waited at her desk, his insides churning. He heard Benson's muffled voice, and then Jill opened the door and leaned inside the doorway. In a moment she turned back to Adam and said, "Did you hear that, Mr. Burke?"

Adam walked toward her. "Yes, Jill. Thank you."

When the door closed behind him, Adam smiled and said, "Did you have a successful trip, sir?"

"Sure did," said Benson, rising from his desk to offer his hand. He invited Adam to sit down and then returned to his own chair. "Well! The first items brought to my attention when I came in this morning were the cases you handled so beautifully while I was gone. Jill left the reports on top of my desk along with all the others. But yours were at the top of the stack. Well done, Adam. Well done."

"Thank you, sir."

"Now, before you bring up your reason for wanting to see me, please allow me to bring up my subject first."

"Of course."

"Adam, I've given a great deal of thought lately to the fine work you've been doing, and I've decided that you should become a partner in this firm. And as you become a partner, I will see to it that your annual income doubles over what it is right now. How about it? You ready to get your name put on the sign out front?"

"That's . . . that's quite an offer, sir."

Benson chuckled. "I thought it would appeal to you. And you've earned it, son."

"Mr. Benson, this actually brings up the

reason I wanted to see you this morning."

"Oh?"

"Yes, sir. I want you to know that I deeply appreciate the offer you just laid before me, but —"

"But what?"

"I can't accept it, sir. You see, I wanted to talk to you this morning so I could give you my two week notice."

Benson's bushy eyebrows arched. "Two week notice? You're leaving us?"

"Yes, sir. Not because I'm unhappy working for the firm, Mr. Benson, but because I'm going out West to establish my own law firm."

"Your own law firm?"

"Yes, sir."

Benson's brows knitted together in a frown. "And exactly where are you going to establish it?"

"North Platte, Nebraska. The chairman of North Platte's town council, a Mr. William Dauntt, encouraged me to come. There's no law office in the town right now. The people there have to travel a hundred and twenty miles one way for legal help."

"Have you been there?"

"Well, I took a trip all the way to California with my uncle right after I graduated from Harvard, sir. Our train stopped in North Platte, but we didn't get off and actually see the town. On that trip I fell in love with the West. It's been calling me back ever since."

"Adam, I'm disappointed. I very much wanted you as a partner in this firm." A smile broke across Benson's face. "But I have to admire your pioneer spirit. I started my own law firm once, and I can understand your desire to do so."

"I'm glad you feel that way, Mr. Benson."

"Now, what about your wedding? Wasn't that set for late October?"

"It was, sir, but the wedding's off."

Benson's eyebrows arched again. "Off? You and Philipa aren't getting married?"

"No, sir. We had a falling out over my desire to move to Nebraska, so it's all over between us."

"Hmm. Well, I'm sorry to hear that, Adam. But I certainly wish you the best."

On Tuesday morning Joseph Mason lay in bed, still under the effects of the whiskey.

Rachel stood over him and said, "Since you're in no condition to do it, I'll go into the office and tell them about Mama . . . and while I'm downtown I'll wire our relatives, letting them know about Mama's death and that the funeral will be on Saturday."

Joseph scrubbed a palm over his face. "S-s-saturday? How do you know it'll be Saturday?"

"I went to the Harrison Brothers Funeral Parlor and made the arrangements. Mama's body is probably already there by now."

Joseph frowned. "Why Saturday? Couldn't the funeral be soo-sooner?"

"Not if we want to give our relatives time to get here."

"Oh. Of course. You sending wires to everyone?"

"Yes. Some won't be able to come, of course, but at least they should know that Mama died."

Joseph nodded, wincing from the pain in his head.

Esther Holden, Joseph's sister, was the first of the relatives to arrive. She came to the Mason mansion late on Thursday afternoon, having taken a hired buggy from the railroad depot.

Joseph and his sister had always been very close, even after she married Clayton Holden. Things changed somewhat when Esther and Clayton became Christians. Although Nancy and Rachel had not embraced the "Jesus business" — as Joseph put it — they didn't seem to be as uncomfortable around the Holdens as Joseph was. Nancy had corresponded with them over the years, and even more so with Esther when Clayton joined the Confederate army at the outset of the Civil War and was killed at the Battle of Shiloh in April 1862.

As a child, Rachel had spent some time with her Aunt Esther and had learned to love her. Esther was a bundle of energy and one of the kindest people Rachel had ever met. She was always busy with her home, her church, her neighborhood, and anyplace else where her tireless help was needed. She had a deep, abiding faith in Christ, and her countenance showed the peace that was in her heart.

When Rachel turned sixteen, she and Esther began writing to each other and had developed a strong bond between them. Rachel was glad now to be able to turn the reins over to Esther with her propensity for organization and detail.

Millie, the maid and cook, had returned that morning from her visit to relatives. After the initial shock of learning about Nancy's death, she went back to her duties, finding some relief in the mundane tasks of cooking and cleaning.

In spite of Millie and Esther's protests, Rachel joined in and helped them.

Saturday was sunny and warm with a bright azure sky covering Philadelphia like a canopy. The funeral was well attended by friends, acquaintances, and people of the business world. Relatives had come from far and near and were a comfort to the grieving husband and daughter.

Esther was a tower of strength for Rachel during the service. At the graveside, Esther placed herself between Joseph and Rachel, ready to offer a strong arm to lean on.

After the brief service, everyone was invited to the Mason home for refreshments. The guests gathered in the backyard, where Joseph and Rachel greeted them and accepted their heartfelt condolences. Aunt Esther was the perfect hostess, seeming to be everywhere at once.

After a short time, Joseph excused himself to a couple of relatives and made his way toward the back door of the house. Although he had sworn to himself not to drink while his sister was staying with them, he was feeling more and more as if he would never make it through this day without it.

Esther caught a glimpse of him looking over his shoulder as he passed through the door, and she prayed silently for him. Her brother and niece needed God's love and grace so badly, but they couldn't experience these until they knew Jesus as Lord and Saviour. Only then could they know the truth of Psalm 30:5, "Weeping may endure for a night, but joy cometh in the morning." Esther thumbed away a tear, and turned back to talk with relatives she had not seen for a long time.

When the guests were preparing to leave, Rachel looked around for her father. Her heart sank when she could not find him, and she hurried into the house and up the stairs to her father's room.

Joseph lay on his bed, a whiskey bottle in his hand. He looked at her with droopy eyes and waited for her to speak. But Rachel wheeled about and slammed the door behind her.

Rachel let the departing guests believe that her father was so overcome with grief that he had gone to his room. Finally, only Rachel, Esther, and Millie remained. Millie went to work gathering plates, cups, and glasses from the backyard.

Esther looked at her niece and said, "Is my brother really in his room because he couldn't face people any longer, or has he got his friend up there with him?"

"His friend?"

"The bottle."

Tears filled Rachel's eyes, and Esther gathered her in her arms, holding her tightly for a moment. "Has he been on the stuff again, or did it start when your mother died?"

"When Mama died. He was doing so well until then."

"I'm sorry you have to live with this."

"Aunt Esther, why don't you sit down and rest? I'll help Millie clean up."

"Not without me, you won't."

In a short while the yard and house were in shipshape condition. Millie prepared a pot of tea, and Esther and Rachel sat down together in the kitchen, each with a cup of hot, spicy tea in front of her. The long, emotion-filled day had taken its toll. Rachel's face was lined with fatigue and sadness, and her mind seemed far away.

"Rachel, let's talk about your precious mother," Esther said. "You've been strong and stoic through these past days, but deep in your heart I know the pain of your loss is almost beyond bearing. Tell me some of your fondest memories of your mother."

Tears began to spill down Rachel's cheeks and her chin quivered. Esther rose from the table and took her niece by the hand.

"Come, sit over here." Esther led Rachel to a small settee. "Talk to me, honey. Tell me some sweet memories you have."

Rachel sniffed. "This is not a memory, Aunt Esther, because I can't remember it. But one thing that has stood out in my mind about Mama is how she risked her life to bring me into the world."

"Yes. And she often said she would do it

again if it meant having a wonderful daughter like you."

"Daddy said that the first time Mama held me after I was born, she kept saying how much she loved her little baby girl."

"Mm-hmm. I know about that."

Rachel's face pinched. "Mama — Mama —"

"Go on, honey. What about her?"

Rachel sucked in a sharp breath and looked at Esther through a wall of tears. "Daddy and I saw Mama alive for the last time on Sunday night. Aunt Esther, the very last words I heard my mother say came when Daddy and I were about to leave her room. She looked at me and said, 'I love you, my precious little girl.'"

Esther stood up and gathered her niece into her arms, holding her head against her bosom, as Rachel gave vent to the anguish she had kept locked away since the day of her mother's death. While Esther held Rachel tight and let her weep, she fervently asked the Lord for guidance.

After some time, the weeping abated. Rachel raised her head and pulled away a little, and Esther took a handkerchief from her sleeve and dried the remaining tears from her niece's face.

Rachel smiled slightly and said, "How can I ever thank you? What would I have done if you hadn't come?"

Esther's own eyes were shining with unshed tears. "I wouldn't have it any other way, sweetie. And I'll stay with you and your daddy as long as you need me."

"I love you, Aunt Esther."

"I love you too, Rachel." Esther let a few seconds pass, then said, "I'm glad for those last words from your mother. You'll have those to hang on to for the rest of your life."

"Yes. I'm so glad, too. That's something no one can take away from me."

Esther Holden stayed at the Mason home for a few more days. Once when she and Rachel were alone in the house, Esther asked her, "Do you remember some of the things I wrote you in my letters, things about the Lord and living our lives for Him?"

"I do, and I appreciated what you said and the Scriptures you quoted. But Daddy . . . well, he told me I needed to be careful about such things. I believe in God, don't get me wrong. I just haven't made up my mind what I believe about those things."

"Well, you go right ahead and think about it some more. And if you ever care to talk about it, you just let me know."

"I will, Aunt Esther. And thank you for caring about me."

One night after Rachel had gone to bed,

Esther took advantage of a brief moment before Joseph turned in to talk to him about his need to know Jesus and to have his sins forgiven. Joseph listened politely for a few minutes, then told his sister he simply wasn't interested in what she had to say about it.

By the time Esther boarded the train for Memphis, she knew Rachel was thinking about her salvation, though she had not been able to lead the girl to the Lord.

On Friday afternoon, September 28, George Benson and his partners, the other lawyers in the firm, and the office staff threw Adam Burke a surprise going away party just before closing time. The next morning, Adam boarded a train at the Philadelphia train station. He sat next to a window in the first car behind the baggage coach. The first destination was Chicago. There he would change trains and board one bound for Cheyenne City, Wyoming.

Adam opened the envelope that contained his tickets and a schedule of the stops between Philadelphia and Chicago. A second schedule showed the stops beyond the Windy City. He studied that schedule and saw that his train would stop at Rock Island, Illinois; Des Moines, Iowa; Omaha, Grand Island, and Kearney, Nebraska. The next stop after Kearney was North Platte.

As the train rolled across Pennsylvania, Adam noticed two young couples sitting ahead of him — a couple on each side of the aisle. He thought again of when he first met Philipa and how he quickly had fallen in love with her. He thought of the dreams of married life they had told each other and of so many happy times. He thought of the last time he had seen her. He could still see the hatred in her eyes when she threw the engagement ring at him.

Adam sighed. *Maybe right now some nice girl in North Platte is lonely and wondering if some nice young man will come along, sweep her off her feet, and ask her to marry him.*

"Tickets, please!" came the voice of the conductor from the back of the coach. "Have your tickets ready, please!"

Adam pulled the Chicago ticket from the envelope and looked at the schedule again. The words *North Platte* stood out like letters of fire against a night sky.

"Get ready, North Platte. Here comes Adam Burke, attorney at law."

15

With each stop along the way, more passengers boarded the Chicago-bound train, and the coach began to fill up. Adam ate supper in the dining car then returned to his seat just as the train chugged into Pittsburgh. The stop was a long one, but when it rolled out of the station there was no one seated beside him.

The next morning, Adam awakened to the conductor's loud voice. "Ten minutes from Cleveland!" He stretched his arms and covered a yawn, then looked out the window and saw light from the rising sun dancing on the rippling waters of Lake Erie.

The train chugged into the Cleveland depot and squealed to a halt. Adam stood up to stretch his legs, and several passengers filed out of the coach. After some twenty minutes, new passengers began to board.

Soon, almost every seat was filled, but the space next to Adam remained empty. The engine whistle gave a blast, and the bell began to ring when suddenly Adam saw a young woman enter the coach carrying an overnight bag. She made her way down the aisle, looking for a vacant seat. She spotted the empty space next to Adam and stopped, giving him a captivating smile. "Pardon me, sir, is that seat taken?"

"No, ma'am." He stepped into the aisle. "May I put your bag in the overhead rack for you?"

"Why, thank you."

Adam took the overnight bag from her and placed it in the rack above the seat, then said, "Would you like to sit by the window, ma'am?"

"Why . . . yes. If you don't mind."

"I don't mind at all. I've been alone on this seat since Philadelphia. It'll be nice to have some company. My name is Adam Burke, Miss . . ."

"Lila Scott. You're from Philadelphia, I take it?"

The train began rolling out of the station.

"Yes, ma'am."

"And what do you do in Philadelphia, Mr. Burke?"

"Well, up until this past Friday I was with the law firm of Benson, Smith, and Walters."

Lila's eyebrows raised. "You're an attorney?"

"Yes, ma'am."

"What law school did you attend?"

"I graduated from Harvard, ma'am."

"Harvard! Well, I am impressed! So if you're no longer with the firm in Philadelphia, what now?"

"Well, I'm heading west to establish my own firm."

"Oh? Where in the West?"

"North Platte, Nebraska."

"North Platte . . . that should be a nice place to settle down."

"I'm excited about it, I'll tell you that much."

"Have you been there?"

"I took a trip west with my uncle right after I graduated from Harvard, all the way to California. The train stopped in North Platte, and though I didn't get to leave the train and see more of the town, I was impressed with what I saw. Actually, I didn't pick the town because I had seen it before. I recently learned that North Platte doesn't have a law firm. So, they're about to get one, Miss Scott!"

Lila glanced at the countryside rushing by and said, "Mr. Burke, I hate to ask you to move to let me out, but I haven't had any breakfast. I believe I'll go to the dining car."

"Tell you what, ma'am. I haven't had breakfast, either. Would you do me the honor of allowing me to buy your breakfast?"

231

"But you hardly know me, sir."

"That's true, but I'd still be honored if you'd join me for breakfast. And while we're eating I can get to know you better."

Lila laughed. "All right. How can I turn down a gentleman's offer that is so well put?"

Soon they were sitting across from one another at a small table in the dining car.

"All the talk so far has been about me," Adam said. "You haven't told me yet where you're from or where you're going."

"Oh. Well, I guess I owe you that. I'm from Cuyahoga Falls, just south of Cleveland. Born and raised there."

"I see. And where are you headed on this trip?"

"Well, it's not just a trip. I'm going to be living on a cattle ranch a few miles west of Sterling, Colorado."

"Oh, really?"

"Mm-hmm. I'll probably be on the same train as you tomorrow. I know it stops in North Platte. It goes all the way to Cheyenne City."

"That's the one," Adam said.

"I'm getting off at Sidney, Nebraska, and taking a stagecoach south to Sterling."

"I seem to remember stopping at Sidney on my California trip. Sterling can't be too awfully far from North Platte."

"No, I don't suppose it would be." Lila glanced at the people at both ends of the dining car waiting for a table. "We'd better let someone else have this table."

"Guess so," Adam said. He held her chair as she stood up.

When they reached their seats, Adam was about to ask her about the cattle ranch, but she covered a yawn and said, "Excuse me, Mr. Burke. I didn't get much sleep last night. I think I'll put my head back and take a nap."

He grinned and said, "Far be it from me to keep a lady from getting her rest. Let me get you a pillow from the rack."

When Lila was comfortable, she closed her eyes and soon was asleep.

The conductor came through the coach some time later announcing they would be in Chicago in twenty minutes. Lila sat up and rubbed her eyes, then looked at Adam and said, "Please forgive me for being such boring company, Mr. Burke."

"Nothing to forgive, Miss Scott. You could never be boring."

"Will you excuse me? I need to go freshen up."

By the time Lila returned, the train was rolling into Chicago. It chugged to a halt in the large depot, and Adam left his seat and reached up for Lila's overnight bag.

"This bag's a bit heavy. May I carry it to the next train for you? I mean, since I'm taking the same train?"

Lila smiled and said, "I would appreciate that very much. Thank you."

They reached the platform at the front of the coach, and Adam stepped down first, then took Lila's hand to help her down the steps. She smiled her thanks and stayed by his side as he led her to the large schedule board. He quickly found the information they needed, and said, "It says our train will leave on time on track 9. We came in on track 21, so it'll be this way."

Adam and Lila walked through the crowded depot to the area that served tracks 6 through 10. He looked around for a bit, then said, "There are a couple of eating places, and we've got almost two hours before departure. How about lunch?"

"I am starting to feel hungry," Lila said. "But I'll buy my own meal this time."

"Oh no, you won't. As long as I have this opportunity I'm taking advantage of it. Lunch is on me."

"You're awfully kind, Mr. Burke. There should be more men like you in the world."

Soon they were seated at a table in a café. When they had placed their order, Lila said, "It must be exciting to make your living as an attorney. I assume you do court cases as well as wills and that sort of thing."

"Oh, yes. I do wills, corporate set-ups, handle legal documents for all kinds of businesses. I handle lawsuits and criminal cases. The one thing I never enjoy working on is a divorce case. Those are always difficult."

"I can imagine."

"I'd say the most interesting part of my work is the criminal cases."

"Tell me about some of them."

Adam told her the story of Seth Coleman and his acquittal, and that it wasn't until Jake Wilson's confession much later that Seth was completely cleared in everyone's minds. "It was the most exciting and personally satisfying case I've experienced so far in my career," Adam said.

At Lila's urging, Adam told her of other interesting cases he had worked on. When they finished lunch, they returned to the boarding area for the next leg of their journey. Adam picked a bench where no one was sitting close by and said, "How about here? This all right?"

"Certainly," Lila said.

Adam placed her overnight bag next to his. "If it pleases you, I'll sit with you as far as North Platte so I can take care of this heavy bag for you."

"That would please me very much, Mr. Burke."

"Sorry I won't be there to take it down for you at Sidney."

"Maybe there'll be another gentleman nearby who will help a lady with her bag."

They sat there for a moment, watching people pass by.

"Miss Scott, I'm curious . . ."

"About what?"

"Well, I don't mean to be nosy, but you haven't told me why you left Cuyahoga Falls to live on a cattle ranch in Colorado."

"Oh, haven't I?"

"We've been talking too much about me and my career."

"I'm going there to marry a young cattle rancher, Mr. Burke. He recently inherited the ranch when his widowed father died. His name is Jess Powers."

"So I take it Jess is actually from Cuyahoga Falls but moved to Colorado when he inherited the ranch?"

"Oh, no. Jess was born and raised on the ranch. I've never met him in person." Lila smiled at Adam's look of consternation.

"You have never met the man, but you're on your way to marry him?"

"Mr. Burke, surely you've heard of mail order brides?"

"Oh, sure! But I've never met a mail order bride. Nor have I ever met a man who sent for one."

"Well, you won't be able to say that again." She opened her purse and pulled out a small photograph. "This is Jess."

It was a picture of a tall, lanky cowboy. Adam forced a smile and said, "Nice-looking man, Miss Scott. I hope you will be very happy."

The announcement came that it was time to board the train, and Adam and Lila made their way to one of the coaches. They found two empty seats together, and Adam once again placed her overnight bag in the overhead rack.

"And what about you, Mr. Burke?" Lila asked. "Is there a young lady in your life?"

"Not at the moment. I was engaged once, but it didn't work out."

"Oh, I'm sorry."

Adam shrugged. "That's life. Maybe I'll find the girl of my dreams in North Platte."

"Maybe. But don't be surprised if you find young unmarried women scarce there. When the first letter came from Jess, he told me that in the West there are about two hundred unmarried men for every unmarried woman."

"Really?"

"That's what he said. He couldn't find any

eligible young women anywhere around Sterling. That's why he put ads in the Mail Order Bride section of several Eastern newspapers. I won't bore you with the details, but I needed to get away from Cuyahoga Falls because of family problems. So I answered Jess's ad in the Cleveland paper. Everything is working out beautifully for me."

The miles rolled by quickly, and soon the train slowed to enter North Platte. When it chugged to a halt, Adam stood up, took his small bag down from the rack, and said, "Well, I guess this is good-bye, Miss Scott. It's been a pleasure meeting you."

"Likewise. Thank you for all the meals, and for the very delightful company."

"It's been a pleasure, ma'am."

"Mr. Burke, I hope you find the right young woman in North Platte." She paused, then added, "Or maybe you'll have to get your bride through the mail."

Adam gave her a slanted grin. "Good-bye, ma'am."

Adam reached the door, and he looked back and nodded. Lila gave a tiny wave, and he moved out onto the platform. As he stepped down from the train, he mumbled, "Not me, ma'am. I'd never order a bride through the mail."

There were only a few people moving about

as Adam headed for the baggage coach. He was nearly there when he saw two men coming toward him. The short, stout man had a badge on his chest. The other man, who was tall, dark, and hollow-cheeked said, "Adam Burke?"

"Yes, sir. And I think I must be looking at Lincoln County Sheriff Ben Colter and North Platte's town council chairman, Mr. William Dauntt."

"That's right," said the tall man. "I'm Sheriff Colter, but William here borrowed my badge!"

All three laughed, then shook hands.

"I assume you have some baggage to pick up?" Dauntt said.

"Four large trunks, sir."

"I'll take care of it," Sheriff Colter said. "Be right back."

Colter went after a porter to bring a cart, and Adam said to Dauntt, "I know right now that you and I will become good friends."

"Well, I'm glad you feel that way, but why didn't you know it before?"

"I figured you were a good man by the spirit of your correspondence, but since you look so much like my hero, Abraham Lincoln, I know for sure you've got to be all right!"

Dauntt laughed. "I guess I look more like honest Abe than I realize. So many people have told me that."

"It's something to be proud of, Mr. Dauntt. Abraham Lincoln, in my estimation, was the greatest president this country's ever had. Don't misunderstand me. I like Hayes. He's a good man, and I'm sure he'll be a great president. But it was Mr. Lincoln's influence that caused me to want to become a lawyer."

"Well, good for Mr. Lincoln. And I'm honored that God gave me a resemblance to him."

Sheriff Colter returned with the porter and his cart. The four trunks were loaded and taken to the parking lot where they were transferred to William Dauntt's wagon.

"We'll take you to your office after we go to the boardinghouse," Dauntt said. "I've put you with Wallace and Minnie Melroy. Their place is a little bit nicer than the other boardinghouse, and the rooms are a bit larger."

"Fine," Adam said. He was all eyes as they rolled into town and up Main Street. The numerous trees along the street and in the yards were beginning to take on their autumn hues.

Dauntt turned south on Main and pointed in a northerly direction. "Your office is back that way. Right in the heart of the business section."

Adam glanced that way and nodded. "Can't wait to see it."

They went two blocks and turned west off

Main onto a side street. Moments later, they hauled up in front of a large two-story frame building. A fresh coat of light gray paint shone in the late afternoon sunlight. The windows were trimmed in white with black shutters. Tied-back filmy curtains decorated each sparkling window. There was a wide, inviting front porch with a few tables and matching chairs scattered about, and a large porch swing.

Adam took a deep breath. The air was clean. He smiled as he looked at the oversized house. "It's just what I imagined, Mr. Dauntt," he said.

Both Melroys came to the door at William Dauntt's knock. Introductions were made, and the bright-eyed couple welcomed Adam warmly.

Minnie Melroy was tall and almost gaunt. Careworn lines crisscrossed her face, but she had an enchanting smile that lit up her whole countenance and the kindest brown eyes Adam had ever seen. She was dressed in blue printed calico partially covered with a stiff white apron. Wallace Melroy was a mite taller than his wife. His shoulders were a little stooped. As they moved into the foyer, Adam noticed that he walked with a slight limp.

"Your room is on the second floor, Mr. Burke," Wallace said. "You have luggage, I assume?"

241

"Yes, sir. Out in Mr. Dauntt's wagon."

"We'll get it for you, Mr. Burke," Colter said. "You go on up and take a look at your room."

Wallace reached into his pocket, handed a key on a small chain to Adam, and said, "Go ahead, son. Minnie will be right behind you. It takes me a little longer to climb the stairs. I was thrown from a horse when I was seven. Broke this left leg in three places. The limp is because there was no doctor near where we lived. Dad and Mom did the best they could, but the bones weren't set correctly. But when I get to heaven, I'll have a new body . . . no more limp!"

Adam smiled. Key in hand, he bounded up the stairs. When the Melroys arrived at the door, Adam told them how attractive and comfortable the room was. The Melroys explained the boardinghouse procedure to him, including the meal schedule. There was a dining hall next to the kitchen on the first floor where all the tenants ate Minnie's cooking three times a day.

Dauntt and Colter set the last of the trunks in the parlor section of the large room. "Well, Mr. Burke," Dauntt said, "we'll take you to your office if you're ready to go."

"Sure am!" said Adam, his eyes dancing.

As the five of them stepped out of the room

into the hall, Minnie said, "Remember, Mr. Burke, supper is at six o'clock sharp."

"I won't forget, ma'am."

"Sure glad to have you here, son," Wallace said.

"You folks are the perfect example of good old Western hospitality. I found it this way when traveling through the West a few years ago. It was one of the things that made me fall in love with this part of the country."

"You'll love it more the longer you're here," Minnie said. "I guarantee it."

"And I believe it! All right, gentlemen, let's go take a look at my office."

Soon the wagon was entering the business district on Main Street. Adam looked from side to side on the broad thoroughfare, taking in the stores, shops, and professional offices. People on the street waved at Dauntt and Colter, calling out greetings.

Dauntt made a sudden turn onto a side street and a quick turn a few seconds later into an alley. "We're going to take you in the back door," he said. "We have a special reason for it, and you'll understand shortly."

"Okay," Adam said with a grin.

Near the next side street, Dauntt swung the wagon up behind a false-fronted clapboard building that stood on the corner. The entrance faced Main Street. They led Adam inside the building, and he saw a large room at the back and two smaller rooms up front. The place was sparkling clean and smelled of new paint.

"You no doubt noticed," Colter said, "that these quarters make up half the building. The other half is the Lincoln County Land Office. They're nice neighbors; I promise."

"North Platte has two doctors, Mr. Burke," Dauntt said. "Dr. Todd Hill and Dr. Darrell Brown. This side of the building was Dr. Brown's office. His practice outgrew it, so he's relocated in his new clinic on the west side of town. The county owns this building, but I doubt the land office will ever need this side. So you won't have to worry about being moved out."

"As long as you pay the rent!" the sheriff said.

"Yes, sir, Sheriff! Seriously, this is better than I had imagined."

Dauntt grinned. "I'm glad you're happy with it. As you can tell, the entire inside has been painted since Dr. Brown left."

Adam ran his gaze around the interior of the building. "This setup will be perfect. I'll hire a secretary and put her up here on this side as a front office. My office will be in the back. And I'll use this other room for files and storage."

"Now," Dauntt said, "the reason we came in the back way . . . just a little surprise. Come out here."

Adam followed Dauntt and Colter out the front door onto the boardwalk, and Dauntt pointed to a sign in the window. Bold, black letters announced: Law Office to Be Opened Soon.

"Hey, look at that!" Adam said. "I suppose you had that done, Mr. Dauntt?"

"You might say that."

"Well, thank you. That was very thoughtful of you."

Colter laughed. "If you like that, Mr. Burke, look above your head."

Adam looked up and saw a large sign in a fancy metal frame. Both sides read:

Adam Burke
Attorney at Law

The young attorney shook his head. "Gentlemen, I've never been treated so royally in all my life!"

Dauntt laid a hand on his shoulder. "Mr. Burke, we're mighty pleased to have you in North Platte. We know you'll be a wonderful asset to this town and to the entire county."

The three men stepped back into the empty office and closed the door. Adam ran his gaze between them and said, "I assume there's a furniture store in town?"

"Sure is," the sheriff said.

"I'll need to furnish this office and make it functional."

"Ben has to get back to his office," Dauntt said, "but if you'd like to go to the furniture store and browse, I'll be glad to take you."

Adam shook Colter's hand and said, "Thank you, Sheriff, for being half of the welcoming committee. I sure appreciate it."

"My pleasure, sir. We'll get to know each other quite well, I'm sure. If there's anything I can ever do for you, just holler."

When Colter was out the door and gone, Dauntt locked it and said, "All right, Mr. Burke, let's go find you some furniture."

Adam looked at the sign over his office door. "Just think, Mr. Dauntt — my shingle is up!"

When they were rolling down the street, headed north, Adam said, "All I know about you, Mr. Dauntt, is that you're the town council chairman. I never thought to ask you what you do for a living."

William Dauntt laughed and said, "I own the Dauntt Furniture Store!"

16

In early October, Seth Coleman finished his training course in Washington, D.C., and was formally commissioned as a deputy United States marshal. The day after the commissioning ceremonies, he and eleven other men who had finished the course were gathered in a room, waiting to be addressed by Deputy U.S. Marshal Kenneth Fortner, who was in charge of assigning the new recruits to their districts of service.

Among the eleven other men in training, Seth had met Mike Frazier, who was a Christian. They had become close friends in a short time and enjoyed attending church together.

Mike and Seth were sitting together, talking about where they might be sent, when Fortner came into the room. The rumble of voices died out as Fortner took his position before them.

"Men," Fortner said, "you are to be congratulated on graduating from the course. As you know, four of the sixteen men who signed up for the course were disqualified.

"I am here to make district assignments. This group will be assigned to one of two districts. Half of you will be sent to the Austin, Texas, office. From there you will be assigned to a U.S. marshal's office within Texas or New Mexico. The other half will be sent to the Kansas City, Missouri, office. From there you will be assigned to a U.S. marshal's office anywhere in Dakota, Nebraska, Kansas, or points west, all the way to the Pacific coast."

Fortner looked down at a sheet of paper in his hand. "Here are your assignments."

He began by reading the names of the six men who would be sent to Austin. Mike's name was read, but Seth's was not. Seth had thought he didn't care which district they sent him to. He just wanted to get on with his life. However, even though he would be separated from Mike, Seth was relieved that he was not going to Texas or New Mexico. He had developed a fascination for the territory due west of the Missouri River, which was known more as the frontier than the southern extremes of Texas and New Mexico.

When the meeting was dismissed, the men of the two groups told each other good-bye. It was hard for Seth and Mike to part, but they both knew the Lord was guiding their lives.

As Seth headed toward his dormitory room, Bettieann Ralston came to mind. He mentally shook himself and went to his room to begin packing for the trip to Kansas City.

Claude Ralston came awake when he felt Lillian leave the bed during the night. Moonlight was streaming through the window. "You all right?" he said in a hushed tone.

Lillian paused with her hand on the knob. "Just listen."

The sound of muffled sobs came from the room across the hall. "It can't go on like this, Lillian," Claude said. "She's got to go talk to Seth and at least hear him say that he forgives her or that it's all over between them."

"She's been nothing but miserable since she tried to see him the other time. Somehow, after trying once and not finding him home, she lost her courage. I'll go talk to her again. You go back to sleep."

Lillian crossed the hall and entered Bettieann's room. The weeping stopped when Bettieann heard her mother come in, but she was still sniffling as Lillian sat down on the side of the bed.

"Honey, you can't go on like this. You've got to talk to Seth and get this thing settled one way or the other."

"I know, Mother," Bettieann said in a quavering voice, "I've got to quit being a coward and go see him. I've got to face Seth and ask his forgiveness."

"Good girl," Lillian said.

Claude was now standing by the door. "I'll take you to his place tomorrow evening."

"All right, Daddy."

"I think it's *this* evening," Lillian said. "It is after midnight."

When her parents had gone back to their room, a feeling of relief washed over Bettieann. "Please, God," she whispered, "let Seth be lenient with me. Help him to know how truly sorry I am." Her last thought before sleep claimed her was, "Please, Seth . . . find it in that big heart of yours to forgive me."

Bettieann came home from Stinson's Department Store where she worked as a clerk and hurriedly changed clothes. She dressed with care for her meeting with Seth. Though she had a measure of peace inside, she had scarcely been able to keep her mind on her work all day. She was checking her reflection in the full-length mirror when she heard her father come in.

"All right, Bettieann, it's time," she said aloud, looking at herself one last time.

Some twenty minutes later, Claude pulled the buggy up in front of the boardinghouse.

Bettieann was visibly shaking. Claude took both of her small hands in his big rough ones and said, "You can do it, sweetheart. What do you have to lose? At least you'll know you tried. Maybe Seth's just as anxious to see you as you are to see him. I'll be here if you need me."

He let go of her hands and gave her a gentle nudge.

When Bettieann reached the porch step, she stopped and looked back at her father who smiled encouragement at her. She walked through the foyer and down the hall to Seth's door. She rapped on it timidly, her heart beating like a trip-hammer. There were footsteps inside and she swallowed hard when the knob rattled and the door came open. A stranger stood looking at her.

"Yes, young lady?" the stocky, silver-haired man said.

Bettieann took a step back. "Oh! I'm sorry, sir. I . . . I was looking for Seth Coleman."

"He doesn't live here anymore. My wife and I have lived here for three weeks now."

"Would you happen to know, sir, where Seth might have moved to?"

"No, I don't. Maybe the landlord knows."

"All right. Thank you. I'm sorry to have bothered you."

The man smiled. "No bother. I hope you find Mr. Coleman."

Bettieann hurried to the landlord's door and knocked. Seconds later, the door opened.

"May I help you, young lady?" the man said.

"Sir, I am a friend of Seth Coleman. I haven't seen him in quite a while. When I knocked on his door, the man there told me he and his wife have lived there for three weeks."

"Yes, that's right."

"Would you happen to know where Seth moved?"

"Well, not exactly. When he told me he was moving out, he said he was going to Washington, D.C. That's all I know."

"Oh. All right. Thank you, sir."

Bettieann returned to the buggy and told her father what had happened, then asked him to drive her to the police station.

The desk sergeant listened to Bettieann and her father, then said, "All I can tell you is that Officer Coleman applied with the federal government to become a deputy United States marshal. He was accepted and had to go to Washington for training."

"Would anyone here have any more information?" Claude asked. "Like where Seth might be staying in Washington?"

"I doubt it, sir. If anyone would know, it

would be Chief Bennett, and he's out of town for another week."

"All right. Thank you, Sergeant."

When father and daughter returned to the buggy, Bettieann said, "Daddy, I can't give up. There must be a way to find Seth — at least get a letter to him. I've got to contact him. If there's any chance at all that he still cares for me, I have to know it."

"Tell you what, honey. Tomorrow I'll wire the Chief U.S. Marshal's Office in Washington and see if they can put me in contact with Seth. I'll ask them to send the reply to my office. Maybe when I come home from work tomorrow evening, I'll have some helpful information."

Bettieann and her mother saw Claude's buggy pull into the driveway and round the house to the barn. Lillian took hold of her daughter's hand and squeezed it. "Here's hoping, honey."

Bettieann's heart was pounding as she waited for her father to come inside.

When Claude saw the look on her face, he sighed. "Bettieann, I'm sorry. I sent the wire first thing this morning and they sent a reply just after noon. Seth finished his training and received his commission to the U.S. Marshal's office in Kansas City. I wired the Kansas City office, and the marshal there said Seth is en route to a marshal's office somewhere in the west. They cannot give his location to anyone but family members. He suggested I contact Seth's family for the information."

"But Daddy, Seth has no family!" Bettieann buried her face against her mother's shoulder and cried out, "I was such a fool to treat Seth the way I did. How could I have done it? Now I've lost him forever!"

The next day at work, Bettieann had a hard time keeping her composure as she helped customers in the store. Danielle Sharrow, another clerk at Stinson's, noticed that Bettieann seemed troubled and distracted, but she was hesitant to ask her about it. Better to wait a few days, she thought, and see if there was any change. But Bettieann was not sleeping well, and Danielle noted day after day the dullness of Bettieann's eyes and the sorrow in her expression. The following Monday, Danielle decided to talk to her.

At quitting time, Bettieann was working behind the counter in the women's clothing department, putting the day's receipts in a small canvas money bag. Danielle looked around to make sure no other employees were within earshot, then eased up beside Bettieann and said, "Bettieann, I've noticed now for several days that you seem to be carrying a heavy load. I can tell something's troubling you. Is there anything I can do to help?"

Bettieann's lower lip quivered slightly. "It's a long story, Danielle. I very much appreciate your kindness, but I wouldn't want to bore you with my problems."

"Bore me? Honey, I've come to like you very much. I can tell you're hurting. Please don't think I just want to stick my nose in your business. It's not that at all. Sometimes when a person is hurting, it helps to talk to someone else. Especially someone who cares. And I care."

Bettieann blinked at the tears in her eyes. "I really appreciate your concern . . . and maybe it would help to talk to you."

"We'll need some privacy then. How about coming to my apartment for supper? My fiancé picks me up after work and takes me home every day. He'll be here in a few minutes. I'll tell him that you and I are going to spend the evening together and that when we're through he and I can take you home. How about it?"

"I couldn't do it without letting my parents know. How about we do it tomorrow evening?"

"All right. You're on for supper tomorrow

night. I'll have Lance eat with us, then he can do something else until about nine o'clock. That should give us enough time, don't you think?"

"Of course. And Lance won't mind?"

"Not in the least. He'll want me to help you all I can."

"All right," said Bettieann, showing the shadow of a smile. "I'll look forward to it."

The next evening, Danielle prayed fervently in her heart for wisdom and power as she prepared a simple meal with Bettieann's help. Soon supper was ready and on the table, and Lance Denning thanked the Lord for the food. Lance finished eating first and excused himself, saying he would be back about nine.

When Lance was gone, Danielle reached across the small table and took hold of Bettieann's hand. "Let's go sit in the parlor." She led Bettieann to a couch. A Bible lay on an end table within easy reach. "All right," she said as they sat down, "tell me all about it."

Bettieann began to speak hesitantly, but soon a floodgate opened and she told the whole story. When she finished, Danielle said, "Honey, you made an awful mistake, but you mustn't give up trying to find Seth. God knows where he is."

"But how will that help me?"

"God loves you, and there is nothing impossible with Him. He can bring you and Seth together again."

"I believe in God, Danielle, but . . . but I've left Him out of my life, as have my parents. We're not churchgoing people. I sure can't ask for any help from Him."

"Oh, but you can. God loves you so much that He gave His only begotten Son on the cross of Calvary for your sins. He not only wants to save your soul, He wants to be the center of your life. He is already your Creator; now He wants to become your heavenly Father."

Bettieann blinked. "I never heard it put like that before."

"May I show you what the Bible says about it?"

"Of course."

Danielle showed Bettieann the gospel story and what Jesus said about the necessity of becoming a child of God by being born again. As she went from Scripture to Scripture, explaining them and answering Bettieann's questions, she could see that the Holy Spirit was working in the young woman's heart. After a couple of hours, Bettieann Ralston believed the gospel, repenting of her sin and placing her faith in Jesus Christ.

A divine peace stole over her battered heart.

She knew from what Danielle showed her that she had a Helper, a Friend who sticks closer than a brother, and He was now in control of her life.

Danielle showed Bettieann that because she was now God's child, He cared about every detail of her life and was willing and eager to answer her prayers. God knew where Seth was, and He could bring the two of them back together.

The next Sunday, Bettieann went to church with Lance and Danielle. When the invitation was given at the close of the sermon, she walked down the aisle and proclaimed her faith in Christ, and was baptized.

As the days passed, the two young women spent much time in prayer together, asking the Lord to lead Bettieann to Seth if it was His will for her life. They also prayed for Seth's salvation, whether God wanted them together or not.

Claude and Lillian Ralston were amazed at the change in their daughter. The peace and contentment in her deeply impressed them, and soon they were attending church with her.

One late afternoon in the middle of October, Rachel Mason stood over her father as he lay passed out on his bed. Joseph Mason had not been to his office in weeks. Although there were capable men at American Securities Company, Rachel wondered how they were dealing with their employer's absence. Roy Preslan, the company's vice president, had come to the house a few times to talk business with Joseph, but Rachel had a feeling that each time Preslan left he was very discouraged.

Rachel left the bedroom and headed down the hall toward her room. Just then Millie came out of Rachel's room carrying a feather duster and her cleaning supplies.

"Is he still out?" Millie asked.

"Yes. Go ahead and clean around him as best you can, but don't even try to take the bedding off. If he wakes up at all he'll just holler at you."

Rachel sat down at her desk and picked up a letter that had come the previous day from Aunt Esther. Rachel had been writing to her aunt regularly to tell her what was happening with her father. In each letter, Rachel had asked Esther to pray that something would bring her father out of his downward slide.

Esther had always answered each letter promptly, telling her niece that she was praying, but also reminding her that Joseph's greatest need — and Rachel's too — was to be saved. Rachel's aunt always said it in such a kind and loving way that Rachel was not the least bit offended. She knew her aunt meant well, and she loved her sweet spirit.

Rachel's eyes scanned the letter again. She was about to begin writing a response when there was a tap at her door.

"Yes, Millie?" she called.

"Miss Rachel, Mr. Preslan is back. He's waiting downstairs."

"Did you tell him Daddy is not able to see him?"

"Well, ma'am, your father woke up when I was cleaning the room. He's got a bad headache, but he's sitting up in his chair. I thought I should ask you if it was all right for Mr. Preslan to see him."

"Let me talk to Daddy first. If he's halfway sober I'll let Mr. Preslan come up."

Joseph's rheumy eyes struggled to focus on Rachel as she moved to where he sat.

"Daddy, Roy Preslan is here again. Are you up to seeing him?"

Joseph squinted at her and said, "He . . . he was jus' here yesterday. What's he want now?"

"He wasn't here yesterday. It was four days ago. If you'd leave that bottle alone you'd know what day it is."

Joseph's head wobbled. "Don' lecture me, girl. An' don' try throwin' my whis-whiskey bottles away any more, either. I bought a good supply, an' I intend to drink every last drop. If you throw 'em away, I'll jus' go out an' buy more. So don' bother yourself."

Rachel sighed. "Do you want to see Mr. Preslan or not?"

Joseph rubbed his aching forehead and said, "Oh, all right. Bring him in."

Rachel moved out into the hall. "Millie, would you go down and tell Mr. Preslan that my father will see him?"

"Yes, ma'am."

Rachel leaned against the doorjamb and massaged her temples, saying in a low whisper, "Aunt Esther, you've got to pray harder."

Preslan reached the top of the stairs and hurried toward her. "Hello, Rachel. Is . . . is he talkable?"

"To a degree. I hope you can get through to him."

"I have to."

"Well, he's expecting you. At least he was a few seconds ago. I'll go in with you and make sure."

Rachel entered the room with Preslan on her heels.

"Daddy, Mr. Preslan is here. Do you remember that you said you would see him?"

Joseph looked at her blankly. His head bobbed as he said, "Course I remember. How are you, Roy?"

"Physically I'm fine, sir. Mentally, not so good. That's why I've got to talk to you today."

Joseph's eyelids drooped, and he gestured toward a straight-backed chair. "Grab that chair over there."

Rachel excused herself and stepped into the hall. She left the door open an inch or so and pressed her ear close to the opening. It wasn't long until she learned of the terrible shape the company was in. Many of the employees feared the company was going to collapse and had taken jobs elsewhere, which meant a loss of customers. This past week, the company could not meet payroll, and many more had given notice that they were leaving.

Rachel could tell that Preslan sincerely cared what happened to the company and was trying to get through to her father's whiskey-clouded brain. But by her father's mumbled response she gathered that he either didn't grasp what he was being told or didn't care.

Soon Preslan was on his way toward the door. Rachel took a few steps back and pretended that she had come from further up the hall.

Preslan looked at her and shook his head. "He's in bad shape, Miss Rachel."

"How well I know."

Rachel walked him downstairs to the door and thanked him for coming, then went back upstairs, feeling sick to her stomach. She must start making cutbacks in household expenses and do everything she could to avert financial ruin. Although Cecil was out of the hospital, he was still recovering in a sanitarium. The doctors had informed her that he might never be able to do the gardener's job again. She would just have to take care of the garden herself. If things got really bad, she might even have to let Millie go. But at least she would do everything in her power to find Millie another job.

Her mind flashed back to the tragedy that had started this downward spiral. She hoped the man who had run her mother down on that stormy night was miserable.

17

Late in October, Adam Burke was looking through the filing cabinet near his desk when he heard the front door open. He looked up to see his new friend. "Well, good morning, Bill. Nice to see you."

"You too," said William Dauntt. "Just thought I'd stop by and see how you're doing, now that you've been here a few weeks. How's it going for you?"

"It's going well. I'm enjoying the furniture and other office items I bought from you, and as for clients, I'm picking up new ones just about every day. Sometimes I've picked up several in one day. Word's beginning to spread to the small towns all around and to the out-lying ranchers and farmers. Looks like I'm going to do well in North Platte."

"Glad to hear it. I'll be needing some legal work done in a few weeks myself. I'll be in to see you about it."

"It'll be my pleasure to serve you, Bill."

Dauntt eyed the file cabinet. "So how

soon'll you be looking for a secretary to take over that kind of work?"

"The way it's going, it won't be long. So far I'm able to keep up with the filing and correspondence, but soon I'll be wanting to pass that work on to some young, bright-eyed secretary."

"It may take you a while to come up with one. Most of the married women aren't wanting to work outside the home. You'll probably have to find a single girl somewhere."

Adam chuckled. "And those are few and far between. I met a young lady on the train on my way here. She was going on to Colorado as a mail order bride."

"Yeah?"

"She warned me that single ladies were scarce as hen's teeth out here. I'm beginning to believe she knew what she was talking about. I've had my eye out for some female companionship, but so far I haven't found it. All the young ladies who aren't yet married seem to be spoken for."

A lopsided grin curved Bill Dauntt's mouth. "Well, Adam, maybe you'll have to get yourself one of those mail order brides and put her to work as your secretary!"

Adam shook his head. "Oh, no! I'm not going to marry some gal I ordered through the mail."

"Well, it may get pretty lonely, son."

"One of these days some pert little gal will come to North Platte looking to marry a handsome, dashing attorney."

Dauntt laughed. "Well, even if she did, where would she find an attorney like that?"

Adam laughed as his friend waved jauntily and left the office. He went back to his filing. When that was finished, he began work on a will he was drawing up for a middle-aged rancher and his wife.

On Monday of the next week, Adam carried some mail to the Wells Fargo office, where it would be put on a stagecoach and taken to the post office in Grand Island. As he neared his office to return to work, he saw a group of townsmen standing in front of the county land office in friendly conversation. Some of them he had met; others were strangers. One of the men he knew motioned to him and said, "Adam, come over here and meet these fellas."

Within minutes, Adam had two new clients. He set appointments for them to come to his office and started to excuse himself when one of the group looked across the wide, dusty street and called out, "Hey, Patch! How you doin'?"

The man gave a quick wave and hurried inside the store. The sign above it read North Platte Clothiers. The brief glimpse Adam had of the man showed him a black patch over his left eye.

"Patch live here in town?" Adam said, turning back to the group.

"Sure does," one of the men said. "Patch Smith. He owns North Platte Clothiers."

"Just about all the merchants and businessmen in town have come by my office to welcome me to North Platte, but I haven't met Mr. Smith. Guess I'll take a minute one of these days and go introduce myself."

"I'm surprised he hasn't dropped in on you. He's a right friendly fellow."

"Probably been too busy," Adam said. "So what's his real name? I assume he picked up the name Patch when he lost his eye."

"I don't rightly know his real name. Patch is all I've heard since he came here."

"That's been a lotta years too," another man said.

At that moment a well-dressed man came out of the clothing store and headed across the street.

"Well, look who's back," one of the men said. "Howdy, Preacher!"

The others in the group greeted him and asked about his trip to Chicago. Adam learned that he was pastor of the town's only church, and his name was Tom Gann. He was a rugged-looking man with an angular face, square jaw, and a kind look in his gray eyes.

Gann shook Adam's hand and said, "I understand I'm a little late for this, Mr. Burke, but welcome to North Platte. As you can tell, I've been out of town for a few weeks."

"Yes, sir," Adam said, "and thank you for your words of welcome. The folks here have made me feel a part of the town already."

"Good. I just saw Wallace and Minnie Melroy in the clothing store across the street. They told me you're living in their boarding-house."

"Yes, sir. They're wonderful people. I understand they're members of your church."

"And very good ones, too. I want to extend an invitation to you, Mr. Burke. How about visiting our services next Sunday?"

"I'll attend sometime soon, Pastor. Can't promise about this coming Sunday, but one of these Sundays, I'll come."

"Fair enough. Well, it's been nice to meet you." Gann shook hands with Adam again, said a few departing words to the other men, and headed down the street.

"Well, good morning, ladies!" said a man in the group.

Adam turned around to see two women

coming along the boardwalk. The resemblance between them was strong enough that they had to be mother and daughter. Adam was promptly introduced to Madge and Olivia Dahl. Madge and her husband Bert owned the Bar-D Ranch a few miles south of town.

"So where's Bert?" one of the men said, looking around.

"He'll be along in a few minutes," Madge replied. "He's picking up some grain at North Platte Feed and Supply. Olivia and I are going to the bank. We heard that one of the tellers is leaving, and Olivia's going to apply for the job."

Adam stepped closer to the pretty girl and said, "Miss Olivia, I'll need to hire a secretary sometime soon. Would you be interested? I was just thinking that if you were interested in bank work you no doubt could learn to do law office work."

Olivia looked at her mother, who was smiling, then said, "Well-l-l, I —"

"I'll pay you ten dollars a week more than the bank would . . . to start."

Olivia's eyes lit up. "I heard the bank starts inexperienced tellers at twelve dollars a week."

"Then I'll pay you twenty-two," said Adam, using his most charming smile. "How about it?"

"All right. You'll have to teach me a lot, I'm

sure. But I promise I'll give you my best."

"I have no doubt about that. How soon can you start?"

Olivia looked at her mother. "Well, honey," Madge said, "you did promise Evalena that you'd be the maid of honor in her wedding."

"But I could come right back instead of staying with Aunt Bertha and Uncle Charlie, couldn't I?"

"Of course. I'm sure they'll understand. You might've had to do the same if you'd taken the bank job."

Olivia turned back to Adam. "Could I start a week from today, Mr. Burke?"

"That'd be great. Let's see, that will be November 5. I open the office at eight o'clock. Could you be here by seven-thirty?"

"Of course."

"It'll only be for the first day. After that, you can come in at ten minutes before opening time."

"That'll be fine, sir. Thank you! I'll be here at seven-thirty a week from today. Anything I need to bring?"

"Just your bright smile. I have everything else you need at the office."

"Well, honey," Madge said, "we'd better get going. We still have to go to the bank so I can make the deposit. Your father plans to pick us up there."

"Oh, I can't wait to tell Papa and Russ about the job!"

Madge smiled at Adam. "Thank you, Mr. Burke, for giving Olivia the job. The extra money will be a great help."

Adam returned to his office elated. Finding a secretary had been much quicker and easier than he had anticipated. And it wouldn't hurt the firm to have such a lovely young lady in the front office either. Not one bit.

After spending a few days at the Chief United States Marshal's office in Kansas City, Seth Coleman boarded a train bound for Omaha. He sighed with pleasure as he took a seat beside the window in the last passenger coach and watched other passengers saying good-bye to friends and relatives. The other five deputies who had traveled from Washington to Kansas City with him had been assigned to offices farther west. Seth was satisfied to be stationed at Omaha. He wondered if Adam Burke had realized his dream of establishing his own law firm in North Platte.

Soon the train was rolling northward out of Kansas City. The conductor entered the rear of the coach and began collecting tickets.

For a while, the train followed the east bank of the Missouri River, then the river passed from view. Seth laid his head back, closed his eyes, and saw the face of Bettieann Ralston. This brought a flood of memories to his mind. The more he tried to push them away, the more vivid they became.

He opened his eyes, sat up, and gazed at the Missouri hills rushing by his window. Soon the Missouri River came back into view, and shortly thereafter the conductor passed through the coach announcing the next stop, St. Joseph. Soon the train was chugging into the St. Joseph depot, and Seth watched the crowd on the platform as new passengers began to board. Suddenly he spotted a familiar face just outside his window. Dave Harmon!

Seth had been part of a team of police officers who chased Harmon through the streets and alleys of Philadelphia after he had robbed a bank and wounded a bank employee. It was Seth who finally cornered Harmon, disarmed him, and arrested him. Harmon had been sentenced to fifteen years in the federal penitentiary near Scranton but had escaped from the prison almost a year ago.

Harmon was in close conversation with three other men, and it appeared they were going to board the train. Seth wondered if Harmon was now into robbing trains. He studied Harmon's three friends and memorized their faces and what they were wearing. As soon as the train started rolling, he would take a little walk to see if Harmon and his friends had spread out into all three cars.

When the voice of the conductor began calling for all passengers to board, Harmon and his friends moved out of Seth's line of sight. Seth removed his badge and put it in his shirt pocket. A well-dressed man carrying a valise sat down beside him. Seth greeted him then turned his attention back to the situation with Harmon and his cronies.

Sure enough, one of Harmon's cohorts entered the coach and took a seat near the front. Moments later, the train rolled out of the depot.

From the corner of his eye Seth saw the man next to him open his valise and take out a Bible. "Ah," he said. "I see you love the same Book I do."

"There's no Book like it. I'm Ken Myers," the man said, extending his hand. "I pastor a church in Omaha that believes this Book from cover to cover. In fact, we even believe the cover because it says Holy Bible."

Seth chuckled. "Well, amen to that! I'd like to talk to you some more, Pastor Myers, but I have a little errand to do first. I'll be back in a bit. Excuse me, please."

Seth squeezed past Myers and stepped into the aisle. He walked past Dave Harmon's friend and casually glanced down at him. The man seemed a bit nervous.

Seth stepped onto the platform of the swaying coach and passed into the next car. He paused at the door and studied the backs of the men's heads. If Harmon was in this car, Seth would have to get past him without being recognized. It took only seconds to spot another one of Harmon's pals, but Dave Harmon was nowhere to be seen. The robber was seated alone near the front.

Seth proceeded to the first passenger coach, paused just inside the door, and did his study again. Dave Harmon was on a seat near the front, sitting by the aisle. An elderly woman sat beside him, looking out the window. Directly across the aisle was Harmon's other cohort, sitting alone.

Seth turned around and left the coach, heading back toward his own car. Myers looked up from his Bible when Seth stopped at the seat, then squeezed past him to sit down.

"Pastor Myers, I'm a deputy U.S. marshal," Seth said, leaning close to the preacher and keeping his voice low. He took the badge from his shirt pocket momentarily for Myers to see. Seth quietly explained the situation, including the fact that the robbers were spread out, ready to go into action.

"I need your help, Pastor. It could involve

some danger, but I've got to keep these four from robbing the train, and at the same time I've got to arrest them."

"You can count on me," Myers whispered. "I was a combat leader in the Civil War. I know about danger."

Seth pointed out the robber near the front door of the coach. "I could take him out right now, but if I did I wouldn't have the goods on him. I have to let him show himself as one of the robbers. All I ask is that if there's any way you can overpower him once he shows himself — without endangering any of the passengers — do it."

"There's an empty seat directly across the aisle from him," Myers said. "I'll move up there."

"I'm going up to the lead car again," Seth whispered. "Pray for me."

Myers nodded. "You go ahead. I'll change seats in a minute."

Seth made his way past Harmon's cohort and moved out onto the platform. Harmon's man in car number two was still in place. As Seth passed him, he prayed, *Lord, help me to be able to take care of this one somehow. Please don't let any of the passengers get hurt.*

When Seth entered coach number one, he saw that Harmon had left his seat and was not in the car, though the other robber was still in his place. Seth suspected Harmon was headed toward the engine. He opened the door and stepped out onto the platform. Harmon's man eyed him and waited a few moments before getting up to follow him.

As soon as Seth was on the platform, he caught a glimpse of Harmon inching across the catwalk on the side of the coal car, gun in hand. Seth moved to the ladder on the rear of the baggage coach and was starting to climb it when he heard the door of the car behind him open. He looked back and saw Harmon's man glaring at him.

"Where you goin'?" the robber demanded.

Seth grinned and moved toward him. "Just curious. I saw some guy heading toward the engine, and I wondered what he was doing."

The man clawed for his gun, but Seth moved with lightning speed and sent a hard fist to the man's jaw. The punch bounced the robber off the door of the coach. When he rebounded, Seth hit him again, and the man went down in a heap.

Seth grabbed the man's gun and tossed it off the train. He used the man's own belt to bind his hands behind his back, then dragged him into the coach.

He flashed his badge to the passengers and said, "Folks, I'm Marshal Seth Coleman. This man and his cohorts have a train robbery planned. If a couple of you men will keep an eye on him, I'd appreciate it. I've got to move fast."

Seth dashed through the coach, opened the back door, and stepped onto the platform. Moving into car number two, he saw Harmon's man just as he got out of his seat and pulled his gun, telling the passengers they were being robbed. Before the robber could completely clear leather, Seth struck him square on the jaw. The passengers looked on stunned as the man's feet left the floor. He bounced off the edge of a seat and landed flat on his back, out cold.

Seth picked up the robber's gun and said, "This man and three others were planning to rob the train. I've got one of the others already subdued. Will a couple of you men take this guy's belt and bind his hands behind his back for me? I've got to keep moving." Seth turned to go back toward the engine car.

The wind whipped Seth's face as he bent low and made his way forward on the roof of the baggage coach. When he reached the coal car, he stepped onto the catwalk, pinned the badge on his chest, and drew his gun.

Dave Harmon's back was squarely toward Seth when he reached the end of the catwalk. Harmon was holding his gun on the engineer and fireman.

Seth leveled his gun on Harmon's head and shouted, "It's all over, Harmon! Toss the gun out in the field!"

Harmon whipped his head around to find himself looking down the muzzle of Seth Coleman's Colt .45. His eyes went from the black muzzle to the shiny badge to Coleman's face. "You!" he gusted, eyes bulging.

"Yeah, me! Throw the gun off the engine. Now!"

Harmon hesitated.

"I mean it!" Seth growled.

Harmon reluctantly tossed his gun off the train.

When the train pulled into Omaha, Pastor Ken Myers and U.S. Marshal Seth Coleman followed the other passengers toward the front door of the coach.

"If you need a ride to the U.S. marshal's office, I can take you there," Myers said. "One of the men from the church is picking me up."

"Thanks, but Chief Houser is supposed to meet me."

"I know him well. He lives next door to the parsonage. In fact, here he comes now," Myers said as they stepped out of the coach.

Frank Houser was a robust man of sixty. As he drew up, he noted the badge on Seth's chest, glanced at Myers and said, "Seth Coleman, welcome to Omaha! Is this outlaw next to you your prisoner?"

Myers laughed.

Seth shook Houser's hand and said, "Pastor Myers isn't my prisoner, Chief, but I've got four men tied up in the caboose. I need to get them to the Douglas County jail."

Houser was surprised to learn about the foiled train robbery but was glad to know that no passengers had been hurt. He chuckled to learn that Myers had coldcocked the robber in coach number three the moment he moved to the front of the coach and pulled his gun.

The man Myers was expecting arrived, and Myers introduced Earl Chambers to Seth. Then he turned to the law officers and said, "Is there anything I can do for you gentlemen?"

"You've done your part," Houser said. "I'll contact Sheriff Bowman and get those robbers off the train and transported to the jail."

"Robbers?" Chambers said. "What happened?"

"I'll tell you on the way home, Earl," Myers said.

Seth extended his hand to Myers. "Pastor, I can't wait to hear you preach. If you can preach as good as you punch, it's got to be good."

"I'll look for you, Deputy."

The pastor and Earl Chambers walked away, and Chief Houser said, "We'll get you settled in a boardinghouse as soon as we get your prisoners settled in their cells, Coleman. Tomorrow morning you'll meet some of your fellow deputies, and within a day or two I'll have you working with one of the more experienced men who'll take you with him on an assignment and show you the way we do it here."

"I can't wait, sir," Seth said.

"On the other hand, maybe I should have you teaching the other deputies how to stop a train robbery!"

18

On Monday morning, November 5, Adam Burke got up at dawn, excited about Olivia Dahl's first day on the job. He stood in front of the mirror, carefully using the straight-edged razor to shave, and thought about how Olivia had been delivered almost magically into his life. He was sure she would make a good secretary. Her bright eyes displayed a keen intelligence as well as a vivacious personality. And she wasn't wearing an engagement ring.

Adam splashed water on his face and grabbed a towel, then looked at himself in the mirror. "Who knows, ol' pal. Maybe something will develop."

He dressed in his best suit and tie and put on the shoes he had shined to a perfect gloss the night before. After an excellent breakfast downstairs in Minnie's dining room, Adam left for work. He reached the office just after seven o'clock. At seven twenty-five, a wagon pulled up out front and moments later the door opened.

"Mr. Burke?"

"Good morning, Olivia. Welcome to the Adam Burke law firm."

Adam showed Olivia around the office, acquainting her with the files and explaining what her job would entail, and that she must keep everything she learned about clients and their businesses confidential. He was pleased at how quickly she caught on to all his instructions.

The day went well as clients came and went. Olivia was excellent with people, and she had a special charm about her.

The last client booked for the day left just before four o'clock. When Adam came into the front office, Olivia was at the file cabinet, putting client records in place. She had already tidied up the office and had it looking even better than when she had arrived that morning.

"Sure looks nice in here, Olivia," he said. "And you handled yourself well with the clients."

"Thank you, Mr. Burke."

"Looks like you've got things ready for tomorrow. Even though your quitting time is five o'clock, you can leave early today if you want."

Olivia glanced at the grandfather clock in

the corner and said, "Russ won't be here to pick me up until five, Mr. Burke. That'll give me time to dust your desk and do anything that's needed in your office. If it's all right for me to go in there, I'll take care of it for you."

"Of course," he said, pondering what she had just said. "Russ? Is that your brother?"

"Oh, no," she said, giggling. "Russ is my fiancé."

It took Adam a few seconds to get his breath. "Oh . . . your fiancé. I didn't realize you were engaged."

"I guess I didn't mention it last week. You remember when Mother thanked you for giving me the job and said that the extra money would be a great help? Well, Russ and I are trying to put aside money for when we get married. Right now he's getting together enough money to buy me an engagement ring. We probably won't be able to get married for another year or so, but my salary is going to help."

"What does Russ do for a living?"

"He's a ranch hand at the Box K Ranch, which is close to ours. Just so you'll know, Mr. Burke, Russ and I talked about it after you hired me. We don't plan to start a family until we've been married a couple of years. So you'll have me around for some time yet."

Adam forced a smile. "Well, I'm glad to

hear that." He excused himself and went into the storeroom, staying there while Olivia dusted his office and straightened it up.

Russ Kline showed up at five o'clock, and Olivia introduced him to her new boss. When they drove away in the wagon, Adam stepped back into his office, sighed and said to himself, "Well, at least I've hired a good secretary."

The next day, Adam had already seen four clients by the time he came out of his office late in the morning. Olivia was busy at the filing cabinet.

"Since there aren't any more appointments till this afternoon, Olivia, I'm going across the street to the general store to pick up some things. If somebody should come in, tell him I'll be back shortly."

"Would you like me to go over to the store for you, sir?"

"No, thanks. I'll take care of it."

Adam started toward the general store, which was across the street and a few doors down. He paused to let a ranch wagon pass, then headed for the boardwalk. He happened to be looking toward North Platte Clothiers when the door opened and Patch Smith started outside. Adam decided he might as well introduce himself to the merchant and veered toward him, but Smith abruptly retreated into the store. Adam stopped at the edge of the boardwalk and shook his head, then headed toward the general store.

Adam suddenly stopped, wheeled about, and headed back toward the corner. When he stepped inside North Platte Clothiers, he saw Smith standing near the back, talking to a man. Smith caught a glimpse of Adam, said something to the man in a low voice, and disappeared through an office door. When the man turned around, Adam recognized him as Jack Brady.

"Well, hello, Adam!" Brady called.

"I didn't realize you worked here, Jack," Adam said as they shook hands.

"Didn't I tell you that day we met at the café?"

"No."

"Guess it slipped my mind. What can I do for you?"

"I've been meaning to come over here and introduce myself to Mr. Smith. I've been in town almost a month and he's the only merchant I haven't met."

"Well . . . uh, Mr. Smith is quite busy right now, Adam. He can't be disturbed."

"I see. Do me a favor?"

"Sure."

"Tell Mr. Smith I'd like to meet him sometime soon. He's welcome to come over to my office . . . or I can come back over here. Ask him to contact me at his convenience, will you?"

"All right. I'll give him the message."

Adam thanked Brady and left the store. As he walked toward the general store, the thought wouldn't leave his mind. He and Smith had met before. But when and where? And what had happened that would cause the man to avoid him?

After making his purchases, Adam crossed the street and noticed two young women, employees at the bank, coming along the boardwalk. The ladies spoke to him in a warm and friendly manner, and Adam greeted them in turn, then went inside his office.

Olivia, who sat near the window, smiled at him and said, "Those girls were sure friendly to you!"

"Just western hospitality, dear secretary. That's all. I happen to know that both of them are engaged to be married."

He carried his purchases into his office and set them down. When he turned around, Olivia was standing at the door. "Yes?"

"Mr. Burke, you haven't mentioned whether there's a young lady in your life. I don't mean to stick my nose in where it doesn't belong, but you seem rather lonely. Is there someone back in Philadelphia? Someone who might be coming here to become your wife?"

Adam sighed. "There was someone in Philadelphia, but she didn't want to leave there and come to this little western town. Excuse me. 'Dried up, dusty, backwoods, little cow town.'"

"I'm sorry, sir. I see I've touched a sensitive nerve. Please forgive me."

"Nothing to forgive. I appreciate your concern."

"I just don't like to see you so lonely, Mr. Burke. I know this much . . . you'll make a good husband to some fortunate young lady someday."

Adam sighed again. "I sure would like to meet that young lady you just mentioned. You're right. I am lonely. I believe there's somebody for everybody, Olivia, but I'm getting a little impatient. I'll turn twenty-five in a few months. I should be a married man."

"Well, Mr. Burke, there's a way to find that young lady."

"And how's that? Hang a sign on my back that I'm available?"

Olivia giggled. "Well, not quite. Many men out here are finding their wives through the mail order bride system."

"I know that's true. But I'll find my bride another way."

The friendship between Bettieann Ralston and Danielle Sharrow grew close as time passed. Bettieann knew she had much to learn about the Bible and God's will in her life, and she drank in every Sunday school lesson and sermon at church. But she also leaned on Danielle to teach her.

Danielle and Bettieann had many discussions about Christian growth and walking close to the Lord. As they prayed together for Seth Coleman's salvation — wherever he was — Danielle made sure Bettieann understood that even if she found Seth, she must not marry him until he became a Christian.

The two young women had become almost inseparable. Bettieann was included in many of the things Danielle and Lance did. At the same time, Lance tried to get Bettieann interested in some of the young men at church who were showing interest in her. She thanked him for his desire to help her social life, but she could not give up on finding Seth.

One night in late November, Lance drove Danielle and Bettieann across town to attend a revival service. They found a pew and were about to sit down when a voice called, "Bettieann! Hello!"

"Ruth! How are you?"

The two women embraced, then Ruth said,

"I'm so glad to see you here for the service."

"And I'm glad to be here. Let me introduce you to my friends."

Bettieann introduced Ruth Nelson to Danielle and Lance and explained that Ruth had worked at Stinsons and had witnessed to her on several occasions. She then told Ruth that Danielle, who now worked at Stinsons, had recently led her to the Lord.

"Oh, Bettieann!" Ruth cried. "I'm so glad!" Then to Danielle, she said, "Thank you for leading her to the Lord."

"The pleasure was mine," Danielle said, smiling.

Ruth turned back to Bettieann and said, "You used to date Seth Coleman, didn't you?"

"Why . . . yes."

"Were you still dating him when he became a Christian?"

"He . . . he became a Christian? When did this happen?"

"Shortly before he left for Washington, D.C. Some of our members led him to the Lord. He was baptized here."

Bettieann turned to Danielle with tears in her eyes. "Did you hear that? Seth's saved! The Lord has already drawn him!" She turned back to Ruth. "I know Seth has be-come a deputy U.S. marshal and is somewhere in the West, but I don't know where. Do you know how I could get in touch with him?"

"Sorry, I don't."

"Would the people who led him to the Lord know?"

"I have no idea, but I'll find out. Be back later."

The music started, and everyone took their seats. Soon the song leader had the crowd on its feet, singing a rousing gospel song. Bettieann had stayed at the end of the pew, on the aisle. She was singing with joy in her heart when she felt a hand on her shoulder.

Ruth bent close to her ear and said, "I talked to the Sheldons. They haven't had any contact with Seth since he left. They don't know where he is."

"Thank you for trying," said Bettieann, squeezing Ruth's hand.

"Danielle, I'm so glad we came tonight," Bettieann said as they drove across town after the service. "It's so good to know that Seth has become a Christian too!"

"That is good news, isn't it. I told you before . . . the Lord knows where Seth is, and though it looks impossible, He can bring the two of you together. Praise the Lord, He's already taken care of Seth's salvation!"

"Yes, I'm delighted about that," Bettieann said, "but I'm still having a hard time understanding how God can bring us together."

Lance had been quietly listening to the conversation as they drove home. He chuckled and said, "God created the universe; He certainly can handle anything that happens in it!"

"The Lord will work out everything in your life and bring you to the joy and happiness He has for you, Bettieann," Danielle said. "It may be with Seth, and it may not. But whatever your heavenly Father does in your life will be right. So often we think we have everything all worked out the way it should be, but we must be careful not to get in the Lord's way of bringing about His will. We must trust Him and desire that the outcome — whatever it turns out to be — will glorify Him."

Bettieann sank to her knees beside the bed and prayed for God's help in understanding His Word and His ways. With a willing spirit she prayed for God's will to be done, and for the strength and grace to accept His will if it was not in His plan for her and Seth to be together.

She turned down the covers, propped the pillows against the headboard, and climbed into bed. She remembered a passage her pastor had preached on, and she opened her Bible to Psalm 63 and found the verse she had marked during the sermon. Her eyes misted as she read, "Because thou hast been my help, therefore in the shadow of thy wings will I rejoice."

A newfound serenity flooded Bettieann's soul and a smile formed on her lips as she slipped down into the blankets and quickly fell into a restful sleep.

The new year came, and as the early days of 1878 passed, Deputy U.S. Marshal Seth Coleman was making his mark as a federal lawman.

On a cold day in late January, Seth rode into snow-laden Omaha, leading a horse carrying a dead man draped over the saddle. When he entered the U.S. marshal's office he found the chief in conversation with another deputy. Both turned to the door when they felt a blast of cold air and smiled when they saw him.

"So how'd it go, Seth?" Frank Houser asked.

"He's draped over his saddle out there, Chief," Seth said tossing a thumb over his shoulder.

"Wouldn't let you take him alive, huh?"

"No, sir."

"Come on into my office."

When the two men were in Houser's office, the chief laid a hand on Seth's shoulder. "I can't tell you how pleased I am with your work. You've proven yourself a brave and proficient lawman. I've lost count of how many outlaws you've brought in since you pinned on that badge . . . and I'm not including those train robbers you captured on your way here."

"Guess I've lost count too, sir."

"You've been out there tracking Kingman for better than a week in that cold weather. I know you've got to be worn out. Take three days off, okay? Get some rest."

Seth grinned. "I'll just do that, sir. Thank you."

Seth entered his room at the boarding-house, hung up his hat and sheepskin coat, and took off his gun belt. He had yet to get used to the quiet and solitude of the place. *I expect to be lonely when I'm out trailing outlaws, but when I come home, I want a pair of loving arms to welcome me.* Seth had hoped there would be some available young women in the Omaha church but had found that those old enough to marry were all taken.

At church on Sunday, Shane and Sandra Keeler came up to Seth and shook his hand.

"Remember what we agreed on before you went out the last time, Seth?" Sandra said.

The young deputy grinned. "Mm-hmm. You said that the first Sunday I was back I was invited to your house for Sunday dinner."

"How about it?" Shane asked. "Can you come today?"

"Sure. After what you've told me about Sandra's cooking, I've been licking my lips in anticipation!"

At dinner, the Keelers told Seth they had just learned that Sandra was going to have a baby.

"Wonderful!" Seth said. "You two have impressed me since the first day I met you."

Shane cocked his head. "Oh? In what way?"

"You seem so happy in your marriage. I hope that's the kind I have someday."

Shane chuckled. "Well, our marriage came about somewhat different than most folk's. There were people in the church who said we'd never make it."

"Why's that?"

"I was a mail order bride, that's why," Sandra said. "Shane moved to Omaha from southern Illinois when he got the job here. He was twenty-one at the time. He soon found that eligible young women just weren't around."

"Of any kind," Shane said. "Of course, I only wanted a Christian girl. I expected to find some unmarried, unattached girls in the church, but they just weren't there. So I talked to Pastor Myers about considering a mail order bride. He told me he had seen it work for several Christian young men. He told me to be very clear up front that I only wanted a Christian girl, that none others need write to me."

"I won't go into my side of the story right now, Seth," Sandra said, "but when I read the ad in the mail order bride section of the *Columbus Sentinel* — Columbus as in Ohio, that is — I was looking for a man of the same caliber."

"The doubters in the church have changed their minds," Shane said. "I suggest you talk to Pastor Myers and pray about it, Seth. If you feel led of the Lord to do so, just go down to the *Omaha News*, tell them you want to put mail order bride ads in at least a dozen newspapers in the East, North, and South, and see what happens."

Seth entered his room that night after talking to Pastor Myers following the evening service, pondering what both the pastor and Shane had said. He dropped to his knees beside his bed and asked the Lord to show him if he should try to find a mail order bride.

Seth continued to pray about the matter as he took another assignment from Chief Houser. When he returned ten days later with two outlaws in tow, he went home and wrote out his ad, laying out his specifications the same as Shane had. He explained what he did for a living, since he knew many women shied away from marrying men who wore a badge.

The next day he took the ad to the *Omaha News* office, and with their help, placed ads in a dozen papers, including the *Philadelphia Enquirer*. As he left the newspaper office, he asked the Lord to give him the wife He had chosen for him . . . even as He had done for Shane Keeler.

19

The door to Adam's private office opened, and Olivia Dahl heard his clients express their appreciation for his help. The middle-aged couple preceded Adam into the main office where Adam laid a folder on Olivia's desk, saying to her, "I have the will worded to Mr. and Mrs. Videen's satisfaction, so it's ready to be copied. I told them you would have it ready within a couple of days."

Olivia smiled at the couple. "You can drop by day after tomorrow and I'll have it ready."

Adam helped Mrs. Videen put on her coat then walked the couple to the door. They thanked him and stepped outside, and Adam glanced across the street and saw Patch Smith in front of his store, talking to a couple of men. Adam said good-bye to the Videens, and when he looked back at Smith, the man was watching him but quickly looked away.

There's something strange going on, Adam thought to himself. It had been almost three months since he'd asked Jack Brady to tell

Smith he would like to meet him, but Smith had never responded nor shown any interest at all in making his acquaintance.

Adam headed back to his office for his coat. "I'll be back in a few minutes," he said to Olivia. He closed the front door and looked across the street. Patch Smith and his friends were gone. When Adam entered North Platte Clothiers he saw that both Smith and Jack Brady were busy with customers. Adam caught Brady's eye, but Smith's back was toward him.

Adam went to the men's section and began looking at the dress shirts, all the while keeping an eye on Smith. When Smith turned toward the counter to complete the sale, he saw Adam and froze for a second, then hurriedly proceeded with his tasks.

He must know me from somewhere, Adam said to himself. But the look in his eye was one of fear. *A court case in Philadelphia?*

Adam stared at Patch Smith. The man's face was scarred on the left side where the patch covered his eye. Adam was sure that if he had ever met the man in court he would remember him. No, it wasn't in a courtroom. There was something about the way Smith carried himself . . . the way his shoulders —

Adam's eyes widened in disbelief. There

was a buzzing inside his head, and his stomach went sour.

". . . that you like, Adam?"

Adam blinked and turned to the man standing beside him. "What did you say, Jack?"

"I said, do you see anything here that you like? You know, the shirts."

"Oh . . . yes. I . . . they're all really nice." Adam tried to watch what was happening at the counter while he slowly looked over the shirts, his heart pounding. "Let's see. I'll take this one . . . and this one. And I saw another one my size over here that I liked."

Adam saw the customers at the counter leave. Patch Smith glanced at Adam then hurried to the rear of the store and went through a door.

"I'll take these, Jack." Adam said, picking up the third shirt.

The purchase was made, and Adam Burke went back to his office. Olivia looked up from her desk when he came in and did a double take.

"Mr. Burke, are you all right?"

He paused, clutching the paper bag to his chest. "Hmm?"

"Are you all right? You're so pale. You look like you've seen a ghost."

"Oh, well . . . I'm not feeling so good, Olivia. Sort of came on sudden while I was in the clothing store. I just need to sit down for a few minutes. I'm sure I'll be all right."

"Can I get you some water?"

"I have water in my office, thanks. I'll be fine in a few minutes."

Soon Adam was pacing back and forth in his office. "Why? Why did he have to be in the very town I chose to make my home? Why?" A tap on the door brought him to a halt.

"Mr. Burke?" came Olivia's worried voice.

Adam wiped a shaky palm over his face and forced himself to calm down. "Yes, Olivia? Come in."

"Are you sure you're all right?"

"Yes, I'm fine."

"Dean Robinson is here for his appointment."

Adam looked at the wall clock behind his desk. "Oh, of course. Send him in."

That evening, when Adam entered the boardinghouse, Wallace Melroy was standing in the foyer.

"Hello, Adam. Busy day?"

"Quite busy, Mr. Melroy."

"I'm glad to see you doing so well. Picking up clients daily, I suppose."

"Just about."

"Minnie will have supper on in about five minutes. Beef stew tonight."

"Ah, Mr. Melroy . . . I've had kind of a sour stomach all afternoon. Think I'll skip supper tonight."

"I'm sorry to hear that."

"I'll be all right by morning, I'm sure. Tell Mrs. Melroy I'll see her for breakfast."

"Will do."

As soon as he was in his apartment, Adam tossed the package of shirts on the end table and sat down on the couch. His hands were shaking. Bitter memories flooded back.

He was still on the couch some time later when a knock on the door invaded his thoughts. He glanced at the clock on the wall. Almost 8:30. A second knock came, and when he opened the door, a wave of revulsion washed over him.

"You finally figured out who I am, didn't you?" Patch Smith said, his face pale.

Adam's jaw tightened. "Patch Smith, huh? I suppose you changed your name when you ran off with that Murray woman!"

"Yes. Patch came naturally," he said, nodding solemnly, "but I put the Smith on me."

"So what happened to the Murray woman? I haven't seen you with a female."

Patch cleared his throat softly. "She left me for another man before we even got to the Missouri River." Tears began to spill down Patch's cheek. "I did a terrible thing, son. I've paid for it over and over all these years. How is . . . how's your mother?"

There was a long silence. Then Adam's voice came out rough and guttural as he said, "She's dead because you deserted her. It took a while, but she finally died of a broken heart."

Patch wept harder, shaking his head. "I'm so sorry, Adam. I made a horrible mistake. A horrible mistake."

Adam only glared at him.

"When I saw the sign go up over the door across the street, with your name on it, I knew you had followed through on your ambition to be an attorney. At least I figured there probably weren't two Adam Burkes in this country who were attorneys. I . . . I'm proud of you, son."

Adam gave no response.

"I knew I should leave town, but I just couldn't bring myself to do it."

"If I'd known you were here, I'd never have chosen North Platte," Adam said.

Patch wiped his wet cheek. "I deserve every bit of the hatred you feel toward me. You don't know how many times I wanted to go home and ask your mother to forgive me and take me back . . . and to ask you and your sisters to forgive me. But I just couldn't work up the courage to do it. Only recently, something happened in my life that had me just about ready to head for Boston. Then I saw your sign go up. I —"

"Would've been too late."

Patch sniffed and wiped more tears. "Where are your sisters?"

"As if you care."

"I do care, though I know you find that hard to believe. I've wanted to cross the street and beg your forgiveness a hundred times since the day you first arrived in North Platte. Tonight I couldn't stand it any longer. That's why I'm here. Please, son . . . will you forgive me for deserting you?"

"If you can resurrect my mother and give her back to me, I'll forgive you, but not until then."

"But that's impossible. There's no way —"

"When I need clothes I'll buy them elsewhere. If Patch Smith ever needs an attorney he can find one someplace else. I won't tell anybody in this town who Patch Smith really is because I'd be so utterly ashamed for them to know your blood flows through my veins. You go on and live your life, and I'll live mine. If we cross paths, it'll be my mistake."

Gordon Burke looked down and said, "I don't blame you for feeling this way. It would mean everything in the world to me if you would forgive me, but I don't deserve your forgiveness." Then he turned and walked away.

Bettieann Ralston was thrilled when her parents walked the aisle on a Sunday morning and opened their hearts to the Lord. Since she had become a Christian, Bettieann's favorite day of the week was Sunday. When Monday came she was eagerly looking forward to Sunday again. It was the same with her parents, now that they were saved.

Bettieann had met several young men at church, but she politely turned down offers for dates. She had placed her burden about Seth in God's hands and wanted to give Him ample time to work. She knew the Lord would give her peace if it was ever time for her to look for another young man.

Bettieann entered Stinson's on a Monday morning and found Danielle Sharrow beside herself with excitement.

"You look awfully happy this morning," she said, smiling.

"Oh, I am!"

Bettieann waited for Danielle to go on, but when nothing else was said, she squinted at her and said, "It's a secret, I guess."

"At the moment it is."

"Well, how long do I have to wait to find out what you are so animated about?"

"Looks like it'll have to be at lunch. It's time for the store to open now. If you'd gotten in a few minutes earlier, I could've shared it then."

"Sorry. I ran into a couple of friends outside. If I'd known you had this big exciting secret to share, I'd have put them off till later."

Danielle laughed. "It'll be hard to keep it in, but believe me . . . you're going to like what I have to share with you!"

Soon customers were streaming through the doors, and the two friends were kept busy for the morning. When the clock on the wall indicated it was noon, and there were clerks in place to cover the lunch hour, Danielle grabbed Bettieann by the hand and said, "Come on, let's go to lunch."

They hurried down the street toward their favorite café, and Bettieann said, "All right, Miss Big Secret. Let's hear it!"

Danielle was almost giddy. "What have we been praying about for months?"

"That the Lord would let me find Seth."

"Let's get our table, then I'll reveal my big secret!"

When they were seated and had ordered, Danielle pulled a newspaper from her coat pocket. "Yesterday's late edition of the *Philadelphia Enquirer*," she said, turning to the classified advertisement section and handing it to

Bettieann. "Here . . . I've marked a special ad. Read it."

Deputy U.S. Marshal Seth Coleman entered the boardinghouse after returning from a long chase of an outlaw gang. He and three other deputies had trailed the gang for a week, finally cornering them, and were able to bring four of the six back alive. Chief Frank Houser had given his deputies three days off.

Seth paused at the mailboxes in the foyer and opened his expectantly. He smiled when he saw at least half a dozen envelopes that had to be responses to his ads. He had already received eight letters from young women, but none of those seemed right.

He entered his room and sat down at a small table and began to sort through his mail. Suddenly he stopped and stared at the familiar handwriting on one of the envelopes. The name Bettieann Ralston was in the upper left-hand corner.

On a dreary day in early March, Rachel Mason was going through the mansion one room at a time, making a list of objects to sell. Income from the American Securities Company had been almost nil since employees had started leaving two and three at a time.

Rachel had been forced to let the cook go.

She had done her best to make ends meet and keep them afloat financially. And she had watched her father sink deeper and deeper into despair. The more whiskey he consumed the farther down he went.

In late afternoon Rachel went to the kitchen to prepare supper. Roy Preslan had picked up her father that morning. Roy had come by the previous night, saying that Joseph had to sober up and come with him to the office in the morning. They had to meet with the other officers of the company on a most serious matter.

The meal was about halfway prepared when Rachel heard her father shuffle into the kitchen. She turned to look at him and said, "Supper will be ready in about half an hour, Daddy."

Joseph slumped onto the nearest chair.

Rachel moved to where he sat and said, "Well?" The smell of alcohol made her back away a few steps.

Joseph covered his face with his hands. "American Securities is no more. I have nothing but heavy personal debts. We'll lose the house, for sure. I don't know what we're going to do."

Rachel dropped onto a chair at the table, burst into sobs, and buried her face in her hands. "Why? Why is all of this happening? I just can't take anymore, Daddy! I just can't take anymore!"

Joseph stared at her helplessly, tears slowly gliding down his cheeks. When the sound of Rachel's weeping became unbearable, Joseph got to his feet and placed a quivering hand on her bent head. Rachel raised her head and looked into his eyes.

"I'm sorry, Rachel," he said softly.

Her father's touch brought solace that had been sorely missing for so long. She suppressed her sobs and sat quietly soaking in the feel of Joseph's hand on her head, bringing comfort to her heartsick soul.

After several minutes, Rachel looked up at him and said, "Daddy?"

"Yes, honey?"

"You said you don't know what we'll do since we're going to lose the house."

"Mm-hmm."

"Aunt Esther has enough house. I'm sure she'd let us move in with her until you're able to get a job. Things will be better in Memphis, Daddy. You'll be away from this house where you have so many memories of Mama. I know you'll be able to quit drinking then. Is . . . is it all right if I write Aunt Esther, tell her what has happened, and ask if she will take us in?"

"Yes," he said nodding. "Go ahead."

★ ★ ★

In Memphis, Tennessee, Esther Holden waited for a reply to her telegram. Upon receiving Rachel's letter, Esther wired them the same day, saying that they were more than welcome to come and live with her. She asked them to let her know as soon as possible if they were coming, and when.

And while she waited, she prayed. She asked the Lord to use the devastation in Joseph's life to bring him to Jesus. And she prayed for Rachel, that she would be convicted of her need to be saved and that the Lord would soon draw her to Himself.

Esther was elated when the return wire came, informing her that Joseph and Rachel would arrive at the Memphis depot on Saturday afternoon, March 23.

Although Esther's house was immaculate, she went about busily making preparations for their arrival. Her gentle heart wanted to soothe their hurts and give them a peaceful place to recuperate from their losses.

The white one-story frame house had four bedrooms. It sat on a large lot some distance from the street. In the summer, Esther's flower gardens were the talk and envy of the neighborhood, as were the delicious fruits and vegetables she grew. The early spring buds were just appearing on the trees, and the crocus and daffodils were tentatively poking their heads through the soil, seeking the warm rays of the sun.

On Saturday afternoon, March 23, Esther took one last look at the rooms she had prepared for Joseph and Rachel, gave a satisfied nod, and went to the barn for her horse and buggy.

Rachel and her aunt were in the kitchen after Rachel had put her things away in her room. Joseph was lying down in his room.

"Aunt Esther," Rachel said, "I'm nineteen now. I'm going to find a job so I can pay you for our room and board."

Esther hugged her and said, "That won't be necessary, honey. Unless you want to get a job to occupy yourself. But you don't have to buy any groceries, and I certainly don't want you and your father paying me rent for living here. I was left well off financially when I sold the farm after your Uncle Clayton was killed."

"I appreciate your generosity, Aunt Esther, but I am going to get a job, and I am going to at least pay for our food. It isn't right that we come here and sponge off of you."

Esther stroked Rachel's soft cheek and said, "All right, if it will make you feel better."

"It will. And . . ."

"And what, honey?"

"And I really believe this change of scenery will help Daddy stop his drinking."

"I'm praying that what my brother finds here will give him victory over that horrible bottle, Rachel. And I believe the Lord is going to bring it to pass."

20

Danielle Sharrow was just pulling the cash drawer from the safe for the new day's business when she saw Bettieann Ralston come through the door. Danielle lifted her eyebrows. "No letter yet?"

"Hasn't been enough time for my letter to get to Seth and a return letter to come back. I only sent my letter a week ago."

"Well, they should come up with a faster way to move the mail."

"What, for instance? Have birds carry it?"

"Wouldn't be a bad idea!"

Bettieann took off her light coat and put her purse under the counter. "I will get edgy, though, if I don't hear from him by this time next week."

"Me too," Danielle said.

Bettieann hit her forehead lightly. "I think both of us are forgetting that we've put the whole matter in the Lord's hands. We're not supposed to get edgy. We're supposed to stay out of His way and let Him work."

"You're right. The old flesh does tend to get in the way sometimes, doesn't it?"

They unlocked the doors, and a crowd of customers flowed in.

"Well, here we go again!" Danielle said.

"Brace yourself. The spring fashions are in, and our regular customers know it!"

It was just after lunch when Danielle and Bettieann returned to their department and relieved the clerks who had filled in for them. They were standing behind the counter, looking for customers to help, when Danielle spotted Lillian Ralston.

"Look, it's your mom."

Bettieann's mother was smiling from ear to ear. "Something just came for you, honey!" she said, opening her purse.

"It couldn't be a letter from Seth," Bettieann said. "There hasn't been time."

"Not a letter. A telegram!"

Bettieann squealed and grabbed the yellow envelope from her mother's hand. "Mother, Danielle, I hope you understand, but I'd like to read this alone. I'll be back in a few minutes." They watched her disappear into the powder room.

"This has got to work out for her," Danielle said. "I couldn't stand it if —"

"Now, Danielle," said Lillian, laying a hand on her arm. "It's going to be all right.

It's in God's hands."

Danielle shook her head. "There I go again. This seems to be my day to let the old flesh take over. Your daughter and I have become such good friends, Mrs. Ralston. I love her so much. But you're right. No matter what the telegram says, it's going to be all right."

Two women looking at dresses motioned to Danielle. She excused herself to Lillian and hurried to assist them.

Lillian browsed about the ladies' department, glancing every minute or so toward the powder room. After some ten minutes, she began to get worried.

On her way to help more customers, Danielle brushed by Lillian, glanced toward the powder room, and said, "I wonder what's taking her so long?"

"I don't know. But if she's not out here in five more minutes, I'm going in there."

At that moment, Bettieann stepped out, holding the telegram. She halted just outside the powder room door and set her tear-filled eyes on her mother.

Lillian rushed to her. "Honey, are you all right?"

"Yes, Mother! Oh, yes! Please. Come in here so I can tell you about it."

Lillian noticed Danielle looking back toward them as she waited on a customer. Lillian smiled at her and nodded, then followed her daughter into the powder room.

"Oh, Mother! Seth's first words in here are that he still loves me as always. He said because it seemed that it was over between us, he was using the mail order bride system to find a good Christian girl to marry. He says I'm forgiven, and tells me how happy he is to know that I have been born again. He wants —" Bettieann choked up. "He wants me to come to Omaha as soon as possible. We will marry as soon as I arrive, if it's all right with me."

Lillian felt her own eyes fill with tears.

Bettieann drew in another shuddering breath. "What does Seth mean 'if it's all right with me'? I'd marry him this minute if he were here!"

On Wednesday, March 27, Seth Coleman paced back and forth at the Omaha depot, waiting for the train from Kansas City to arrive. Before leaving his room, he had taken extra care with his grooming. He was slick and polished to a "fair-thee-well."

There was a white carpet of early spring snow on the ground, but it was melting under the bright sunshine.

Seth had never been so excited. The only time he could remember being more nervous was when the jury was out to decide his fate in the Lawrence Sheldon case. He paced to the end of the platform, made a quick pivot, and bumped into Byron Tucker, proprietor of one of Omaha's general stores.

"Whoa!" Byron said. "You a bit anxious, Deputy Coleman?"

"You might say that, sir. The young lady I'm going to marry is on the train coming in."

"Well, what do you know! Gettin' married, huh? Congratulations."

"Thank you, sir."

"I've got to keep moving," Byron said. "Bring your bride into the store real soon so Nellie and I can meet her."

"Will do, sir." Seth went back to pacing.

The train made a long curve as it followed the west bank of the Missouri River. Bettie-ann Ralston caught a glimpse of Omaha's business section in the distance. She kept willing the train to go faster, yet she was apprehensive about seeing Seth again. Although in his telegram he had assured her of his forgiveness, she knew she wouldn't be at peace until she could see him face to face and apologize in person.

She opened her purse and took out a small hand mirror. She pushed a few stray curls back into place and pinched her cheeks to give a little blush to her pale face. The train was pulling into the depot as she put the mirror back and closed her purse. She looked out the sooty window at a maze of faces. Suddenly her eyes fell on Seth.

He also caught sight of her, and a huge smile lit up his face. Bettieann waved as the train ground to a squealing halt. She took a deep breath, grabbed her small satchel, and headed for the door and toward the love of her life.

Seth met her at the platform of the coach, opening his arms to lift her off the bottom step. Then he whirled her around and carried her away from the crowd before setting her down.

"Welcome home, sweetheart," he said, looking into her misty eyes. "I love you."

"And I love you," she said, dropping her satchel to wrap her arms around his neck.

Seth kissed her soundly, then before he could say a word, she said, "Oh, darling, I'm so sorry for what I did. I was such a fool to doubt you when you told me you were innocent. I was so upset that day at the jail. I'm sorry for saying I had stopped loving you when I really hadn't. Please let me hear you say I'm forgiven, Seth. Please tell me —"

"Sh-h-h!" He placed a forefinger on her lips. "Bettieann, you already asked for my forgiveness, and I told you in my telegram that I had forgiven you. That settles it."

"But . . ."

"I said, that settles it. Just like when the Lord forgives us when we ask Him to. He never brings our sins up to us again. Sweetheart, let's just move on and enjoy our life together."

Bettieann wrapped her arms around his neck again. "You wonderful, wonderful man! I love you so much!"

They kissed again, then Seth picked up her satchel. "I assume you have luggage in the baggage coach?"

"Uh-huh. Four trunks. Do you still want me?"

Seth laughed. "I'll take you! Trunks and all!"

Seth put Bettieann in a hotel close to his boardinghouse, then took her to the office to meet Chief Houser and the deputies who happened to be there. Houser told her how much he appreciated such a fine lawman as Seth, and congratulated them both on their upcoming marriage. He surprised them by telling Seth he was giving him a week off with pay for his honeymoon.

Seth took Bettieann back to the hotel so she could unpack and freshen up. He picked her up an hour before suppertime to take her to the parsonage and introduce her to Pastor and Mrs. Ken Myers. Again, Bettieann was welcomed warmly.

The pastor took them to his office and spent a few minutes talking about the wedding, and marriage in general, showing them some Scriptures on the subject.

Later, as they were eating together at the hotel restaurant, Seth set loving eyes on Bettieann and said, "I have a little surprise to show you in the morning."

"What kind of a surprise?"

A boyish grin curved his mouth. "Our house."

"Our house?"

"I rented it the day you wired me to say you were coming."

"Well, you stinker! I figured since you took three of my trunks to your boardinghouse, we'd be living in your room."

"You'll love the house, I guarantee you! And someday when we've been able to put away a little money, we'll buy us one of our own."

"Oh, darling, I can hardly believe this is really happening!"

"Well, it is. Believe me." He paused, then said, "Since we have a week for our honeymoon, how would you like to take a little trip for a couple of those days?"

"A trip? To where?"

"North Platte."

"That's west of here, isn't it?"

"Almost three hundred miles. It's right at the spot where the North Platte and the South Platte come together and become the Platte River. It empties into the Missouri just a few miles south of where you sit at this moment."

"Well, thank you for the geography lesson, Deputy Marshal Seth Coleman."

"You're quite welcome."

"I'll go anywhere with you, darling; you know that. But why have you chosen North Platte for our little trip?"

"I want you to meet a very good friend of mine."

Her dainty eyebrows lifted. "You have a friend way out in North Platte, Nebraska?"

"My attorney in the Lawrence Sheldon trial."

"Oh . . . Adam Burke! His name was mentioned in all the newspapers. I'm sorry to say that Adam Burke had more faith in your innocence than I did."

Seth reached across the table and patted her hand. "That is in the past. Adam was planning to open up his own law firm in North Platte, and I want us to go see him, if he's there. If he's not . . . we'll have had a nice little honeymoon trip. I owe him a lot,

Bettieann, and I want you two to meet each other. Besides that, he was about to get married the last time I saw him. I'm sure you've heard of Philip Conrad III, who has the big law firm in Philadelphia."

"Oh, sure."

"Adam was engaged to Philipa Conrad, his daughter."

"So we'll be hobnobbing with the elite in North Platte, will we?"

Seth laughed. "Well, I guess you might say that. Is it all right with you, then, if we go?"

"Certainly, darling."

Three days later, Seth and Bettieann were married by Pastor Ken Myers in his office. Mrs. Myers and one of the church deacons were witnesses.

Adam Burke walked to work on a bright, clear morning and arrived at the office just as Olivia Dahl's fiancé pulled his wagon to a halt at the hitch rail.

"Good morning, Olivia, Russ," Adam said.

Both returned the greeting as Russ hopped out of the wagon and helped Olivia down.

Adam unlocked the front door of the office and held the door for Olivia. As she moved past him he looked across the street. Gordon Burke stood on the boardwalk alone, watching him. Adam turned his back and closed the door.

It was almost noon when Adam came out of his office with a client and noticed a man and woman seated on the other side of Olivia's desk. He could see the young woman's face, but the man's back was to him.

"I'll have Olivia get your papers in the mail right away, Mr. Snelling," Adam said. "You should hear back from us within about ten days."

"Fine," Snelling said, and headed for the door.

"Mr. Burke," Olivia said, "these people want to see you. I told them you wouldn't be able to until this afternoon, but the man is wearing a badge and insisted that you see them as soon as you came out of your office."

The man stood up and turned around. "Hello, counselor."

Adam could hardly believe his eyes.

Bettieann and Olivia looked on with pleasure as Seth Coleman and Adam Burke embraced and pounded each other on the back.

Adam turned to Bettieann, then looked at his friend. "All right, Seth, who is this lovely lady?"

"I want you to meet my new bride, Bettieann!"

"Your new bride? When did this happen?"

"Yesterday. We're on our honeymoon. I'm

working out of the Omaha U.S. Marshal's Office."

Adam shook his head in wonderment. "Omaha! So you met this pretty girl in Omaha, huh?"

"Well, no actually. It's a long story."

"Hey, I want to hear it right now. I don't care how long it is. Can I take you to lunch?"

"I think we could handle that," Seth said, smiling at Bettieann. She nodded her head and smiled.

Over lunch at one of North Platte's cafés, Seth and Bettieann told Adam the whole story.

"My, my, my," Adam said, shaking his head. "It's nothing short of a miracle that you two got back together. And now, here you are husband and wife!"

"We give the glory to God," Seth said. "Only He could have done this."

"Yes," Bettieann said. "To God be the glory!"

Adam hesitated a moment, then said weakly, "That's for sure."

Adam put his friends up in North Platte's finest hotel, and that evening they had supper together in the hotel's café.

"Adam, I recall that the last time I saw you there was a wedding date set with Philipa

Conrad," Seth said while they were eating.

Adam nodded. "Long story. I'll make it short. Philipa broke off the engagement. She didn't want to come to Nebraska with me. To her, this part of the country is the back woods. This is where I had my heart set on living the rest of my life. So, I came alone."

"Well, I'm sorry it didn't work out."

"It's all for the best. Philipa is definitely a high society girl. She belongs in the East."

"Any young ladies in your life?"

Adam looked glum. "None. Unattached or unmarried young ladies are hard to come by in these parts. All these months I've been in North Platte I've found no prospects."

"Well, you know that Bettieann and I were brought together again by the mail order bride system. Maybe you ought to put some ads in newspapers back East. Might find you a good wife that way."

"I made the bold statement not long ago that I would never order myself a bride through the mail. But it's making more sense now. Maybe I should put some ads in some papers. I'm beginning to think if I don't, I'll be a bachelor the rest of my life."

The next morning, Adam put Seth and Bettieann on the train for Omaha and told them to come back and see him when they could. Seth gave Adam their address and told him to let them know when he found the right young lady. He and Bettieann wanted to come to the wedding.

Rachel Mason was working in a Memphis flower shop and enjoying it immensely. She had made many friends in the stores and shops around the area. She loved living with Aunt Esther, who was such a kind and caring woman and always seemed to look for the good in everyone and every situation. She certainly lived what she believed.

Rachel willingly went to church with her aunt and listened politely to the preacher, though she still clung to what her father had taught her about life, death, and eternity. And she was never so rude as to turn away whenever the dear woman talked to her about Jesus Christ. Her life with her aunt was pleasant and good.

The one flaw in Rachel's world was her father. His drinking was getting worse instead of better. Most days he was so drunk there was no communication between them at all. She thought about going elsewhere to get away from the situation, but each time it crossed her mind she reminded herself it wouldn't be right to saddle Aunt Esther with her father. And even if she could do that, where would she go? Young ladies couldn't just strike out on their own. She had no other family who could take her in.

There seemed to be no way out.

On a mild April evening, after helping Aunt Esther clean up the kitchen after supper, Rachel took a shawl, went out onto the front porch, and sat down in the big swing.

Her thoughts drifted back to happy days when her mother was alive and her father had conquered the bottle. Tears brimmed her eyes and left tracks on her cheeks as they spilled down and dripped off her chin.

Esther Holden left her brother passed out in his room and went in search of her niece. When she reached the parlor, she heard the squeak of the front porch swing. She eased up to the window and saw Rachel weeping.

Esther moved into the hall and took her shawl off its hook, then quietly opened the front door. Rachel was startled when Esther laid a hand on her shoulder. Her head whipped around and she quickly brushed away the trace of tears on her cheeks.

Esther rounded the swing, sat down beside Rachel, and took the girl's soft hand in her own. "Honey, I know you're feeling downcast and mixed-up. Let's talk about it, okay?"

Rachel looked away.

"Sweetie, two heads are better than one. And a burden shared is always halved."

"Aunt Esther, I don't want to put any more strain on you than my father has done already," Rachel said, staring straight ahead.

"But I love you, and I want to help if I can. It would be easier for me to know the problem and help you with it than to worry and wonder what is wrong."

Tears gathered in Rachel's eyes again, and with a trembling voice she began to talk about the burden her father's drinking had put on her. She talked about the few young men she had dated, and that each time one came to the house, her father had embarrassed her, and the young man had not returned.

She had come to the point where she was ashamed to have anyone know he was her father. She had never mentioned him to anyone she worked with at the flower shop. She had even considered running away, and would have if she had somewhere to go.

Esther put an arm around her and hugged her close, telling her they would work out a solution together.

Rachel broke into sobs, but managed to tell Esther how selfish she felt because she wanted to run away from a bad situation.

Esther held her niece and asked God for wisdom as she patted the girl's hand.

Soon Rachel pulled herself together and Esther reached out to cup the girl's chin in her hand, gently turning her head to look into her eyes.

"Rachel, dear, I understand what's going on inside you. There's nothing selfish about wanting to get away from the shame and heartache your father has brought on you with his drinking. You're nineteen years old . . . a young woman. You want a life of your own, and that's how it should be."

Aunt and niece continued to talk in hushed tones for a long time, thinking of and discarding many possible solutions. They didn't come to any perfect answer, but Rachel felt as if the weight of the world had been lifted from her. She hugged her aunt and thanked her for talking to her.

The night air that drifted through the city from the Mississippi River had dropped the temperature considerably.

"A nice cup of tea would warm us, don't you think?" Esther said shivering.

"Sounds good."

They both finished two cups, then Rachel hugged her aunt, bid her good-night, and disappeared down the dim hall.

Esther went to her room, dropped to her knees beside the bed, and asked God for strength and wisdom. She thanked Him for His mercy and patience with the lost and begged for the salvation of Joseph and Rachel.

Her mind went to a favorite passage from the Psalms: "Wait on the LORD: be of good courage, and he shall strengthen thine heart: wait, I say, on the LORD."

Esther wept as she prayed, "Help me, Lord, to wait on You and not to faint. Please help me to pray in faith, believing."

With an open, trusting heart, Esther Holden left her burdens with the One whose yoke was easy and whose burden was light.

21

"Rachel, did you hear about the devastating fire that wiped out one of the shipping companies on the docks last night?" Esther Holden asked.

"My coworkers at the flower shop were talking about it today," Rachel said. "Sounded pretty bad."

"I read about it in the paper while you were in your father's room trying to get him to eat some supper. You can take it to your room and read it if you want."

"I'll do that. I didn't get much food down him, either. Just a little beef broth. Do you suppose when he gets too weak to get out and walk to the store for his whiskey, maybe he'll sober up?"

"Maybe. I'm sure not going to buy the stuff for him."

"Trouble is, he's probably got bottles stashed in places around here we haven't even thought of."

Soon niece and aunt bid each other good-night and went to their rooms. Rachel got into her nightgown, turned the bed covers down, and propped up the pillows against the headboard. She opened the newspaper and read the front page story of the fire at the docks, then browsed through the rest of the paper. She came to the classified section, and her eyes landed on a page that carried ads for mail order brides. Rachel's mind raced as she ran her eyes up and down the columns.

This is it! This is my way out!

Men from nearly every western state and territory had placed ads, and she carefully studied each one. She took a pencil and marked the ads she would respond to. Then she doused the lantern and slipped between the covers.

Rachel felt a strange excitement. Surely one of those men would find her interesting enough to want her for a bride. Even if the situation wasn't perfect, it would have to be better than her life now. She told herself she would lay down one restriction in each letter: She would not marry a man who was a drinker.

Rachel decided not to tell Aunt Esther what she was doing. When letters from the men started arriving, she would have to come up with some kind of explanation. She felt a bit guilty at the deception but reasoned that if one of the men got serious, she would discuss it with her aunt before making any final decision.

By the end of the first week of May, letters began to arrive. To Rachel's amazement, Aunt Esther did not question her about them. The letters were lying on her dresser each day when she came home from work, and night after night, Rachel wrote replies to the men whose letters interested her.

One night she opened a letter from a young attorney in North Platte, Nebraska. When she read the name Adam Burke, it sounded familiar, but she decided there was no way she could know a man who lived in Nebraska. There was a warmth and a sincerity to Adam Burke's letter that was lacking in the others, but in order to keep her options open, she sent replies to other men too.

As the days passed, Rachel waited eagerly to hear back from each of the young men . . . and especially from Adam Burke.

During the first week of May, Adam Burke began to receive letters from young women — and some not so young — interested in becoming his mail order bride. After he had received seventeen letters, Adam decided to write to the two girls he liked best. One lived on Long Island and the other in Roanoke. He mailed his replies at the Wells Fargo office, picked up his mail, and headed home, sifting through the day's letters. There were four more responses to his ad. The one on top was from a girl in Jersey City; the second was from Portland, Maine; the third from Milford, Delaware; and the fourth from Memphis.

When he saw the name on the envelope from Memphis, he stopped in his tracks.

A buggy passed by and someone called out, "Hello, Mr. Burke!"

Adam recognized a client and waved. Then his eyes went back to the envelope he had placed on top, and he read the name aloud: "Rachel Mason." His mind was already trailing back to Philadelphia and the terrible tragedy that took place there. The last name of the woman he had accidentally killed was Mason . . . Nancy Mason. He moved on down the boardwalk, muttering, "Surely there couldn't be any connection. Rachel Mason lives in Memphis."

When Adam arrived at his office, Olivia had some papers for him to sign. It was an hour before his next appointment, so Adam secluded himself in his office and read the four letters. He quickly dismissed three of them but was intrigued with the letter from the nineteen-year-old girl in Memphis, Rachel Mason.

He dashed off a reply, telling her that although he had received several letters, so far hers was the one that captivated his interest. He told her that he was from Boston, had graduated from Harvard University Law School, and after working in a law firm for three years, had come to North Platte to start his own practice. He explained that business was good and that he would be able to offer her financial security. He decided to wait to tell her that he was also the recipient of a large portion of an estate connected to Boston Clothiers. He told her as much about himself as he felt he could, and enclosed a photograph that had been taken barely over a year ago.

By May 14, Rachel Mason had received a reply from seven out of thirteen men in the West whose ads she had answered. Three more came that day while she was at work, and Esther laid them on her dresser as she had the others.

Esther was in the hall when Rachel came in the door after work.

"Hello, honey," Esther said. "How'd it go today?"

"Fine, Aunt Esther."

"Tired?"

"A little. How's Daddy?"

"He's out in the backyard, taking in some sunshine."

Rachel nodded and started toward her room.

"You received three more letters today, Rachel. You . . . ah . . . have me a bit puzzled."

"I do?"

"Mm-hmm. How is it you have male friends from way out west?"

"Aunt Esther, I haven't meant to be sneaky but . . . well, you've heard about the mail order brides, haven't you?"

"Of course. Have . . . have you been —"

"Yes, I have. I've decided that I've got to get away from Daddy and have a life of my own."

Esther folded her niece into her arms and held her close. "Honey, I feel so bad that things have gone like this in your young life. And I understand why you're doing this, I really do. But I have to be honest about it. I have some misgivings. But I can't tell you what to do."

"Thank you for understanding," Rachel said, pressing her head against Aunt Esther's shoulder.

"Rachel, you've had several letters come. Have you found any that interest you?"

"Some. I've written back to those men, and I'll just have to wait and see what develops. I

. . . I really was going to talk to you about it if I found a man I was interested in. Honest."

Esther drew back, looked her niece in the eye, and said, "I'm sure you were. At least let me give you my opinion when you think you've narrowed it down."

"I will. I promise."

Two days later, Rachel received Adam Burke's letter. Her heart told her this was the man she should marry, especially when she saw his photograph. He was handsome and had kind eyes. In his letter, Adam told her that if they decided they were for each other, he would write to her parents, asking permission to marry her. And if she did come to North Platte to be his bride, he would provide her a room in the town's nicest hotel until they had gotten to know each other and decided if they would marry. He wanted her to be sure she liked him and the town before they proceeded any further. If they did marry, there was a justice of the peace in town who would perform the ceremony.

Rachel's heart pounded. She picked up Adam's first letter and carried them both to her aunt, who was sitting on the top step of the back porch selecting flower seeds to plant in her riotous garden. She smiled as Rachel sat down beside her, then glanced at the letters.

"I think by the look in your eyes you've found one you're really interested in."

"Yes! Oh, yes! His name is Adam Burke. He's an attorney with his own law firm in North Platte, Nebraska. He graduated from Harvard University Law School."

Esther's eyebrows arched. "Harvard! Really?"

"Yes, and here's his picture."

Esther studied the photograph. "Handsome fellow. I like his eyes."

"Me too," Rachel said. She extended the letters toward her aunt. "Please. Read them."

Esther looked at Rachel's bright face and sparkling eyes and saw happiness that hadn't been there since before Nancy died. She brushed the dust from her hands and reached for the letters. She thoroughly read them both, then read them again.

Rachel waited and watched.

For a long moment Esther Holden stared out at the backyard, taking in the flowering trees and the lawn that still sparkled with dew. In her heart she was talking to the Lord, and when His peace stole over her, she turned to Rachel with a smile on her wrinkled face. Tears twinkled in her pale blue eyes.

"Child, I've prayed long and hard over this situation, and from the happiness I see written all over your face, this has to be the answer I've been waiting for. If it's my blessing you're wanting, then you have it, and I'll do anything I can to help you."

Rachel let out her breath, grabbed her aunt, and hugged her hard. "Thank you, Aunt Esther, for always being there for me and for understanding my need to go on with my life." She looked into her aunt's kind face and said, "My only regret is leaving the care of my father to you."

"Honey, listen. You have a right to live your life to the fullest. Your father and I have lived ours as we have chosen. Now it's your turn. My brother and I will do just fine, and you know I will stand by him and care for him as long as necessary."

"Thank you." Rachel managed a faint smile. "You saw that Adam said he would write my parents and ask them for permission to marry me. What should I do about that?"

Esther thought a moment. "The best thing is to be honest right up front. Tell him your mother is dead and that your father is a hopeless drunk. Better he knows it right now. Just tell him a letter to your father isn't necessary." Esther stroked Rachel's cheek. "Come on, now. Let me see that happy face I saw a few minutes ago. We need to get busy. We have much to do and a wedding to look forward to."

Again Rachel placed her arms around her

aunt's shoulders and said softly, "I love you, Aunt Esther."

Esther kissed Rachel's cheek. "I love you too, honey."

That evening, Rachel wrote back to Adam Burke and sent a photograph of herself. She explained that she had written several other men but he had interested her more than any of them. She would not make another move until she heard back from him.

As her aunt had suggested, she told him that her mother was dead and explained the situation with her father. Finally, she told him she was accepting his proposal as of this letter, and if he still wanted her to come, to please write as soon as possible and let her know.

Adam Burke was full of joy as he mailed a letter to Rachel Mason, enclosing a check to cover her travel fare and any other expenses. He asked her to wire him the date and time she would arrive at the North Platte railroad station. At the bottom of the letter he thanked her for the photograph, saying she was even more beautiful than he had imagined.

Adam then went to a retired man in town who had a large lot for sale in the nicest part of North Platte. He bought the lot, then went to the office of Donald Wiersby, a homebuilder. Wiersby showed him several sets of plans for houses, and when Adam saw the one he liked best, he wrote a sizable check and told Wiersby to begin construction as quickly as possible.

Only recently had Adam told his secretary that he was putting ads in the newspapers for a mail order bride. As he entered the office, smiling broadly, she said, "My boss looks awfully happy today. Got a secret?"

Adam laughed. "I haven't told you that a certain young lady in Tennessee and I have been getting serious, have I?"

"Well, no, you haven't. Let's hear it."

Adam explained all about Rachel Mason.

"Mr. Burke," Olivia said, smiling broadly, "I can't tell you how happy I am for you!"

The door opened and Pastor Tom Gann came in, saying he wanted to set an appointment with Adam to discuss some legal matter. Adam invited him to meet with him now, since he didn't have an appointment scheduled for another two hours. Gann rushed home to get the necessary papers, and when he returned, the two men went into Adam's office.

The work was done within an hour. Gann pulled out his checkbook and asked what he owed Adam. While he was writing the check, he said, "Adam, you've lived in North Platte for quite a while now, but you still haven't visited the church . . . even though you've told me you would."

"I really intended to come, Pastor. I just haven't made it yet."

Gann handed Adam the check and said, "I'd like to ask you a question."

"Sure."

"Let's say you were to die suddenly today. Where would you go? Heaven or hell?"

"Well, I sure hope I'd go to heaven."

"You hope?"

"Well, yes. I certainly wouldn't want to go to hell."

"So you do believe there's a hell?"

"Sure. God's got to have a place to put the souls of really bad people. Like John Wilkes Booth and other cold-blooded murderers . . . and people who start wars."

"Adam, people don't go to hell because they're bad. And people don't go to heaven because they're good."

Adam's brow furrowed. "They don't?"

"You told me your next appointment is a little more than half an hour from now. Could we talk about this until then?"

"Well, I suppose . . . sure."

Tom Gann took a small Bible from his pocket and read passages about the sinful nature in all human beings. In God's sight, no one was good. Then he turned to passages about Jesus' death and resurrection, explained the gospel plainly, and showed Adam that unless he repented of sin and believed in the Lord Jesus, he would spend eternity in hell. He was about to press Adam for a reply when Olivia tapped on the door and told her boss that his next client was there.

Adam rose from his chair and said, "Thank you for letting me do the work on those papers for you, Pastor."

"I'm just glad you're here so I don't have to go to Grand Island anymore." As he headed for the door, he added, "And that invitation to come to church still stands. You're welcome any time."

"I know that. Thanks again for coming in."

On May 30, Rachel received Adam's letter and the check. She showed them to her aunt, then went to the railroad station and bought her ticket. She stopped at the Western Union office and sent the wire to Adam, telling him when she would arrive in North Platte.

That evening after supper, Joseph was fairly sober, and Rachel told him in front of Esther about replying to the mail order bride ads, and that she had found the young man she was going to marry.

"You can't be serious!" Joseph said. "Why

not find a man here in Memphis and get to know him before you go off accepting a marriage proposal? How can you possibly know whether you want to marry this Adam Burke? You're not even in love with him. You need to marry a man because you love him, not just because he offers you financial security."

"But Daddy, Adam is going to put me up in North Platte's finest hotel until we can get to know each other and have a chance to fall in love."

"Well . . . maybe. But I still don't want you heading off to Nebraska, of all places."

"Well, I'm going, whether you want me to or not. I can't stand it anymore seeing you drink yourself to death. I had hoped that moving here to Memphis would make a difference, but it hasn't. I just can't live like this anymore."

On the day of Rachel's departure, Joseph went to the railroad station with his sister and daughter. Tears ran down his face as he watched his daughter climb aboard the train. Esther stood beside him, once again asking the Lord to bring Rachel to Himself, in his own way and His own time.

On Tuesday morning, June 4, 1878, Rachel's train pulled out of Des Moines, Iowa.

The sun was just peeking over the eastern horizon. This was the day! At four o'clock this afternoon she would meet the man she was sure was to become her husband.

It had been a beautiful trip so far, even though saying good-bye to her father and her aunt had been more difficult than she had imagined. But once the train pulled out of the Memphis depot, and she had time to settle in and compose herself, she found that she was looking forward to the trip with great anticipation.

As the train rolled across the Iowa corn-fields, Rachel laid her head back and closed her eyes. Aunt Esther's words kept running through her mind in rhythm with the clacking wheels: "Now it's your turn . . . now it's your turn . . . now it's your turn . . ."

Soon they crossed the trestle that carried them over the Missouri River, and the train pulled into Omaha. After a thirty-minute stop, they were rolling westward once again.

Rachel became aware of a vast change in the terrain as the train raced across Nebraska. It was quite a contrast to Tennessee . . . even to Pennsylvania. In this land where trees were scarce, a person could almost see forever. She enjoyed the scenery and the touch of freedom the wide open spaces seemed to bring. Though she was a little weary, her spirits were buoyant, and excitement filled her veins. The train was moving at a good clip, but the time seemed to drag.

Rachel opened her purse, took out a book, and tried to read, but found that she couldn't concentrate. She put the book away and took out pencil and paper to write a letter to her aunt and her father.

The train slowed and finally ground to a halt in Grand Island, and some passengers got off and others got on. Soon the train was on its way with three more stops before it reached North Platte. Rachel closed her eyes and laid her head back. The rhythmic click of the wheels soon lulled her into a light slumber. She stirred slightly when the train stopped at Kearney, Lexington, and Gothenburg. But each time she went back to sleep.

Rachel was suddenly awakened when the brakes of the train squealed and the train came to a stop. She heard an excited child say they were in North Platte. She sat up, blinking, and rubbed her eyes. A few passengers around her were picking up their hand luggage preparing to leave the train.

"Oh, dear," Rachel said to herself in a low voice. "How could I have slept so long? Now there isn't even time to freshen up before I meet Adam!"

She used the window for a mirror as best she could, hastily patting her hair into some semblance of order, then put on her small straw bonnet and tied the pretty bow under her chin. She stood up and tried to shake out the wrinkles in her blue travel suit, then picked up her overnight bag.

She took a deep breath and said, "Guess I'm ready as I'll ever be."

Adam had arrived at the station a half hour before the train was due. He passed the time either pacing the platform or gazing down the track, eager to catch the first sight of the long-awaited train.

He had just answered a friendly greeting from a client who was passing through the depot when he heard the whistle and saw smoke billowing skyward. His heart started beating double-time.

When the engine hissed and the wheels screeched to a halt, Adam positioned himself so he could see the small platforms on each of the three passenger coaches. He was scanning every face when suddenly the face he had been searching for was directly in front of him.

He hurried to the side of the coach and stopped. Rachel was on the bottom step, recognition showing in her eyes. Both of them stood stock still for several seconds, then smiles lit up their faces.

"Hello, Rachel. Welcome to North Platte." Adam gave her his hand and helped her down onto the platform. They stood looking into each other's eyes, not sure what to do next. Finally, Adam said, "Rachel, may I have permission to embrace you?"

She met his soft gaze and nodded. Adam's strong arms went around her, and Rachel knew deep inside that he was the man for her.

Adam loaded Rachel's trunks into his buggy and helped her onto the seat. "I'll take you to the hotel in a little while," he said, "but first I want to show you something."

She smiled at him. "Whatever you say. What am I about to see?"

"Well, I hope you won't think me too presumptuous since we agreed that we'd give it time before we marry. You know . . . see if we are really for each other. But I . . . ah . . . went ahead and bought some land to build a house on, and as you will see, they've started construction on it."

"Oh," she said, secretly pleased. "I'm sure it's going to be nice."

Rachel let her gaze roam over the town as they moved along Main Street, liking what she saw. Soon Adam guided the buggy onto a side street. After going two blocks, he swung up and stopped by the lot.

"This is it," he said. "What do you think?"

The foundation of the house was finished and two sides were already framed. Several graceful cottonwood trees decorated the yard. The house fit nicely between two rows of trees so that none of them would have to be sacrificed.

"It's beautiful."

"Like you . . . only in a different way." Adam reached beneath the seat and pulled out three large sheets of paper. "These are the plans. Let me show you."

Rachel listened as Adam explained the detailed drawings. The house was two storied, not too large, not too small. Immediately, Rachel started decorating it in her mind. Adam traced the outline of the yard with his finger and explained how it would look when it was landscaped.

"Oh, Adam," she said in a voice just above a whisper, "I don't think you're presumptuous at all." Her eyes shone with unshed tears. "How wonderful to have a home of my own. Thank you for being so thoughtful."

"I'm so glad you're here," he said, touching her hand. "If this works out and you decide that you want to go ahead and marry me before the house is built, there are some houses for rent all over town. We can live in one of those until our house is finished."

Rachel looked into his eyes and said, "I feel like I'm dreaming."

"Yes, me too. Would you like to see my office before I take you to the hotel?"

"I'd love to."

It was just before closing time when Adam pulled the buggy up in front of his office. As he was helping Rachel down, he glanced across the street and saw his father standing on the boardwalk. As usual, there was a pained look on Gordon Burke's face, but this time there was also curiosity.

They headed for the office door, and Adam introduced Rachel to several people who happened to be walking by. Rachel was warmly welcomed by all those she met in North Platte.

The following week was a blissful one for Adam and Rachel. They enjoyed each other's company, and after each time they were together they were even more convinced they were meant for each other.

One evening they were eating together at the hotel café, and Adam looked up to see Pastor Gann and his wife, Barbara, come in. The Ganns spotted them and headed toward their table. Adam introduced Rachel and explained that she had come from Memphis to marry him.

The pastor told Rachel in a light manner that he had been trying to get Adam to visit the church but had been unsuccessful. He invited Rachel, suggesting that maybe she could get him there. Rachel smiled and said maybe she could.

The Ganns left then and went to their own table, and Rachel said how nice they were and that sometime soon she and Adam should attend a service as a courtesy to them. Adam agreed.

After supper, Adam and Rachel took a moonlight ride to their new property to see how the construction was progressing. They were happy to see the entire structure had been framed up and the roof was going on.

Adam brought Rachel back to the hotel and held her hand as they mounted the stairs to the second floor.

"Thank you for a delightful evening," Adam said as they drew near her door. A sweet silence descended over them, and they looked deeply into each other's eyes.

The pleasant touch of Rachel's lips was still with Adam when he stepped inside the boardinghouse. He found Patch Smith talking to Wallace Melroy. Patch's back was toward him, but Wallace saw him come through the door and said, "Here he is now, Patch."

Adam's father turned around.

"Patch was wanting to see you, Adam," Wallace said. "I was just telling him I thought you'd be here soon."

"Sure, Mr. Smith, come on to my room."

When they stepped into the apartment and the door was closed, Adam said coldly, "What do you want?"

"I need your mercy, Adam. I'm begging you to forgive me. I'm your father. I want to be close to you."

"You didn't want to be close to me when you ran off with that Murray woman. You didn't want to be close to my sisters or my mother. Receiving my forgiveness for what you did is impossible."

Gordon turned to the door and took hold of the knob. "I heard that the young lady who came to town is here to marry you," he said, looking back at his son.

"She is."

"She's beautiful, son. I hope you'll be very happy together."

When the only reply was silence, Gordon stepped out of the room, closed the door, and walked away. Tears ran down his cheeks unchecked.

22

By the first week of July, Adam Burke and Rachel Mason knew they were deeply in love and it was time to set the wedding date. They agreed on July 17.

Construction on their home was coming along, but it was far from finished, so they rented a small furnished house to live in until construction was completed. The day after they set the wedding date, Adam spoke with the justice of the peace and made arrangements for the ceremony, then went to the rented house where Rachel had been scrubbing floors, cleaning the kitchen, and washing windows.

Rachel laughed when Adam took her in his arms to kiss her. "Are you sure you want to get that close? I'm awful dirty."

"If the dirt is on you, it has to be clean and wonderful. I love to kiss clean and wonderful dirt!" They kissed three or four times, then Adam said, "It just came to me this morning as I left the justice of the peace that you might like to have a new dress for the wedding. There are a couple of dress shops on Main Street where you could get fitted and have them put a rush on getting it done."

Rachel smiled. "I'm way ahead of you, darling. Before I left Memphis, Aunt Esther made me a beautiful dress for the wedding. All I need to do is go to the millinery shop and buy a hat."

Adam kissed the tip of her nose. "Pretty sneaky, aren't you?"

"What do you mean?"

"You had your mind made up before you came that this arrangement was going to work."

"Sneaky or not, the dress is ready. I saved some money from working at the flower shop for my trousseau."

"Oh, no, you don't. Your groom is paying for that." Adam took out his wallet and stuffed an uncounted wad of bills into her hand. "If you need more, just holler."

"You're such a wonderful man."

"As long as I can keep you believing that, everything will be great."

"Is it all set with the justice of the peace?"

"All set. The ceremony will take place in Mr. Waldron's parlor at four o'clock on the seventeenth."

"Oh, Adam, I'm so happy!"

"You can't be any happier than I am!" They kissed again, then Adam said, "We need to talk about the honeymoon." She looked deep into his eyes, waiting for him to proceed. "Since I'm the only lawyer in town and business is booming, would it be all right if we put off the honeymoon till later?"

"As far as I'm concerned, we don't need a honeymoon. I'll be as happy as possible just being Mrs. Adam Burke."

The next day Rachel went shopping on Main Street, and people on the boardwalk greeted her warmly, which added to her happiness. She entered North Platte Clothiers and glanced at the young man who was busy with a customer at the counter. He excused himself to the customer and said, "Hello, ma'am. Looking for something particular?"

"Yes, sir. The ladies' department."

"Right over that way," he said, pointing. "My name's Jack Brady. If I can help you, please let me know. I'll be through here in a couple of minutes."

Rachel thanked him and headed toward the ladies' department. She had barely begun to look around when a man with a patch over his left eye approached her. He smiled at her and said, "I'm Patch Smith, ma'am, the proprietor."

"I'm happy to meet you, Mr. Smith."

"I believe your name is Miss Rachel Mason?"

"Why, yes, it is."

"And you're here to marry our fine attorney, Adam Burke."

"Right again."

"Let me welcome you to North Platte, Miss Mason."

"Thank you, sir."

"Now, is there anything I can help you with?"

"What I need, Mr. Smith, are hat, gloves, and shoes to complete my wedding trousseau."

"I believe you'll like our selection," Patch said. "Where would you like to start?"

"Let's go for the hat, first."

Rachel made her choices and went to the counter, where Patch tabulated the sale and began wrapping the items for her.

"We have a nice jewelry department over on this side of the store, Miss Mason. I would like to —"

"I'm really not in the market for jewelry right now, Mr. Smith. Maybe some other time."

Patch smiled. "Maybe I should have come at this another way. What I would like to do is give you something from the jewelry case as a wedding present."

Rachel's face flushed. "Oh, Mr. Smith, I can't let you —"

"Please?"

"Well, I —"

"Please let me do this. I would be honored."

Olivia Dahl looked up from the paperwork before her as Rachel came through the door. "Looks like you've been shopping," she said with a grin.

"Some things for my trousseau. Is Adam busy?"

"He's working on some business contracts for a client, but he's alone. I'm sure he'll be glad to see you."

Rachel knocked on the door and was received with open arms. Adam closed the door, kissed her soundly, and said, "Find everything you wanted?"

"I did. May I show them to you?"

Adam oohed and aahed at the hat, shoes, and gloves, then said, "Did you get these all at the same place?"

"Yes. At the clothing store across the street."

"Oh . . . that's nice."

"And I got something else there, too." She took a small box from her purse and opened it. Inside was an exquisite brooch.

"It's beautiful, sweetheart! That will look really good on just about anything you wear. I always want you to buy anything you want."

"But I didn't buy this. That nice Mr. Smith gave it to me for a wedding present. I tried to talk him out of it, but he wouldn't listen. Wasn't that a sweet thing to do?"

"Ah, yes. It sure was. I'm surprised he would do something so . . . thoughtful."

"Well, I'll get out of here and let you go back to work," Rachel said, closing the small box and returning it to her purse. "Would it be all right if I buy some materials so I can make some things for our new house? I'll need some muslin, embroidery thread, and hoops."

"Sure. Buy anything you want."

"You've been so generous in every way, Adam. I'd like to contribute something to our new home when we get it finished and move in."

Adam took her in his arms and kissed her. "You're the most wonderful thing that's ever happened to me."

That evening when Rachel was alone in her hotel room, she wrote a thank-you note to Patch Smith, then wrote to Aunt Esther — the third letter since she arrived in North Platte. She told her aunt they were getting

357

married on July 17 and asked her to tell her father about the wedding.

Adam was superbly happy that night, lying in bed. He even breathed a prayer, thanking God that he had found the girl of his dreams. He was glad he hadn't given in to Philipa and stayed in Philadelphia. Sooner or later their marriage would have fallen apart. But he would always be happy with his wonderful Rachel, and he was living in the West where he belonged.

The next morning Adam went to the Western Union office and sent a wire to Seth and Bettieann Coleman in Omaha telling them of their wedding plans. Four hours later, a Western Union messenger came to Adam's office with a telegram informing him that Deputy Coleman was tracking outlaws in western Nebraska and was not expected to return for some time. The chief U.S. marshal had contacted Mrs. Coleman, and she sent her congratulations, saying that she would advise her husband of the wedding upon his return.

July 17 was a glorious summer day in Nebraska. Wayfaring breezes tufted the tall grass on the prairie and made the leaves in the trees dance jauntily. The cobalt blue sky stretched endlessly in every direction.

Adam drove his buggy toward the hotel to pick up Rachel. He looked resplendent in his best black suit, white shirt and black tie, and shoes so well polished he could see his reflection in them.

Rachel was no less than dazzling in her soft butter-yellow dress of fine cotton broadcloth sprigged with tiny green leaves. A wide sash of the same green cinched her slender waist and tied in a graceful bow in back. White eyelet lace trimmed the modest rounded neck and elbow length sleeves. A natural straw hat nestled atop her glossy hair.

At four o'clock, the bright-eyed couple stood before Justice of the Peace James Waldron radiating happiness. Witnessing the ceremony were Mrs. Waldron and Olivia Dahl.

When the justice pronounced them husband and wife, Adam sweetly kissed Rachel's lips. The Waldrons congratulated them with a smile and a handshake, but Olivia hugged them both and kissed Rachel on the cheek.

Rachel tucked her hand in the crook of Adam's arm and he escorted her toward the door, then stopped to look back and say with a mock frown, "Back to work, Miss Dahl."

"Slave driver!" she said, laughing.

Adam had made a reservation at the hotel's

café for the one room they had for private occasions. He and Rachel had an hour before dinner and decided to take a drive outside of town and just enjoy each other's company.

Rachel held on to her husband's arm as the horse trotted west along the south bank of the North Platte River. A few months ago she had thought she would never be happy again. But now, here she was, sitting beside her husband . . . the love of her life. A wondrous future awaited her.

She leaned close to Adam and whispered, "I love you."

He took the reins in his left hand, put his arm around her, and pulled her against him. "I love you too, beautiful lady."

God has been so good to me, Rachel thought.

They sat down at the table in their private dining room, almost too excited to eat. When dinner was over and they left the café arm in arm, Adam and Rachel looked toward the spectacular sunset. The lowering sun was painting the broad prairie a brilliant red that stretched as far as the eye could see.

Rachel's hand found Adam's as she said, "What a perfect ending to a perfect day."

Adam helped her into the buggy, kissed her softly, and said, "Perfect because today Adam

360

Burke became the most blessed man on the face of the earth."

He climbed in beside her and put the horse in motion. They drove through the dusty streets of North Platte toward their little rented home and their new life together.

On Friday, when Adam came home from work, a pleasant aroma met him at the door. It hadn't taken long for him to learn that Rachel was an excellent cook. Now he tiptoed to the kitchen door and peeked in. Rachel was sitting at the kitchen table, reading a letter. Her hands were trembling, and she was sniffling.

He went to her quickly and said, "Honey, what's the matter?"

She looked up at him through a film of tears. "I'm crying happy tears, darling. Look here." She took out a check from Aunt Esther's envelope. "My precious aunt sent us a hundred dollars as a wedding gift."

"Well, that was awfully nice of her. We'll have to write and thank her."

Rachel laid the check back on top of the envelope and picked up a second letter. "And this is from Daddy."

Adam's eyes fell on the envelope. The return address was the same as Esther Holden's, but a gasp escaped his lips when he saw the name Joseph Mason.

"What's wrong?" Rachel said, frowning up at him.

"Nothing. It just surprises me that you got a letter from your father. You know . . . being an alcoholic and all. What does he say?"

"Here. I'd like you to read it."

Adam began reading. Joseph's handwriting was sharp and clear as he told his daughter that within days after she left for Nebraska he came to the end of his rope, and for the first time he listened as his sister told him the gospel and they read together from the Bible. For the first time in his miserable life he saw what Jesus had done for him on the cross. Esther had led him to the Lord on June 6. Immediately after opening his heart to Jesus, he had thrown away every liquor bottle.

He went to church with Esther the next Sunday and was baptized. He had not touched a drop of alcohol since the day he got saved. Jesus had not only saved his soul from hell but had taken away the power of alcohol over him. He was free in body and soul.

He had been offered a job at a Memphis brokerage firm. With his years of experience as owner of American Securities Company, he felt he would do well there. He told Rachel how sorry he was for not having been a good father. He asked her to forgive him and told her he loved her. He also asked her to greet his new son-in-law for him.

Adam's insides were churning. Nancy Mason's husband, Joseph, had owned the most successful brokerage firm in Philadelphia — American Securities Company.

He handed the letter back to Rachel. "I'm glad your father found a way to overcome his drinking problem."

"My aunt has long been a Christian. She's talked to me about being saved many, many times. Daddy taught me to stay away from that 'religious fanaticism' from the time I can remember, but now I'm wondering if there really isn't something to it. I expected that any day Daddy would die from his drinking but . . . his letter sounds so wonderful. I can hardly believe the change." Rachel left her chair and went to Adam, putting her arms around his neck. "Honey, are you all right?"

"Yes. Yes, I'm fine. I'm just . . . so overwhelmed to hear this good news about your father."

"You go get washed up. Supper will be on in fifteen minutes."

"We haven't talked about church or that sort of thing, Adam," Rachel said while they were eating. "What do you think? Daddy's change is really marvelous. Is there something

363

to it? Believing in Jesus and being saved, I mean." Adam seemed preoccupied and didn't respond. Rachel reached across the table to grasp his hand. "Honey, are you sure you're all right?"

"Oh. Uh . . . yes. I think there just might be something to it. Pastor Gann has talked to me about it at length, and I've thought about Jesus on the cross a lot since then. It could be everything Pastor Gann says it is."

Later that night as they lay in the darkness holding each other, Rachel said, "Adam, would you like to know more about becoming a Christian? There's been such a change in Daddy, what Aunt Esther has been telling me all these years has to be true. Why don't we go see Pastor Gann tomorrow and let him explain it some more?"

"Maybe we ought to go to church Sunday, like we told Pastor Gann we would."

"I think that would be a good thing to do."

Rachel awakened the next morning tired and listless from a troublesome night. She and Adam sat at the breakfast table barely picking at their food, and she could tell Adam had not slept well either.

Rachel kissed Adam and sent him off to work, then cleared the table and did her morning chores. All the while the words of her father's letter kept running through her mind. She poured herself a second cup of coffee and read the letter again. She stared out the kitchen window at the white clouds drifting on the high winds, and recalled Aunt Esther's letters and their conversations over the years.

Suddenly, Rachel knew she couldn't wait till Sunday. She undid her apron, tidied her hair, and hurried out the door.

Deputy U.S. Marshal Seth Coleman guided his horse down Main Street at the west end of North Platte. His chase had led him almost to the Nebraska–Wyoming border before it came to an abrupt end. He had decided to see Adam Burke on his ride back to Omaha, and planned his route through North Platte.

Seth spotted his friend coming toward him on the boardwalk. He put the horse to a fast trot, removed his hat and waved it, calling, "Adam! Hey, Adam!"

Adam was caught momentarily off guard, then smiled at seeing his friend and waved back. He left the boardwalk and headed into the street.

As Seth slid from his saddle, he noted a man sitting on a horse in line with the bank's front door. He was holding the reins of two other horses.

Just then, Adam rushed up and slung an arm across Seth's shoulders. "It's so good to see you, friend. I wired you that I'd found my mail order bride and was getting married on the seventeenth. Your office said you were chasing outlaws in western Nebraska."

"That's right. I left a couple of dead outlaws with the Kimball County sheriff. Thought I'd come through here and see how you were doing. I'm really glad to hear that you're married!"

Suddenly, gunshots came from inside the bank. Seth moved with catlike speed and grabbed the man in front of the bank, pulling him off his horse and slamming him to the ground. He shouted to Adam to take cover.

Two men carrying smoking guns and a canvas bag bolted from the bank. Adam froze in his tracks.

"Adam! Take care of this one!" Seth shouted.

Adam darted to the man on the ground and drove a hard punch to his jaw. A bullet hummed past his ear. It stunned him a bit, but he managed to hit the man again with enough power to drop him cold.

When Adam looked up, he saw the other two robbers lying on the ground with bloody shoulders. Seth was picking up their guns, and two male bank employees picked up the money bag. By the time Sheriff Ben Colter arrived, everything was under control. He holstered his gun and listened as people on the street told him what Adam Burke and the deputy U.S. marshal had done.

While Colter was shaking hands with Seth Coleman, Adam felt something moist running down his right jaw. He put a hand to it and realized his ear was bleeding.

"Adam, you've been hit!" Seth said.

"A bullet hummed past my ear, but I didn't feel anything." Adam pulled a handkerchief from his pocket and pressed it to his ear.

The bank president joined them, telling Sheriff Colter that no one inside the bank was hurt. The robbers had only fired into the ceiling to frighten everyone into submission.

"Adam," Colter said, "you need to let Doc Holcomb have a look at that. I'm glad it isn't worse."

"What about these two over here, Sheriff?" one of the bank employees asked. "They've both got bullets in their shoulders."

"I'll need some of you men to take them to Doc. I'll haul the one Adam laid out to the jail and lock him up."

Seth stayed with Adam while Dr. Harry Holcomb treated the wounded ear and put in two stitches. "Mr. Burke, you just about left this world today," Holcomb said as he bandaged Adam's ear. "If that bullet had been an inch and a half closer, they'd be digging your grave right now."

The hair bristled on Adam's neck. "That was close, wasn't it?"

"Too close," Seth said. "Your new bride came within an inch and a half of becoming a widow."

Adam was shaken, though he tried not to show it as he and Seth walked out of the doctor's office. "I'd like you to meet Rachel," Adam said. "Do you have time?"

"I've got to be back on the road in a little while, but if we can go see her right away, I'd sure like to meet her."

"Our house isn't far. Come on."

Seth led his horse as they walked, and Adam talked about the ads he had put in several newspapers. He explained about the letters that came from young ladies in several parts of the eastern United States, but how Rachel's letter captured him the moment he read it.

Seth tied his horse at the front porch and followed Adam to the door. When they moved inside, Adam called, "Rachel, I have somebody here I want you to meet! Where are you, sweetheart?"

No answer came, and Adam went out to

the backyard. Not finding her there, he searched the rest of the house. He then told Seth to wait in the parlor while he went to the closest neighbor. He returned in minutes.

"The neighbors said they saw Rachel walking toward Main Street earlier this morning. She could be in any store in town. It might take some time to find her."

"Probably be easier just to let her come see us," Seth said. "I can wait a little longer before riding out."

"Good. I hope she gets back before you have to go. In the meantime, I need your help."

"I'd be glad to help anyway I can."

"You told me before you left for Washington, D.C., that you had been born again."

Seth's face lit up. "That's right."

"The pastor here has talked to me about it, but I've been foolishly putting it off."

"Well, I think we both were reminded today that a person never knows when he might be snatched out of this life."

"That's exactly why I brought it up." Adam touched the bandage on his ear. "If I had been killed today, I'd be in hell right now. God has given me a warning, and I'm not going to reject His Son any longer. I want to be saved, Seth. Will you help me?"

The day was getting older, and Rachel still

had not come home. Finally Adam walked Seth to his horse and they embraced, pounding each other on the back. Seth mounted his horse and looked down from his perch with a grin.

"Oh. I almost forgot to tell you. We're putting a U.S. marshal's office in North Platte. Be about six months. Now that I know you're here, I'll make application to work out of this office. I'm sure Rachel and Bettieann will become friends, just like you and me."

"I have no doubt of that," Adam said.

Seth put his horse to a trot. When he reached the corner he paused and waved. Adam wiped tears from his eyes and waved back.

23

Adam Burke's heart was filled with joy as he entered the house. He glanced at the clock on the mantel and realized he had been gone from the office a long time. By now Olivia had probably heard of the shooting. He must go back to the office and let her know he was all right.

Adam left the office again a little past 3:30 and headed for home. If Rachel wasn't home by this time, he would search through town until he found her. He felt a little nervous about telling Rachel he had become a Christian, but as he pondered their recent conversations he thought she would want to be saved, too.

As he drew up to the house, the front door was open. He hurried across the porch and into the house, calling her name.

"Adam, darling!" Rachel called from the kitchen. "What are you doing home this early?" She came through the kitchen door with flour on her hands and stopped when she saw the bandage on his ear. "Adam! What happened?"

He took her in his arms and kissed her, saying, "I'm not hurt bad, honey. I'll be fine."

"I'm glad it's not serious, but what happened?"

"You haven't heard about the bank robbery?"

"No. I've been at the Gann home since this morning. Barbara and I heard some shots, but we thought it was probably someone just outside of town hunting rabbits or pheasants."

Adam told her about the attempted bank robbery and of the part his friend Seth Coleman played in foiling it. In the exchange of shots a bullet grazed his ear.

"That bullet was too close. You could've been killed!"

"I know. It was a close call."

She wrapped her arms around him and held him close for several minutes. Then she eased back and looked into his eyes. "Would you come into the kitchen, darling? I'm making bread, but I need to talk to you. It's very important."

Adam sat down at the kitchen table. Rachel placed the dough in the oven, then wiped flour from her hands and sat down facing him.

"Adam, I told you a moment ago that I was at the Gann home."

"Yes. What were you doing there?"

"I . . . I had a bad night last night. Didn't sleep much."

"I know what you mean."

"The reason I couldn't sleep was because I was so troubled about the things my aunt has talked to me about over the years. I couldn't wait till Sunday to get right with God. I went to the parsonage to talk to Pastor Gann. He wasn't there, but Mrs. Gann . . . Barbara . . . asked if she could help me. I told her I was there because I wanted to be saved, Adam. I hope you understand."

"I most certainly do."

Rachel sighed, a look of relief on her face. "Barbara took me through the Scriptures to make sure I understood. Adam, I took Jesus as my Saviour. I'm a Christian now."

"I'm happy for you, honey." There were tears in Adam's eyes as he reached across the table to grasp her hands. "Now, let me tell you a story."

The words tumbled from Adam's mouth as he told Rachel he had brought Seth to the house to meet her, and while they were waiting, Seth had led him to the Lord.

"Seth told me the first thing to do now is to let Pastor Gann know what happened and to tell him I want to be baptized."

"Adam, Pastor Gann came home while I was still there. I'm already set to be baptized Sunday morning. Oh, praise the Lord! We can be baptized together."

On Sunday morning, Adam and Rachel entered the church building and were greeted warmly by the people standing in the vestibule. They walked into the auditorium to find seats, and Adam's eyes strayed toward a row of pews near the front. His heart lurched when he saw his father turned in the pew, looking at him. *My father in church?* Adam couldn't ever remember seeing his father inside a church.

Rachel saw Patch and waved at him. "Hello, Mr. Smith!"

Patch stood up, smiling at her as she came to greet him. "I received the thank-you card," he said. "It was kind of you to send it."

"And it was very kind of you to give me this beautiful brooch."

"It looks nice on you."

Rachel looked around to see if Adam was behind her and saw him across the room, motioning her to come. She excused herself to Patch and went to sit beside her husband.

When the service was over, Patch joined the long line of people who came by to welcome the new couple into the church. When it was his turn, Patch shook Adam's hand and smiled, then welcomed them both and moved on.

"I feel such a peace in my heart since I let Jesus come in," Rachel said as she and Adam lay in the darkness about to go to sleep.

"Wonderful, isn't it?"

"Uh-huh. Adam . . . could we talk a minute?"

"Of course," he said, rolling toward her.

"There's something I want to talk about that was too difficult for me before."

"What's that?"

"Mama. You probably wondered why I never told you about how or when she died, or anything."

Adam swallowed with difficulty. "Well, yes. But I told myself I would just wait till you brought it up. I didn't want to cause you any unnecessary pain."

"You're sweet."

"Sometimes."

Rachel smiled. "Anyway, I haven't told you very much about my life. You see, Daddy and I haven't lived in Memphis very long. We're from Philadelphia originally. Mama's name was Nancy . . . I don't think I ever told you that."

"No."

Rachel told him the whole story. "And the . . . the scum who ran her down didn't even have the decency to stop! Just left her lying in the mud to die!"

That night Adam did not sleep. The next morning he pretended that everything was all right, but he was torn up inside.

Adam and Rachel studied their Bibles daily and memorized Scripture to hide the Word of God in their hearts. Rachel was filled with joy at the beginning of each day and often recited Psalm 118:24 to Adam when they woke up: "This is the day which the LORD hath made; we will rejoice and be glad in it."

Adam rejoiced over his newfound faith too, but the secret he carried was slowly crushing him. Rachel loved Adam with her whole being, and she sensed deep within that he was gravely troubled.

During supper one evening, Rachel had to tell Adam twice that they couldn't go into the country for a picnic on Saturday evening because a family in the church had invited them over.

"Darling, is something troubling you?" she said.

Adam pressed a smile on his lips. "Why would you ask that?"

"I'm your wife. I love you. And I sense that

you're worrying about something."

"Just pressure from the load I have at the office," he said, rising from his chair. He leaned over and hugged her. "Business is too good . . . if that makes sense to you. I'm about to the place where I've got to hire another attorney to join the firm."

This scene was repeated often as time passed. On each occasion, Adam would assure her that his preoccupation was only work pressure and nothing more. Each time, Rachel tried to believe him, and for a short time she felt better. But as his preoccupation continued, a growing apprehension came over her.

One morning after Adam had gone to work, Rachel sat down at the kitchen table, bowed her head, and asked God to give Adam the courage to tell her what was troubling him.

Day after day, Adam's conscience ate at him. He struggled to keep his secret hidden, convinced that he must never tell Rachel that it was he who had run her mother down.

But one Sunday night, when Pastor Gann preached from Romans 12:17 that Christians must be honest in all things, Adam felt as if someone had set the pew on fire. The Spirit of God bore down on the things he was keeping from Rachel. He became even more uncomfortable when the pastor talked about husbands and wives being honest with each other.

Adam was on edge when the service was over. Others had gone to the altar under conviction from the sermon, but Adam had refused. He and Rachel were on their way to the door, shaking hands with people, when they came upon Patch Smith. Patch greeted Rachel, and as usual, shook his son's hand. "How about me taking you and this lovely young lady to supper one of these nights?" he said.

A scowl clouded Adam's features, and he replied, "We're too busy."

Rachel's eyes widened and her mouth fell open. "Adam! What has gotten into you?"

Adam hurried toward the door, passing by people who were trying to speak to him. Rachel laid a hand on Patch's arm and said, "I'm sorry, Mr. Smith. I must ask you to forgive my husband. He's been under a lot of stress lately. He's not been himself."

Patch watched his son disappear through the vestibule door. "I'm sorry to hear that. Adam ordinarily has a very pleasant manner about him."

"Yes. I'm hoping he'll soon get back to his old self."

Rachel found Adam waiting for her outside, and they started walking home beneath a starlit sky.

"Adam, I know you're under stress and all, but I have to tell you that what I saw in there was uncalled for. Mr. Smith was trying to do something nice for us."

He put an arm around her. "You're right. I don't know why I snapped at him like that. I'll apologize to him, okay?"

"Okay. You owe him that. Thank you."

For the next three weeks, Adam Burke's conscience battled with the sermon on honesty and the secrets he was keeping from Rachel. The Word of God's convicting power was cutting him up inside. Now he knew why the Bible called itself the *sword* of the Spirit.

Adam worked hard at stifling the conviction in his heart. Many times he asked the Lord if he should hurt Rachel with the truth . . . and possibly hurt their marriage. Every time, one line of Scripture burned through his mind: "Provide things honest in the sight of all men."

It was almost midnight on Sunday, four weeks since the sermon on honesty. Adam let out a cry and sat bolt upright in bed. Rachel came awake instantly and reached out to touch him. Adam let his mind reach back and grasp the nightmare. He was racing the buggy down the lightning-lit street on that fateful night in Philadelphia. When he felt the horse jerk to one side and felt the right wheel go over something, he let out the cry that had awakened him and Rachel.

Rachel slipped out of bed and lit the lantern on the small table next to it. Adam's face was beaded with sweat. She went to the wash-room and returned with a towel.

"What were you dreaming about?" she asked.

When he did not reply, she leaned down on the bed facing him and pressed her head against his chest.

"Adam, I love you," she said softly. "What-ever this is, you've got to share it with me. I'm your wife. I love you with all my heart. I want to help you, but I can't unless you tell me what it is. Please don't pass it off again as work pressure. I know better. Come on. Let me help. Tell me."

Adam took a deep breath and sent a silent prayer heavenward, then took hold of Ra-chel's shoulders. There was a quaver in his voice as he said, "I am the man . . . who was driving the buggy that struck your mother on that stormy night."

It took his words a few seconds to sink it. When they did, Rachel's hand leaped to her mouth. She closed her eyes. When she finally opened them again, she looked at him as if he had slapped her.

He took hold of her hand. "I knew this was going to hit you hard, honey. I . . . I tried to keep it to myself, but hiding it from you has become unbearable. I didn't want to hurt you."

A tear trickled down her cheek and fell into her lap. More tears followed. She did not speak but continued to look at him as if in a daze.

"Rachel, you must believe me. The storm was violent. You should remember that. Lightning, thunder, rain pouring down. Your mother must have stepped into my path without realizing it. I didn't even know I'd hit her until it came out in the paper the next day. Honest. I'm not a heartless beast. I did not know I had hit her!"

Rachel jerked her hand from his, staring hard at him.

"Please. You've got to believe me. I watched the paper to see how it was going for your mother. When it appeared that she was going to be all right, I went to the hospital to see her and was told that she had just died. I could see no reason to contact her family, nor to go tell the police I was the driver of the buggy that hit her. It would've served no purpose. Do you understand?"

Rachel said nothing.

"The papers never gave your name. I didn't know you were her daughter when I wrote to you. I only learned your father's name when his letter came. Since then I've carried this thing, trying to hide it so I wouldn't hurt you."

Adam and Rachel looked into each other's eyes. Hers were full of pain, his with love and suffering of soul. Adam reached for her, but she drew back.

"Don't touch me!"

"Rachel, we can't let this thing tear us apart."

Rachel clenched her fists and closed her eyes. Adam reached out and took her hand. She jerked it from him and rasped, "I said, don't touch me!"

"I love you, sweetheart," Adam said, leaning close. "You must believe that."

"How could I have done this?" she said, staring at him through her tears. "How could I love and marry the man who killed my sweet mother?"

"Rachel, it was an accident! I didn't even know I hit her."

"Even so, when you realized it was my mother, you should've been honest and told me."

"Yes, I should have. But please understand, it hit me like a bolt of lightning when I realized it was your mother. I found you in Memphis. The Mason family I knew about lived in Philadelphia. I was stunned when I realized who Nancy Mason's daughter was."

Rachel was silent for a moment, then she said, "I need to be alone."

Adam nodded. "All right. I'll be in the parlor."

The night passed slowly while Adam sat in the parlor, enveloped in darkness. When dawn came, he had heard nothing from Rachel. He went to the bedroom and found her sitting in the same position as when he left hours before.

"Why don't you lie down and get some sleep?" he said.

She looked at him with glassy eyes. "I want to be alone."

"I have to go to work, honey. Will you be all right?"

"Of course. I'll be alone."

Barbara Gann opened the front door of the parsonage and saw Adam standing there. "Well, hello, Adam. You look awfully tired. Working too hard these days?"

"Not really, ma'am. I'm sorry to bother you, but is the pastor in?"

"He's in his office at the church."

"Would it be all right if I knock on his door? I need to talk to him."

"Of course. Go right ahead."

Tom Gann smiled when he opened his office door to find Adam Burke. "Hello, Adam. Pleasure to see you here. What can I do for you?"

"Pastor, I need your help."

"Well, come in and sit down."

Adam sat in front of Gann's desk and told him the whole story, beginning with the night he struck Nancy Mason with his buggy in Philadelphia.

"I can't get her to talk to me, Pastor. She just keeps saying she wants to be alone. I worked till noon and went home, and she was still in her nightgown and told me she wanted to be alone. I couldn't get her to eat anything. What can I do?"

The preacher sighed. "Rachel seems to like my wife. How about if I bring Barbara to the house and let her talk to her?"

"Fine. I'll try anything."

"We'll be over right after supper."

"All right, sir. I really appreciate it."

"Before you go, let's pray for Rachel and ask the Lord to help her see that she needs to let Him heal the breach between you."

Gann led them in prayer, then walked Adam to the door and laid a hand on his shoulder. "It may not seem like it right now, Adam, but you did the right thing in telling her. It's always right to obey the Word of God, which you did. We've laid this situation in the Lord's hands, and now we must trust Him to take care of it."

The Ganns arrived at the Burke house, and Barbara went into the bedroom and talked to Rachel. She was even able to get her to eat a little food. When Barbara came out of the bedroom two hours later, she suggested that she move into the house for a few days so she could feed Rachel and talk with her. The pastor and Adam agreed. Adam said he would stay at the hotel and come by the house a couple of times a day to check on Rachel.

This went on for over a week. Rachel stayed secluded in the bedroom and refused to see anyone but Barbara. She was eating better and letting Barbara pray with her and read Scripture to her, but she still didn't want to see Adam.

When Rachel had been secluded in the bedroom for two weeks, Barbara met Adam in the parlor on his morning visit and said, "Good news. The Lord is answering prayer. I've finally been able to persuade her to talk to my husband. I'll go get him after I feed her some breakfast."

"No need," Adam said. "I'll go tell him Rachel's ready to talk."

It was shortly after nine o'clock when Pastor Gann knocked on the Burkes's door. Barbara met him with a smile on her face. "She's still in the mood to see you, honey. I think you can help her."

The Ganns entered the bedroom together. Rachel was sitting in an overstuffed chair by the window, wearing a robe, and Barbara had brushed her hair.

"Good morning, Rachel," Gann said.

She smiled up at him. "Good morning, Pastor."

"Thank you for letting me come and talk to you. We've all been concerned about you, you know . . . especially Adam."

Rachel stared blankly at him.

"Rachel, do you love your husband?"

"Do I love Adam?" She looked out the window a moment, then back at the pastor. "Adam cut my heart out, Pastor. How can I live with the man who killed my mother? How can I look at him day after day, knowing what he did? Not only did he take my mother from me, he took my father too. The only way my father could cope with Mama's death was to drown himself in whiskey. We lost everything, Pastor! Everything!"

Gann leaned close to Rachel, looking into her eyes. "The tragedy of your mother's death was terrible for you, I know. Adam has already told me about your father losing the business and all . . . but he also told me your father has recently been saved and is off the bottle."

A smile graced Rachel's lips. "Yes, that's true."

Gann cleared his throat. "Rachel, if you shut Adam out of your life, you will be making a monumental mistake. He loves you. The two of you have a great future ahead of you if you will only give your marriage a chance. Will you let me bring Adam in so I can talk to both of you at the same time?"

Rachel swung fearful eyes to Barbara.

"I'll be right here too, honey," she said.

Rachel licked her lips nervously, looked back at Gann, and nodded.

He patted her hand. "I'll go get Adam. I don't know how his appointments are set up for today, but I'll be back with him as soon as possible."

A half hour later, Adam entered the bedroom ahead of the pastor and found Barbara standing over Rachel, who was still sitting in the overstuffed chair. Rachel finished drinking a cup of water and handed it back to

Barbara, smiling her thanks. When Rachel looked at Adam, her smile faded.

"Hello, sweetheart," Adam said softly. "You're looking beautiful today, as always." He sat down in front of her with the pastor beside him. Barbara was seated beside Rachel.

"Rachel," Gann said, "I want to help both you and Adam. You know that, don't you?"

She nodded without meeting his gaze.

Pastor Gann reminded Rachel of the mercy Jesus had shown her in forgiving her and washing away all her sins in His blood. He opened his Bible and read several passages of Scripture about Christians being merciful and forgiving those who have wronged them. He then asked Rachel to read Matthew 5:7 aloud, reminding her that they were the words of Jesus Himself.

Rachel took the Bible from the pastor's hands and read with a steady voice, "Blessed are the merciful: for they shall obtain mercy."

"What Adam needs from you now, Rachel, is mercy. He needs your forgiveness."

Rachel looked at the verse again, then said to Adam, "The only way I'll forgive you is if you'll bring my mother back to me." Then she turned to Barbara and began to sob.

Adam sat without moving for a moment, then jumped out of his chair and said, "Pastor, I have to go somewhere right now. It's very, very important. Will both of you stay here with Rachel? I won't be gone long." Adam bent over his wife and said, "Rachel, I love you. Nothing can ever change that."

24

Patch Smith was working in his office at North Platte Clothiers when there was a tap at the door. "Yes, Jack?" he called, looking up from paperwork.

Jack Brady leaned in and said, "Adam Burke is here. He'd like to see you."

Patch rose from his chair. "By all means, send him in."

Jack left the door open, and a few seconds later, Adam came in and closed the door behind him. "Dad, I need to talk to you."

Patch rounded the desk and picked up two straight-backed chairs from by the wall. "Here, son. Sit down." Then he opened the door and called to Jack, telling him he was not to be disturbed. "What can I do for you?" he said, sitting down to face Adam.

"Well, first you can listen while I tell you a long story. Do you have time?"

"I have however long it takes."

Adam's voice broke several times while he told his father the whole story, from the night he hit Nancy Mason with the buggy until the shattering moment when he told Rachel she was married to the man who had run her mother down.

"Pastor and Mrs. Gann are trying to help us. They're with Rachel right now. But something happened a few minutes ago that shook me to my bones, and I had to come see you." Tears welled up in Adam's eyes. "Dad, you came to me admitting how wrong you had been to desert your family. You asked me to forgive you, but I refused. When Pastor Gann was talking to Rachel about forgiving me, he showed her verses from the Bible about Christians showing mercy to those who have wronged them. And he had her read the place where Jesus said, 'Blessed are the merciful: for they shall obtain mercy.' Suddenly it struck me. Jesus said it is those who show mercy who receive mercy. I saw it clearly right then, Dad." Adam choked up, then went on. "You admitted how wrong you'd been and you asked my forgiveness. I was so full of bitterness toward you that I refused."

Patch kept his eyes on Adam's face, waiting for his next words.

"I was terribly wrong not to forgive you. I . . . I couldn't wait another minute to come over here and ask you to forgive me."

Suddenly father and son were in each other's arms.

"Then you forgive me too, son?"

"Yes, Dad. I forgive you . . . and I love you."

When the emotions finally subsided, Adam said, "I've got to get back to Rachel. Would . . . would you go with me? She really thinks a lot of you. I know it will mean a lot to her when she finds out you are her father-in-law."

"Rachel," Pastor Gann said, "Adam told me he has already asked the Lord to forgive him. Doesn't the Lord say He forgives us when we acknowledge our sins and the wrongs we have done?"

"Yes, He does."

"Since God has forgiven Adam, by God's grace you can forgive him too." Rachel thumbed a tear from her eye. "Adam has grieved over that unfortunate accident for a long time. And he has grieved over his failure to go to you and your father when he learned he had struck your mother with his buggy. He has had to live with this guilt ever since. But who of us hasn't done something wrong? Who of us hasn't done something that has hurt another? Something for which we are very sorry and would change if we could?"

Rachel looked into Pastor Gann's eyes, letting his words sink in.

"When we confess our sins to the Lord in

392

honest repentance," Gann said, "He is quick to forgive us. First John 1:9 says, 'If we confess our sins, he is faithful and just to forgive us our sins, and to cleanse us from all unrighteousness.' The psalmist says, 'Blessed is he whose transgression is forgiven.' The Lord has shown you mercy by forgiving all your sins, Rachel. Twenty-six times in Psalm 136 we are told that God's mercy endures forever. He is to be praised for that."

Rachel nodded.

"Then what about Rachel's mercy toward the man she loves? 'Blessed are the merciful: for they shall obtain mercy.' "

Rachel sat quietly, with Barbara's arm around her, thinking on the Word of God as her heart embraced its truths. Suddenly she uttered a tiny sigh and bowed her head. The Ganns saw her stiff body relax and her lips begin to move in silent prayer, and they also prayed for the heartbroken girl earnestly asking her heavenly Father for guidance and help.

After several minutes, Rachel raised her bowed head and a small, tentative smile formed on her lips. Just then, they heard the front door open and close.

"Adam's back," Barbara whispered.

Moments later, Adam came into the room with Patch Smith on his heels. Adam looked at his wife, almost afraid to believe his eyes for the change he saw on her face. His throat swelled a bit as he said, "Rachel, I want to introduce you to someone very important to me. I want you to meet my dad. Yes, you heard me right. Patch Smith, whose real name is Gordon Burke, is my father."

The Ganns listened on as Adam told Rachel how his father had deserted his family in the days just after the Civil War, and that he had not seen his father until he came to North Platte almost a year ago, not knowing his father lived here. He went on to tell about the hatred and bitterness he had carried toward his father all these years, and that when he figured out who Patch Smith was, the bitterness was as strong as it had ever been.

"Rachel, when Dad asked me for mercy and forgiveness months ago, I said to him, 'If you can resurrect my mother and bring her back to me, I'll forgive you . . . but not until you do that.' You said virtually the same thing to me when I asked for your forgiveness. I suddenly realized that here I was refusing to have mercy on Dad and to forgive him when he asked for it . . . even as I asked for the same from you. That's why I left abruptly. I had to tell Dad he was forgiven." Adam moved close to Rachel, dropped to one knee, and said with tears in his eyes, "Sweetheart, I am now asking for your mercy and forgiveness."

Rachel's lips quivered. Her eyes were swimming in tears. A tiny sob escaped her lips as she bent over, threw her arms around Adam's neck, and said, "Yes, I forgive you! Oh, Adam, please forgive me for being so unkind to you and for breaking your heart. I'm the one who needs mercy and forgiveness."

After some time, the weeping eased and Rachel kissed Adam's cheek, then stood and walked over to Gordon, who was looking at her with affectionate eyes. Rachel embraced him and kissed his cheek. Suddenly father and son were hugging, with Rachel squeezed in between them.

"There's mercy flowing all over this place!" Pastor Gann said. " 'Blessed are the merciful: for they shall obtain mercy.' Did you know that one of the meanings of *blessed* is to make happy?"

Adam laughed for joy and said, "Well, Pastor, I've never been happier in my life!"